Hometown Cowboy

Kellersburg
Book 4

by

Merrillee Whren

Merrillee Whren
http://www.merrilleewhren.com/

Hometown Cowboy/ Merrillee Whren
ISBN: 978-1-944773-39-7

"Praise be to the God and Father of our Lord Jesus Christ! In his great mercy he has given us new birth into a living hope through the resurrection of Jesus Christ from the dead,"

1 Peter 2:3 NIV

B-beep. B-beep. B-beep. Someone had punched a Call button, and the sound echoed off the pale-yellow walls of the nursing home. Caroline Keller wondered whether she'd ever get used to hearing that noise. This was her first day on the job. Would she eventually tune it out, or would the sound make her want to run to the nurses' station and stop the annoyance?

Although the facility was known for its excellent care, she didn't know how that sound didn't give the residents a headache. Caroline tried to block out the blare as she drew closer to the nurses' station, where two nurses' aides were in an animated discussion.

"I don't want to deal with that man." Maisey Norberg, a petite blond, frowned. Her blue eyes brimmed with anger.

Caroline gave Maisey a sympathetic smile. "Who's the problem? Is that why this noise is giving me a headache?"

Maisey shook her head. "That's Mr. Nash. He's always hitting his Call button by mistake."

"Does that make it hard to know when someone really needs attention?"

"Yes, but we deal with it. At least he's not disagreeable."

"Like the guy you don't want to deal with?"

"Ms. Caroline, maybe you can soothe his ruffled feathers. Nobody wants to deal with him. Every time I enter his room, he's yelling and complaining about something. When I deliver the food, he says, 'I wouldn't feed pigs that slop.'" Maisey huffed as she gripped the cart containing the evening meal.

"He sounds like a challenge." Caroline imagined an older man with a sour disposition. "You still haven't told me who this is."

"Wyatt Bayer." Maisey's frown deepened. "Just because he's some celebrity cowboy, he thinks everyone should bow and scrape to him. Not me."

Caroline tried to hide a smile. Wyatt Bayer, rodeo champ. What was he doing in a nursing home in Kellersburg, Ohio? Sure he'd graduated from high school here in her class, but he'd gone away to college on a rodeo scholarship and hadn't been back, as far as she knew. But then she'd been away at college, missionary training, and then teaching missionary children in Kenya for over six years.

Maybe she should save Maisey from the difficult patient. "If you don't deliver dinner to that room, who will?"

"I don't know, but it won't be me. I've had enough of his foul mood and mouth. No one should have to take the abuse that man doles out every day. There should be a law against people who make life miserable for others."

"I'll save you from this dastardly man." Caroline

placed a hand on the cart. "I can deliver the rest of your meals and tell the residents about my new activities."

"You will?" Maisey's eyes grew wide. "You won't tell my supervisor, will you?"

"It'll be our secret." Caroline winked. "I'll tell him all about the programs I have planned for the residents."

"You're the new activities coordinator, aren't you?"

"I am. Maybe I can get Mr. Bayer to join in. What do you think?"

"I don't know, but thanks for doing this." Maisey grimaced. "You are a brave woman."

Caroline chuckled. "Brave? Questionable. Impetuous? For sure."

"Best wishes." Maisey waved as Caroline pushed the food cart toward the first room on the list for this hallway, the heels of her sensible pumps clicking on the gray tile floor.

Caroline delivered the meals with a smile, told the occupants about the new activities, and gave them each a flyer about times and places for each activity. She approached Wyatt's room. It didn't surprise her that Wyatt was trouble. He'd been trouble in school and had often given her a hard time, teasing her about being a goody-goody. He'd annoyed her from the time they'd been in elementary school until the day they'd graduated. She'd even been surprised that he'd managed to graduate. Now she was more surprised that he was in a nursing home.

Why was he here?

Now he was a "celebrity cowboy," as Maisey

described him. Did his celebrity make him think he was entitled to special treatment? She braced herself for his caustic attitude as she paused outside his room. She'd saved his tray till last.

"Good evening, Mr. Bayer. I've brought you a delicious meal." Caroline purposely didn't look up as she pushed the cart into the room and opened the doors to retrieve his tray.

"It's about time I got my food. You're new. Where's Maisey?"

"You frightened her away with your gruffness." Still not meeting his gaze, Caroline put the tray on the rolling table that went over the bed and opened the dome. "Here you go."

"Caroline Keller?"

"In person." Caroline looked up. Her heart froze as she gazed into his chocolate-brown eyes and took in the five o'clock shadow that shaded his strong jawline. She steeled herself against the reaction. Ever since elementary school, Wyatt had been able to elicit a reaction from her, good or bad. But was this a reaction to Wyatt or a sense of alarm that had happened all too frequently since she'd left Kenya?

"What're you doing here?" He ran a hand over his short dark-brown hair.

Caroline had been asking herself the same question. But this was a job until she could figure out what she wanted to do with the rest of her life. "I could ask you the same."

"Isn't it obvious?" He pointed to the brace on his leg

and a walking cast. "A horse fell on me and broke and crushed a lot of bones in my body. Thankfully, I'm just about ready to get out of this place."

"I don't know. I only deliver meals for frightened CNAs and lead the residents in activities, starting tomorrow. I don't know your medical prognosis, but I do know you should be joining us for some fun."

He looked at her as if she'd asked him to sprout wings and fly. "I'm not a joiner."

"Is that why you stay in your room rather than eating with the other residents in the dining hall? You don't look bedridden to me."

A muscle worked in his jaw as he stared at her. "You don't have a clue about me. The docs told me last week that I'll never be on the rodeo circuit again. They've taken away my life after I've spent weeks going through rehab for nothing."

"I'm sorry to hear that." Caroline didn't miss the resentment in his eyes. She wanted to tell him it wasn't for nothing, but he probably wouldn't accept her assessment.

He picked up the fork on the tray. "Now that you've brought me this so-called food, you can leave anytime."

"Okay, but in the future, think about being nice to the help. They don't deserve your wrath."

"Someone does."

"Not a sweet young woman like Maisey. Be kind. She's only here to help you."

Wyatt narrowed his gaze as he stabbed at the roasted chicken on his plate. "Leave and take your preaching with you."

"All right then. Have a good evening." Nodding, Caroline pasted a smile on her face.

She wished she could say she'd pray for him, but he certainly didn't want to hear that. She'd still pray for him and all the people who had to deal with him. He was hurting, but hadn't he always been hurting? He'd had a rough life as a kid, but hadn't his success made up for that? Or maybe nothing could undo a terrible childhood.

Nothing could undo the hurt in her own life. She and Wyatt had more in common than she wanted to admit.

Caroline pushed the cart to the end of the hallway and found Maisey hiding near the door that led to the courtyard, where residents could sit outside on nice days. Today wasn't one of them. Snow and ice covered the patio. January's chill obviously did nothing to brighten the prospect of an encounter with Wyatt Bayer.

Maisey stepped forward. "Ms. Caroline, did you deliver the meal? Did he bite your head off?"

"I did deliver his meal, but as you see, I still have my head." Caroline hoped she could talk to Maisey about Wyatt and help her understand his attitude.

Maisey laughed. "Ms. Caroline, you're so funny. I remember when you used to teach my Sunday school class before you went away to be a missionary. I always loved how you made the Bible stories come to life."

"Thank you. That's nice to hear." Caroline fell into step beside Maisey as they walked toward the nursing station. "Actually, I went away to college, then to missionary school."

"What do they teach you in missionary school?"

"Are you interested in being a missionary?"

"Not really. I want to be an RN someday, but it'll take me forever because I have to work and go to school at the same time. I'm taking an online class right now, but it's tough. Maybe I'm not smart enough to be a real nurse."

Caroline laid a hand on Maisey's shoulder. "You're smart, and you'll make a great nurse."

"Really?" Maisey let out a big huff of air. "I'm not too sure after having to deal with patients like that cowboy."

"Yeah, sometimes patients aren't all that fun to deal with, but that's any job. You have to deal with people, and people can be unkind. We just have to love them and pray for them."

Maisey smiled. "I wish I could be as good as you."

Caroline let out a halfhearted laugh, knowing she was far from good. She regretted not following her own advice. Her hurt ran deep, and forgiveness was hard to give. "Believe me. I'm not always good. It's hard to follow the example of Jesus and love the unlovable."

"Yeah, when they're like Wyatt Bayer. Why is he so mean?" Maisey shook her head.

"He's unhappy because he's been told he'll never be able to go back on the rodeo circuit."

Maisey widened her eyes. "He told you that? How did you get him to talk? He just yells at me."

"We've known each other since we were kids. He was kind of like that when he was a kid, too. A bit of a bully, but I always felt sorry for him and wished I could help him."

"Why?"

"His parents were drunk most of the time, and he eventually went to live with his grandparents." Caroline remembered how he used to follow her and her friends home from school and threaten them with rocks and curses. After he went to live with his grandparents on their farm, she didn't have to worry about him while she walked home from school.

Maisey shrugged. "Maybe that explains his attitude. But he's rich now, isn't he? Shouldn't that make him happy?"

Caroline shook her head. "Not all rich people are happy. Some are quite miserable."

"I'd like to give it a try." Maisey chuckled. "Maybe I could be one of the happy ones."

"We'd all like to think that." Caroline wondered how rich Wyatt was. Her parents had mentioned that he'd built a new house for his grandparents on their farm. That showed he at least appreciated what they'd done for him. His life had been more settled living with his grandparents, but he'd always been an outsider. He'd marched to his own drummer, being the only kid in their high school who'd taken an interest in rodeo, and Wyatt Bayer was still a mystery.

"Well, I'd better get back to work, or I won't even have a paycheck, much less riches." Maisey waved as she hurried down the hallway to one of the rooms.

Caroline hoped she could encourage the younger

woman in her quest to become a nurse. Everyone needed a little encouragement, even Wyatt Bayer. But he didn't want her advice or anyone else's. What could she possibly do to help him? Maybe she could talk to his grandparents and find out what had happened and how he had come to be here in Kellersburg. On the other hand, maybe she should just mind her own business.

She wasn't very good at that. She liked to help people whether they wanted it or not.

***

Wyatt finished the last of his rubber chicken and watery mashed potatoes, then tossed the fork onto the tray. Why did the food here have to be so bad? He longed for some of his grandmother's good home cooking, but he probably wouldn't get any of that either. He'd been just as horrible to his grandparents as he'd been to Maisey and Caroline today.

He closed his eyes and lay back against the adjustable hospital bed that had him sitting upright. He'd pushed everyone away, even the people he loved the most, his grandparents. They'd been there for him through all the ups and downs of his life, so why had he yelled at them and told them to stay away? He wished he could take it all back, but that wish hadn't made him any kinder to the people who tried to help him here.

But it had all come to a head today when Caroline Keller had looked into his eyes and asked him what he was doing here and told him to be kind.

Why was he here? Where was his life headed? Who was he these days without his livelihood? He couldn't answer any of these questions.

But Wyatt knew one thing. Caroline Keller had fascinated him since he'd been in the same first-grade class with her.

Caroline Keller. Perfect Caroline with her compassionate gray eyes and light reddish-brown hair pulled back in some sort of braid thingy. He'd like to unpin it and let it fall around her shoulders. He'd like to have her look at him without remembering the kid he used to be. He'd like for her to see beyond the cowboy he had become. But he was afraid to let her too close, even though that was what he wanted. Was he crazy?

Caroline had looked at him with compassion, but he didn't want her pity. He wanted her to like him, but he had done nothing to change the way she had probably always looked at him. He imagined she saw him through the prism of his past bad behavior, or maybe his own insecurities made him feel that way.

Instead of saying something civil, he'd lashed out at her the same way he'd lashed out at everyone who tried to help him. Acting like that wouldn't make her see him any differently. Why couldn't he change?

He rubbed his forehead. Would an apology help? He had to admit things couldn't get much worse. He'd alienated almost everyone he knew. Doctors, his few friends on the circuit who'd tried to reach out to him, the nurses and aides here, his grandparents, and finally the woman who had captured his interest since he'd been a foul-mouthed kid trying to get her attention by calling her names and throwing rocks.

How to win friends. Not his gift.

Social skills had eluded him from the time he'd tried to make up for his parents' neglect. Struggling to live down the stigma of his parents being the town drunks had made him something he wasn't proud of. He'd tried to overcome that in all the wrong ways. When he'd been forced to live with his father's parents, he'd had a sense of abandonment. Despite his grandparents' love, he'd felt all alone in the world.

His mother's parents had never been in the picture, as they had died in a car accident when he'd been a baby. Maybe that was why his mother had traded him for a bottle of booze and dragged his dad with her. He hadn't heard from them since he'd gone off to college. He'd made no effort to find them, and they had disappeared from his life. Had it been a mistake to ignore their existence? This injury and time in the nursing home had made him reflect on a lot of things in his life.

So many questions. No answers.

"Mr. Bayer?"

A timid female voice made Wyatt look toward the doorway. "Yeah?"

Maisey stood there, clinging to the doorframe. "Are you finished with your tray?"

"Yeah." *Be kind.* Caroline's words hammered in Wyatt's head. He could do that. He'd let this injury take him back to his rotten childhood, but Caroline's sudden appearance and her advice had reached him when no one else had. The old childhood dream of impressing Caroline Keller sat squarely in his thoughts.

He would change direction right here and now and show Caroline a better side of himself. He was pretty sure what he said to Maisey would get back to Caroline. He could be more than kind. He could take an interest in the young woman and find out about her life.

"Should I take your tray?" Maisey cowered as she gazed at him.

He had caused that look. Was there any way to make amends? Could he talk to her without setting up expectations in her mind? Was that being a little too full of himself? Probably, but he'd had enough women chase him over the years to make him more than cautious. "Yeah, you can take my tray, but first let me say I'm sorry for blaming you for the bad food. You only deliver it."

Surprise registered in Maisey's smile as she sidled into the room. "Thank you for that."

"You're welcome. I'll try to do better." Wyatt tapped his leg. "This makes me angry, and I should know better than take it out on you."

Maisey placed the tray on the cart. "Should I remind you of that the next time you yell at me?"

Wyatt gave her a lopsided smile. "Sure. Tell me to be kind."

"Did Ms. Caroline tell you to apologize?" Maisey wrinkled her brow.

Wyatt chuckled. "You're a smart young woman.

Yes, Ms. Caroline is very persuasive."

Maisey nodded. "She's such an encouraging person. She told me I should reach for my dream of being an RN, even though it may take me forever because I have to work and take classes at the same time."

Everything Maisey had said about Caroline was true. She had encouraged him to be kind, and he wanted to please her. He had to think about her every time he was tempted to let his temper fly. "You should definitely reach for your dream. I think you'll make a great RN. You've managed to put up with me."

"Well, not exactly." Maisey shrugged. "I have to be honest. I kinda complained about you. That's why Ms. Caroline delivered your meal."

Wyatt couldn't help smiling. "Your honesty is refreshing. And thanks for sending Ms. Caroline my way."

"Do you like her?" Maisey narrowed her gaze.

Wyatt wished he hadn't opened his mouth. "Of course. Who doesn't like Caroline Keller?"

Maisey smiled. "Yeah. She's a great person and easy to like. But I was thinking maybe you more than just like her."

Wyatt shook his head. "As my gramps used to say, 'Now you've gone to meddlin'.'"

Maisey laughed. "My grandma used to say that, too."

"Guess grandparents have the same sayings." After the way Wyatt had treated Maisey during most of his rehab here, he marveled that he was actually having a civil conversation with the young woman.

Maisey took a deep breath. "Well, I'd better get moving. I've got lots of trays to collect."

Wyatt nodded. "I'll remember to be kind the next time I see you."

"Thanks." Maisey gave a little wave as she pushed the cart into the hallway.

Wyatt lay back on his bed again. Would Maisey go running to Caroline and tell her about their conversation? Did he care? Yeah, he cared, but why? Did he want to show Miss Congeniality of his high school class that he could be congenial, too? Or was there more, as Maisey had suspected? Sure he'd always been fascinated with Caroline, but not in a romantic sense. They didn't suit in the least. She was too refined for the likes of him. But he sure would like to find out how good it would be to kiss her.

Now that was crazy. She'd probably slap him if he tried something like that.

That first year on the circuit he'd soon discovered he could attract a woman without even trying. He'd learned quickly to avoid the buckle bunnies, women who hung around the cowboys. He didn't want to be a one-night-stand kind of guy, not after his one terrible experience with a young woman that first year.

Now he looked at most women with distrust. But Caroline Keller was a different woman altogether. She had always seemed to have her life in perfect order. She had been generous and encouraging to people even when they were kids. Even him. She hadn't tattled to her parents or other adults about his bad behavior. She'd just ignored him, and he suspected that she'd wished he'd go away. He had to some extent when he'd gone to live with his grandparents. Now he'd like to get to know her a whole lot better. Was this whole scenario taking him back to his childhood dream?

Before he could pursue Caroline, he had to figure out what he would do with his life once he hobbled out of this place. He'd still have recuperation and rehab after this. Maybe he should do some of that joining he wasn't fond of. On the other hand, maybe he should get his head on straight and forget all about going after a woman who was definitely beyond his reach.

***

"That dress looks absolutely marvelous on you. It fits perfectly." Caroline looked at her future sister-in-law, Melanie Drake. "Nathan won't know what hit him when he sees you in it."

Melanie smoothed the ivory satin of the lace-trimmed A-line skirt with the empire waist. "Thanks, but this destination-wedding thing has me a little nervous."

"There's nothing to be nervous about."

"I hope you're right."

"Of course I'm right. Who doesn't want to take off work and get out of this snow and cold to spend a few days where it's warm?"

Pushing a strand of her dark-brown hair away from her face, Melanie gave Caroline a tepid smile. "Guess

I'm an anxious flyer, because I've never flown before. And I can't forget Nathan's plane crash."

Caroline patted Melanie's shoulder. "That was a small plane, and besides, Nathan will be there to hold your hand."

Melanie chuckled as she let Caroline unzip the dress. "That's what he keeps telling me. Ryan and Andrew, on the other hand, can hardly wait to fly in a big plane after Nathan took them for a flight in his plane."

"Your boys are so cute, and they certainly weren't afraid to go up with Nathan after the crash."

"They think Nathan can do no wrong." Melanie's expression indicated that she thought the same as she took off her dress. "Ryan and Andrew are so excited about standing up with Nathan."

Caroline smiled at Melanie. "Nathan is so looking forward to being a dad to those boys."

"They practically adopted Nathan the first time they met him." Melanie nodded and handed the dress to Julianne.

"And he them."

"For sure. And he's so good about helping them remember Tim." Melanie blinked rapidly as tears welled in her eyes. "I can hardly believe God has blessed me with two wonderful men in my lifetime."

"God has blessed our family by bringing you and your boys into it."

"Thank you. I'm blessed to be a part of your family."

"Okay, ladies. I'm sorry I have to break up this

gabfest, but Caroline needs to try on her dress now."
Julianne Frey, Caroline's cousin and manager of the
local variety store, took Melanie's bridal gown and
placed it on the nearby hanger. "I'm so glad your dress
is a perfect fit. No alterations needed."

"Me, too." Melanie let out a happy sigh as she put
her pink dental assistant's uniform, covered in dancing
toothbrushes, back on. "Now it's Caroline's turn."

Julianne held up a navy-blue chiffon dress with a
glittery sparkle of silver. "Caroline, *you* will look
marvelous in this dress."

Caroline manufactured a smile as she thought about
all the bridesmaid dresses hanging in the closet of her
childhood room. Thankfully, she'd been out of the
country for a number of family weddings, or she feared
there might have been more of them. *Always a
bridesmaid, never the bride*. Wasn't that the old saying?
Maybe that was her role. Never to be a bride. And now
there was even more reason why she probably wouldn't
be one.

"It's a beautiful dress."

"Yes, it is. Now let's get you in it so I can see if it
needs any alterations." Julianne held up the dress.

In seconds Caroline stood on a platform in front of
the triple mirror and surveyed her reflection. Only weeks
ago she'd been the bridesmaid in Ashley Hiatt's
wedding. Her good friend from missionary training had
found her true love. Caroline had caught the bouquet at
the reception, and Ashley was sure Caroline would find
her true love waiting here in Kellersburg. But

Kellersburg wasn't exactly a hot spot for eligible bachelors. With the secret she carried, one she couldn't bring herself to share with anyone, being single was probably best, even though the eligible bachelor count had increased by one with the presence of Wyatt Bayer.

She didn't even know why she was thinking about him. She shouldn't judge him on her past experiences with him or even the day she had delivered his meal, because she didn't really know him anymore. Besides, even though Wyatt was definitely an eligible bachelor, he was all wrong for her.

Or maybe she was all wrong for him, or any man. She wasn't wife material. Her life was broken, and she couldn't even talk to her parents about it. God was her only confidant, but the incident that had changed her world had made Him seem far away. Somehow she had to get her life back together.

She definitely shouldn't judge Wyatt just as she didn't want to be judged. It wasn't her place. She should take her own suggestion and be kind, but she had avoided him since the day she had delivered his meal and given him unsolicited advice. She didn't know whether he'd been kind to Maisey or whoever delivered his meals. Maisey hadn't complained since that day. Even after Caroline's prompting, he hadn't joined any of the activities, and she hadn't gone looking for him.

"You look lost in thought." Julianne's statement shook Caroline from her musings.

Caroline gave Julianne a halfhearted smile. "Thinking about work."

"How's that going?"

"Okay, I guess. I haven't been at it long enough to evaluate my success." Caroline shrugged. "I'm looking forward to Elise having her students come to the nursing home to sing. I'm pretty sure the residents will enjoy it."

"For sure." Julianne took a tuck in the fabric at the back of Caroline's dress. "Looks like this one little alteration is all you need. The length is good. So you can take it off."

Caroline stepped out of the dress and handed it to her cousin. "Thanks. I'm looking forward to enjoying some much warmer weather in Florida."

"We all are." A male voice sounded from the other side of the drape covering the opening to the dressing room.

Melanie raced to the doorway and peeked out to the other side of the drape. "Nathan, why are you here? I thought I was going to meet you at the bank."

"Am I in trouble?" he asked with a laugh.

Melanie laughed in return as she stood, holding on to the drape. "No, but you aren't supposed to see me in my dress until the wedding, and Caroline is changing."

"I don't see a wedding dress, just a flash of my favorite pink uniform."

Melanie glanced at Caroline "Should I let your brother in?"

"Yeah. Let him in." Caroline grabbed her purse from the nearby table and slung it over one shoulder.

"Caroline said okay, but if you'd come just a few minutes earlier, I would've had my dress on."

"Whew. I just missed a disaster." Nathan brushed a hand across his forehead as he stepped into the room filled with clothing racks, mirrors, mannequins, and sewing paraphernalia on tables. Melanie glowered as she tried to hide a smile. "You are not funny."

"I've never been accused of being a comedian."

"Nathan, what's going on?" Caroline approached, now dressed in navy pants and a cream-colored turtleneck sweater.

Nathan stepped into the room and put an arm around Caroline's shoulders. "Little sis, I just came to see my bride-to-be. It's hard being away from her."

"Seriously. You never leave the bank this early." Caroline frowned.

"Seriously. I missed Melanie, and we have an appointment to see one of my favorite clients."

"So it is bank business after all." Caroline grinned. "I knew you'd be all about business."

Nathan put his other arm around Melanie and pulled her close. "Melanie, tell my sister that I'm not all about business anymore."

Melanie's gaze flitted between Caroline and Nathan. "Sweetheart, you wouldn't want me to tell your sister a lie, would you?"

Nathan let out a big belly laugh. "I can see where this is going. Two females ganging up on me. Julianne, vouch for me."

Julianne held up both hands. "I'm staying out of this."

"Okay. I can see when I'm beat." Nathan kissed the

tip of Melanie's nose. "You have to admit I'm working on getting better."

"I'll give you that." Melanie nodded as she turned to Caroline. "Be kind to your brother. He deserves it."

Be kind. The same words Caroline had said to Wyatt. She wasn't really being unkind to Nathan, just teasing him, wasn't she? "Okay, big brother. I won't tease you about working too much."

Nathan shook his head. "I think that was still a backhanded way of saying I spend too much time at work, but Melanie will stick up for me."

Melanie kissed Nathan on the cheek. "I guess I'll defend you against your sister."

"Somehow I'm coming out on the wrong end of this conversation." Nathan laughed again and grabbed Melanie's hand. "Let's go to the nursing home and visit Wyatt."

"Wyatt Bayer?" Caroline's mind couldn't wrap around a connection between Nathan and Wyatt.

"Yeah. Wyatt's the client I was talking about." Nathan stood there holding Melanie's hand. "Does he attend your activities?"

"No. He told me he wasn't a joiner."

"So you have seen him since you started working at the nursing home?" Nathan gave Caroline a curious look.

"Yeah, on my first day. I had no idea he'd been so severely injured." Caroline shrugged. "But then, I really never followed his career."

Nathan narrowed his gaze. "You and Wyatt were in

the same class, right?"

"Yeah, but we didn't run in the same circles." Caroline had no idea why discussing Wyatt was so uncomfortable, but uneasiness floated through her mind.

"You should come with us."

"I just came from there, and my workday is over. Unlike you, I know when to clock out."

"Yeah, but this isn't about working. It's about visiting someone who needs some encouragement. It's always nice to have visitors when you're in a nursing home or hospital." Melanie's kind smile matched her words.

Shame for her attitude joined the uneasiness as Caroline stared at her future sister-in-law. Caroline wasn't going to tell Nathan and Melanie about her run-in with Wyatt. How could she get out of this visit without appearing to be unkind? There it was again. *Kindness.* She needed to practice what she preached. "Okay. You've got me there."

"Great. You can ride with us. No need to take more than one car. We'll drop you back by here to pick up your car on our way home." Nathan jangled the keys in his pocket as he motioned toward the front of the store. "We'd better get out of here. Julianne's probably ready to close up shop for the day."

"I am. See you all later, and Caroline, I'll give you a call when the alterations are done so you can try on your dress again to make sure it fits."

"Okay. I'll be waiting to hear from you."

Caroline wanted to know why Nathan considered

Wyatt one of his best clients, but it probably wasn't any of her business. She just had to remember to be kind. But would kindness work on a man who appeared bitter about his present circumstances? Kindness hadn't worked when they were kids—he'd mocked her all the way through high school. Why should things be any different now?

CHAPTER TWO

"You're making great progress, and I think you'll be out of here two weeks from now."

Wyatt stared at the physical therapist, Tina, a short, middle-aged woman with curly medium-brown hair. She had just told him he'd be set free from this place. He should be thrilled, but that meant he'd have to figure out what to do with the rest of his life—he could hardly fathom a life without the rodeo circuit.

"That sounds good." Wyatt produced a smile he didn't feel.

"Of course, that doesn't mean you're all done with these exercises. They are ongoing if you want to get back to normal."

"Got it." *Normal.* What was his normal now? Would he ever get on the back of a bucking horse and stay on for eight seconds? Eight seconds. It could seem like a lifetime on a writhing, twisting thousand-pound animal. Yet people wasted eight seconds hundreds of times a day. He wanted to believe he could ride again, but he'd been told he wouldn't. Could he prove them wrong?

"So I'll send you on your way with the suggestion that you put yourself out there. Quit hiding in your room."

Wyatt scowled. "How do you know I've been doing

that?"

"It's common knowledge."

"But you've never said anything to me before. Why now?" Wyatt wondered whether Caroline had anything to do with these instructions. That was probably wishful thinking. She most likely never gave him a second thought after she'd left his room that day last week. He hadn't seen her once since then, but her suggestion to be kind had made a big difference in his relationship with Maisey. Now she actually smiled and talked to him when she delivered his meals.

"I wanted to wait until you could see the finish line."

"But you said the therapy was ongoing."

The therapist nodded. "Yes, but when your time here is finished, the real world awaits. I want you to be thinking about that. Prepare yourself to get out there when you leave this place."

"I'll consider it." Wyatt pushed his way out of the physical therapy room on his walker. *A walker*. He was twenty-nine, not eighty-nine. Two weeks and he could throw this thing away…right?

"Hey, Wyatt."

As Wyatt neared his room, he turned at the sound of a male voice. "Nathan, what are you doing here?"

"Visiting you, and I've brought company."

Wyatt glanced behind Nathan but didn't see anyone. A good thing. He wasn't sure he wanted company, but he would smile and make nice with the man who had helped to make him a millionaire. "Good to see you. Thanks for coming by. Who's the company?"

"Melanie and my sister, Caroline." Nathan motioned toward the other end of the hallway. "They went to visit Gretchen Hornbacher from church first. They'll be by momentarily."

"Hey, before they get here, I'd like to make a request." Wyatt let Nathan go into the room first.

"Sure. What can I do for you?" Curiosity colored Nathan's expression as he sat in the nearby chair while Wyatt sat on the edge of the bed.

Wyatt glanced toward the door to make sure neither Melanie nor Caroline lurked in the hallway. "There's a young nurse's aide who works here, Maisey Norberg. She told me she'd like to go to school to become an RN, but she can't take too many classes because she has to work. I'd like to set up a scholarship for her. Can you work that out? And I want it to be anonymous."

Nathan nodded. "I should be able to do that, but I need details. Like where she wants to attend school, when she wants to start, things like that. Can you give me that information?"

Shrugging, Wyatt shook his head. "I don't know how I'd get the information without making her suspicious about where the scholarship came from. I don't want her to know."

Nathan rubbed his chin. "Umm, I'll see what I can do. Maybe Caroline can help us out, since she works here."

"I don't want her to know either. I don't want anyone to know. I wouldn't tell you either, except I kind of have to." Wyatt smiled wryly.

"You do." Nathan chuckled as he stood and extended his hand to Wyatt. "I'll try my best to keep this under wraps, but I'm making no promises. It could all go wrong. You know what happened when you tried to surprise your grandparents with their new house."

Wyatt chuckled as he shook his head. "Yeah, Grandpa ran into the contractor, who spilled the beans."

Nathan shook his head. "I didn't see that one coming, otherwise I would've told the contractor the house was a surprise."

"But I know you'll do your best to keep this a secret. You've always done your best for me." Wyatt remembered the first time the two of them had shaken hands in Nathan's office at the bank nine years ago. Wyatt had been Nathan's first client. Their financial partnership had turned out to be one of the best things in Wyatt's life. Nathan had not only helped Wyatt secure his financial future, but he had served as a confidant.

"I try." Nathan returned to the chair. "It's good to see you out and about."

Wyatt tapped the walker. "I'd be happier if I was out and about without this thing."

"It's better than being stuck in your bed like you were in the beginning."

"That's the way I should look at it, but I have to admit, I don't usually think that way."

Nathan sat forward in his seat. "Sorry I haven't stopped by lately. How are things going?"

"I should be getting out of here in a couple of weeks." Wyatt gestured around the room. "I can't say

I'll miss this place."

"I'm sure that's true. It's great that you'll be getting out just in time so you can attend the wedding."

Wyatt didn't understand Nathan's invitation. Sure they had a business relationship, but that hardly qualified him to attend the man's wedding. "You didn't have to invite me. I'm not family."

"This is about friends and family."

Friends? Is that what Nathan considered their relationship? Their biannual in-person meetings and weekly calls about Wyatt's portfolio hardly qualified as friendship in his book. Maybe he should've looked at Nathan as a friend, instead of just a financial advisor and sounding board. "I'm honored you've invited me."

"I figured after being cooped up in this place for months, a few days at the beach would appeal to you, especially since you helped Melanie and me find the perfect venue for our wedding."

"I was glad to do it. No thanks or invitations required."

Nathan tilted his head as he stared at Wyatt. "But I suspect that warm weather and sunshine sound pretty good."

Wyatt couldn't help smiling as he glanced out the window at the snow-covered ground. "You're not wrong there."

"We'll have to see about getting you an airline ticket. So let's get one booked." Nathan pointed to the bedside table. "Grab your tablet."

Wyatt could hardly refuse without seeming

ungrateful for everything Nathan had done. Wyatt swiped the tablet screen. "What day?"

Nathan held out his hand. "I can find a flight for you, if you don't mind."

"Sure. Go ahead." Wyatt gave the tablet to Nathan.

Nathan tapped the screen, then looked up, "First class or coach?"

Wyatt let the choice roll through his mind. What would Nathan think if he knew Wyatt had never been on a plane? He had seen almost every corner of the US. He had driven everywhere in his pickup—in the beginning because he couldn't afford to fly, and later because he enjoyed the time to himself. "If this is the same flight you're on, I'll do the same as you."

"Are you sure you want to fly coach?"

"Yeah." Wyatt opened the drawer on the bedside table. "Let me get my credit card."

"No need. This is on me."

Wyatt shook his head. "I can't let you do that."

"Sure you can." Nathan extracted his wallet from the back pocket of his pants and pulled out his credit card.

"I don't understand why you're doing this."

Nathan finished the transaction and closed the cover on the tablet. "You're all set."

"Thanks, but that was completely unnecessary."

"I want to repay you for trusting me with your investments all these years. It's meant a lot to me."

"I'm the one who should be thanking you." Wyatt couldn't wrap his mind around Nathan's kindness.

"You have a thousand times over."

"Please explain."

Nathan expelled a harsh breath. "It's like this. The success I had with your portfolio helped me prove to my dad that I know what I'm doing when it comes to investments and the bank. You see, my older brother is an extremely successful investment banker in New York City. I've always lived in his shadow. You and your portfolio gave me the opportunity for success in my own right."

Wyatt smiled wryly. "Glad I could help."

Nathan laughed. "You more than helped. You made my career."

"I hardly doubt that."

"Now we have to get you a room." Nathan reached for the tablet, ignoring Wyatt's statement.

Wyatt grabbed the tablet out from under Nathan's hand. "I'll take care of that."

"Okay. I won't fight you, but I'd suggest you do it right away. We only have a few rooms left in our room block."

Wyatt opened the tablet lid. "I'll do it right now."

Wyatt finished booking his room and looked up just as Melanie and Caroline stopped in the doorway. "Come in, ladies."

Melanie approached. "Wyatt, you are looking well."

"I'm doing much better. Thanks."

"Yeah, he's getting out of here in two weeks." Nathan put an arm around Melanie's shoulders as he guided her farther into the room.

Melanie smiled, her eyes lighting up. "That's

marvelous news."

"It is." Wyatt observed Caroline to catch her reaction. She remained near the door and looked as if she wanted to be someplace else. Wishing she could escape or still be visiting Mrs. Hornbacher? Why did he care what Caroline thought? He didn't need her approval, although he had to admit he wanted it. He always had. Annoyed with himself for even thinking about her, he turned his attention to Melanie, whose kindness touched him. Even his sour moods hadn't discouraged her from visiting him. Nathan was a lucky man.

"And that means he's coming to the wedding," Nathan said.

"More marvelous news." Melanie clapped her hands together in a prayerful pose as she turned to Caroline. "Did you hear that? Wyatt will get to come to the wedding."

Caroline stepped away from the door. "I'm sure he'll be glad to get out of this cold weather."

"For sure, as well as out of this place." Wyatt gave her a halfhearted smile. The little pucker between her eyebrows told him she wasn't particularly pleased that he'd be at the wedding.

"And you can attend the Valentine banquet at church." Melanie slipped an arm through Nathan's as she gazed up at him with adoration written all over her face. "Nathan and I will be in the couples' competition to see who knows each other the best. We're the almost married couple."

"Wyatt, aren't your grandparents part of the competition this year?" Melanie gave him a questioning look.

He didn't have a clue. What would they say if they knew he hadn't talked to his grandparents since the day a couple of weeks ago when he'd told them to leave him alone? After the doctors had told him he wouldn't be able to return to the rodeo unless he wanted to chance permanent disability, he'd taken his anger out on his grandparents and told them to leave him alone. They had respected his wishes.

Now he had more bridges to mend before he got out of here. "They haven't mentioned it. What exactly is this competition?"

"It's like that old TV show 'The Newlywed Game.' Only none of the couples are newlyweds." Nathan patted Melanie's arm. "Melanie thinks it'll be fun, but I'm not so sure. What if I don't remember her favorite color or know what she told me two weeks ago?"

Melanie shook her head. "It's for fun, Nathan. I won't care if you don't remember something."

"That's what you say now." Nathan wagged a finger at Melanie.

Melanie smiled back, then glanced at Caroline. "Tell your brother he has nothing to worry about."

Caroline smiled for the first time since she'd stepped into the room. "You two are too cute. Nathan, it's all in fun."

Nathan nodded as he glanced at Caroline. "I'm having a little fun of my own, a surprise for you."

"And what would that be?" Caroline knit her brow.

"It wouldn't be a surprise if I told you."

"You know I hate surprises."

Nathan grinned. "That's why it's so fun to surprise you."

Caroline made a face at Nathan. "If I didn't like Melanie so much, I'd make you pay, Nathan Keller."

Nathan laughed. "You are so fun to tease."

Caroline shook her head. "What am I going to do with you?"

"Be kind." Nathan gave her that big-brother look.

Wyatt chuckled to himself. *Be kind.* Maybe that was the Keller family motto. "Yeah, Caroline, be kind to your brother. He's a good guy. I can vouch for that."

Caroline flashed Wyatt a surprised look. "If he's such a good guy, he wouldn't tease me or plan surprises that involve me."

"How do you know his surprise isn't something you'll like?" Wyatt tilted his head and gave her a wry smile.

Caroline narrowed her gaze. "You're just on his side because you guys like to stick together."

Wyatt didn't realize how much fun it was to spar with Caroline. "Yeah. Us guys gotta stick together, or you women will run all over us."

"I doubt that. I think you're pretty capable of holding your own."

"Seriously?" Wyatt tapped the walker. "You're talking to a guy who can't walk without this thing."

A smile appeared on Caroline's lips, very kissable

lips. Oh wow! Was he in trouble now. Good thing she couldn't read his mind.

"Trying to play on my sympathies?" Caroline asked.

"No. I wouldn't want you to waste your sympathy on me, but just to show you what a good guy I am, I'll make sure your surprise is a good one." Wyatt waggled his eyebrows.

"Were you two conspiring before I got here?" Caroline's gaze flitted between Nathan and Wyatt, then to Melanie. "Melanie, do you know about this surprise?"

Melanie held up both hands. "Not a clue, but I have a fabulous idea. Why don't you and Wyatt go to the Valentine's banquet together?"

"I can't do that. I'm on the setup committee, and I have to be there early to get things ready and make sure the food is coming."

The near horror in Caroline's eyes as she stared at Melanie curdled Wyatt's stomach.

"I forgot about that." Melanie gave Caroline a sympathetic glance.

Was Wyatt the only one who recognized Caroline's reluctance? Were Nathan and Melanie trying to play matchmakers? Wyatt wouldn't mind in the least if they were. He'd welcome their interference, but it was obvious that Caroline didn't.

Melanie gestured toward Wyatt. "Even though you can't go with Caroline, I'll make sure we save a seat so you can sit at our table. Then we can all be together. I'll save a place for your grandparents, too. Does that work for you, Wyatt?"

"Sure." Wyatt smiled, fearful of looking in Caroline's direction. He didn't want to read the unhappiness in her eyes, but he was no coward. He'd wrangled unruly calves and hung on to raging broncs and bulls. He could overcome the reluctance of one pretty woman. "It would be my pleasure to sit next to Caroline."

"Great." Melanie looked over at Caroline. "That will give you and Wyatt a chance to get reacquainted."

"It will." Caroline's smile looked more fake than the faux-leather chair in the corner.

"The banquet is always a lot of fun," Melanie said, oblivious to Caroline's reluctance to join the fun.

"I'm sure Uncle Ray will be in fine form with the karaoke." Caroline's fake smile morphed into a genuine chuckle.

"For sure." Nathan nodded.

"Nathan, are you singing?" Caroline asked.

Nathan hesitated. "Possibly. You know how Uncle Ray is. He likes to keep people guessing. Some of the entertainment is preplanned. The rest is impromptu."

Caroline sent a little glare in Nathan's direction. "That surprise you talked about isn't getting me to sing, is it? Because you know you got all the singing talent in our family. Nobody wants to hear me sing."

Wyatt suppressed a smile. So Caroline wasn't perfect after all. She didn't sing well.

Nathan stepped over and put an arm around Caroline's shoulders. "I don't think you have to worry about Uncle Ray asking you to sing."

"Let's hope not." Caroline hunched her shoulders.

Before anyone could respond, Maisey wheeled a cart into the room. "Hey, Mr. Bayer, looks like you have lots of company. Your dinner is here, if you're ready."

"Hey, Maisey, you know Ms. Caroline here. Have you met her brother and sister-in-law to be?"

Maisey bobbed her head. "I've seen Mr. Keller at the bank and at church. And Ms. Drake has cleaned my teeth."

"Hi, Maisey." Melanie smiled. "No need to be so formal. You can call us Nathan and Melanie."

Maisey bobbed her head again. "I know you guys are getting married soon."

"Less than a month to go, but it can't get here soon enough." Nathan put an arm around Melanie's waist and pulled her close. "This lady has made me a very happy man."

Melanie gave Nathan a peck on the cheek, then glanced around the room. "We'd better get going and let Wyatt eat his dinner."

"You're right." Nathan extended his hand to Wyatt. "Be sure to let me know when you get out of here now that we've got you all set up to attend the wedding."

"I'm looking forward to it." Wyatt didn't miss the way Caroline looked at Nathan with disbelief on her face. Yeah, he was looking forward to it—looking forward to some time with Caroline Keller.

***

The church fellowship hall buzzed with activity as Caroline, along with her cousin Val, instructed the youth group volunteers on how to serve the meal for the Valentine's banquet. Afterward, Caroline made one last check of the room to make sure each table covered in a red-and-white-checked tablecloth had a candle centerpiece.

As she returned to the kitchen, she glanced at the clock on the far wall. People would be arriving any minute. Would Wyatt be among them? In his remaining days at the nursing home, he had never attended any of the activities, and she had never seen him again after that day Nathan and Melanie had gone to visit Wyatt. She didn't know why she cared. He was gone from the nursing home. She tried to tell herself that she didn't care if he showed tonight.

Caroline hadn't missed the pinched look on his face when Melanie had suggested he go to the banquet with Caroline. Then she'd seen relief flood his eyes when she'd said she had to help with the setup. Why did that bother her?

Then there was the matter of the wedding. Wyatt would be at the wedding, too. Caroline still hadn't figured that one out. Even if he was an important client, why would Nathan have invited a client to the wedding? If she asked Nathan, that would only fuel the matchmaking fires. She certainly didn't want to do that.

"Hey, is everything set?"

Caroline turned at the sound of her uncle Ray's voice and smiled. "It is. Are you set up for the singing?"

"You bet." Uncle Ray, tall and slightly rotund with a full head of brown hair, stood in the doorway and motioned toward the small stage at the far end of the fellowship hall. "Are you going to sing for us tonight? You'd look mighty pretty up there on the stage in your red dress."

Caroline let out a sick little laugh as she ran a hand down the skirt of the long-sleeved silk dress. "Thank you, but you know I won't be singing."

Uncle Ray let out a big belly laugh. "You know we got your uncle Carl to sing a couple of years ago at the Memorial Day picnic, and now we can't keep the microphone away from him."

"That won't happen with me. I will spare the guests and not sing."

"I hear there's a young man who will be sitting with you at your table tonight."

Caroline forced herself not to frown. "And where did you hear such a rumor?"

Uncle Ray tapped the side of his head. "I have my sources. You know Julianne and Lukas had their first date at this banquet. Look at them now. Maybe this is the beginning of something for you."

Caroline's stomach curdled. "Uncle Ray, I don't know who's been filling your head with nonsense about me and anyone. It's a total fabrication."

"Hmmm." Uncle Ray rubbed his chin, then chortled. "We'll have to see about that."

"I have work to do." Caroline hoped for the end of this discussion, and she certainly didn't want Val to get wind of it. Or maybe she was already part of the small-town gossip. Caroline hoped not.

"I'm sure you do, but you can't outrun the local grapevine. It'll find you every time. And you know your grandma Addie will have her hand in any matchmaking that occurs. Just look how well she did for your brother."

Caroline couldn't believe she'd even bothered to acknowledge her uncle's assertion. Wyatt hadn't said he was coming. So if he didn't, that would prove her point. But she couldn't ignore the tiny piece of her heart that wanted him to be there tonight. Foolish heart.

"Looks like we're all set." Val came to stand beside Caroline. "What were you and Uncle Ray talking about?"

"He was trying to get me to sing." Caroline chuckled. "That would clear the room. I'll leave the singing to Julianne, Elise, and Nathan. They got all the good singing genes in the Keller family."

"And isn't it interesting that they both married guys who can sing." Val leaned closer. "And did I hear correctly that your date for the evening is Wyatt Bayer?"

Caroline used all her willpower not to show her agitation. She put on her sweetest smile. "Now where did you hear that? If I had a date, would I be here doing setup?"

"Sure. Because he's coming with his grandparents, because he can't drive."

Caroline held her smile in place. "You still didn't tell me where you heard this rumor."

Val pushed a strand of light-brown hair behind one

ear. Her brown eyes twinkled. "I can read the place cards on the tables."

"Just because his name's on a place card doesn't mean he'll be here."

"And why not?"

"I don't keep tabs on him, but I know for sure that I don't have a date with Wyatt Bayer. He might sit at my table because he and Nathan do business together, but that's all. I have no idea whether Wyatt will be here or not."

"Oh, oh, oh. Someone protests too much."

Caroline wanted to roll her eyes, but she just gave a shrug. "Believe what you'd like."

Val put on an impish grin. "I'll believe what I see."

"You won't see anything."

"I'll reserve judgment."

Caroline refused to take the bait. "People will be arriving any minute. I'll help Maisey take tickets."

Ignoring her cousin's laughter, Caroline marched to the entrance of the fellowship hall, where Maisey already sat at the table near the door. "Are we ready?"

Maisey patted the paper lying in front of her on the small table covered in a red cloth. "The list is right here. We check them off as they give us their tickets."

"Do you have a special someone with you tonight?" Caroline fiddled with the nearby pen and wished she could take the question back. Now Maisey would probably ask her the same thing.

"Yeah, Alex Martin."

"I remember him. I used to babysit him when he was

little. It's hard to think of him as grown up."

Maisey wrinkled her nose. "We're really just friends."

"It's good to be friends. Maybe it'll become something more."

Maisey shook her head. "I'm not sure I want that. I just don't see him as more than a friend."

"That's okay." Caroline breathed a sigh of relief. Maybe Maisey hadn't heard the gossip.

"Ms. Caroline, I have the best news."

"What's that?"

Maisey clasped her hands together. "Your brother Nathan brought me this application to fill out today. It's for a scholarship to go to nursing school. He says all I have to do is fill it out and give it back to him, and my schooling will be paid for. Isn't that amazing?"

"Wow! It certainly is." Caroline let her mind wrap around Maisey's good news. Who was giving her a scholarship? "Did Nathan say where the scholarship is from?"

Maisey shook her head. "He said an anonymous donor was giving scholarships to deserving students. So I guess I'll never know. I wish I could thank that person."

"You could write a thank-you and give it to Nathan. I'm sure he'll pass it along."

"Oh, that's a good idea. I can put it in with my application." Maisey's smile covered her whole face. "Thanks for that idea."

"You're welcome." Caroline glanced into the

hallway. "Looks like we have our first arrivals."

In the next few minutes, Caroline and Maisey took tickets and pointed people to their assigned tables. Thankfully, when Nathan, Melanie, Julianne, and Lukas checked in, they didn't mention anything about Wyatt.

Each time the outside door opened on the other side of the hallway, Caroline looked in that direction. She didn't want to think she was looking for Wyatt, but she couldn't deny that she was. He was haunting her just like he'd done in fifth grade when he'd taunted her all the way home from school. His no-show taunted her now.

"Hi, Alex." Maisey's voice brought Caroline back to the task at hand.

"Hey, Maisey. You look nice in your red sweater." Alex smiled down at the young woman.

"Thanks." A blush rose in Maisey's cheeks. "I've already turned in our tickets."

"That's good."

Caroline didn't miss the admiration in the young man's blue eyes as he gazed at Maisey. Caroline wasn't so sure Maisey had the correct read on Alex's intentions. His look said more than friendship. "Maisey, you and Alex go on and find your table. I can handle the rest of check-in."

"Okay. Thanks." Maisey hopped up from her chair. "See you later."

Caroline waved as Maisey and Alex headed toward the tables nearer the stage. They were complete opposites. His tall frame and dark hair contrasted with her petite figure and blond hair. They made a cute couple.

"Hello there."

Caroline's heart skipped a beat as the familiar voice made her turn her attention away from the young couple. "Hi."

Wyatt stared down at her with his expressive dark-brown eyes. A lopsided smile split his face as he turned to his grandparents, who stood behind him. "Gram, Gramps, you remember Caroline Keller?"

George and Denise Bayer nodded and smiled as Denise stepped forward, her graying hair forming a curly cloud around her face. "Yes, I remember you spoke to the ladies' mission group when you were home on furlough from the mission field three years ago. Are you on furlough again?"

Caroline shook her head. "I'm home to stay, and I'm working at the nursing home."

"Oh yes. Wyatt mentioned that. So sorry I forgot." Denise patted Wyatt's arm. "We're so happy that he's finally well enough to come home."

"That's a good thing." Caroline smiled back, glad she didn't have to explain why she was no longer on the mission field. No one knew of the trial she had endured there. Instead of doing what she had promised God, she was doing work she wasn't trained for in a nursing home in her hometown. An icicle of guilt about her decision not to return to her mission left a cold spot in her heart, but the hurt lingered. She was lost in a blizzard of doubt about that decision.

Looking dangerously handsome in his western-cut jacket and red tie covered in cowboy boots, Wyatt held out several tickets. "I'll just get Gram and Gramps settled, then I'll join you."

"That's not necessary."

"Sure it is. We can't just leave you sitting here all alone."

Sure you can. The words sat on the tip of Caroline's tongue, but she didn't say them. What was she to make of his attention, of how he was acting like it was a date? Her breath caught at the thought.

As Wyatt thumped across the fellowship hall with his cane and halting gait, Caroline's heart thumped along with the sound. Who was Wyatt Bayer? The rotten kid who had tormented her on the way home from school? The kid with a chip on his shoulder during their high school years? A world-famous cowboy? A grumpy patient at the nursing home? Or this man who was taking care of his grandparents?

After Wyatt settled his grandparents at the table with Nathan and Melanie, he hobbled his way toward Caroline. She didn't want to stare, but her gaze was drawn to him against her will. His lopsided grin did nothing to slow the rate of her heartbeat. She took a deep breath and forced herself to smile. She would get through this evening. She would.

"Hey." Wyatt sat on the empty chair next to Caroline and leaned his cane against the nearby wall. "Got almost everyone checked in?"

Caroline's heart raced, and she couldn't catch her

breath. For a moment she was back in Kenya on a dusty road in the heat of the day. She gave herself a mental shake. She was not in Kenya. She was here in Kellersburg in the church fellowship hall. Had Wyatt's proximity triggered that flashback? How often would this happen?

She gave Wyatt a sideways glance and hoped she appeared normal as she tried to calm her heart. "A little over half."

"So we've got some work ahead of us." He looked over the list. "How many of these people do I know?"

"You might know my cousins that were all in school at the same time we were. Julianne, Elise, Val, and Carrie." The normal conversation settled Caroline.

"I vaguely remember them." Wyatt's voice trailed away, as if recalling something from long ago.

"So how are you doing since you got out of jail?"

Wyatt chuckled. "Me and my trusty cane are doing great. The physical therapist continues to torture me. She says it's for my own good, but I wonder."

"I'm glad. Not about the torture from the PT, but that you're getting better."

Before she could think of something to say next, several couples arrived and turned in their tickets. She introduced Wyatt to the others, including her cousin Elise and her husband, Seth.

"Hey, you're the one who's on the rodeo circuit, aren't you?" Seth asked.

"Was." Wyatt tapped the top of the cane. "I was injured, and I've been rehabbing here in Kellersburg, where my grandparents live. It looks like my days on the rodeo circuit are over."

Seth shook his head. "I'm sorry to hear that. Are you in town to stay?"

"I'm not sure what my future holds. I'm still working with a physical therapist."

"Tina Forsythe?"

Wyatt smiled. "Yeah. She's a drill sergeant disguised as a physical therapist."

Seth laughed out loud. "For sure. I was in a bad car accident when I first moved to Kellersburg and spent a number of weeks in the nursing home, and Tina was my therapist. So I know what you're talking about. She's excellent. She'll get you into shape."

Wyatt sighed. "Not in good enough shape to get back on the rodeo circuit."

"That's too bad." Seth shook his head. "We hope you'll stick around."

Wyatt hunched his shoulders. "Can't say for sure. I'll think about it."

"Caroline, you should talk him into staying." Elise eyed Caroline with a conspiratorial look.

"I'm sure he can make up his own mind." Caroline wished Elise and Seth would just go to their table and quit trying to pressure Wyatt into staying in town.

Elise tugged on Seth. "We'd better find our table so we don't hold up the line. See you later."

"Sure." Caroline gave a little wave as Elise and Seth walked away.

A pained look crossed Wyatt's face. "Can you tell

me if your cousin is pregnant?"

Caroline chuckled. "She is."

Wyatt tapped the side of his head. "I thought so, but I wasn't going to ask and be wrong."

"Yeah. It's not always a good idea to ask a woman if she's pregnant, especially if that's not the case." Caroline grinned. "The baby's due in September. I believe someone told me they're having a girl. Olivia, their little girl, will love having a sister." Caroline let out a little sigh. "I always wished I'd had a sister, someone to share secrets with. My brothers think I'm Dad's princess just because I'm the youngest and the only girl."

"Aren't you?" Wyatt's eyes twinkled with laughter.

"What makes you think that?" Caroline eyed Wyatt.

"Just a guess." He shrugged. "And what kind of secrets would you share?"

"I don't know. It was a silly wish."

Wyatt gave her a thoughtful glance. "It's not silly. I wish I'd had a brother or a sister to share stuff with, but some families don't get along. So maybe it was just as well that I didn't have a brother or sister."

Caroline nodded, not sure how to respond. She should be thankful for her brothers and the wonderful family she'd grown up in. Wyatt had had no one while he'd been growing up. No one to share the good or the bad.

"Hey, I didn't mean to make the conversation gloomy." He glanced away.

Caroline had never thought of him as someone who

would divulge a wish to her, unless it was his wish for her to stop preaching and go away. What had changed since that day she had delivered his evening meal?

A last-minute flurry of arrivals kept them from discussing any more personal things. Caroline sensed Wyatt's withdrawal, as if he had realized he'd revealed too much.

Finally Caroline tapped the sheet of paper in front of her. "That's it. We've got everyone checked in. Thanks for your help."

"You're welcome," Wyatt said with a slight nod. "You can call on me any time to help."

Caroline gave him a curious glance. "You'd better be careful what you volunteer for. I've got all kinds of jobs I could use you for at the nursing home."

Wyatt gave her a wry smile. "I don't want to hang around that place any more than I have to. Physical therapy is about all I can stand."

Caroline turned to him. "But wouldn't it be fun to help me entertain the residents?"

Wyatt narrowed his gaze. "And just exactly what could I do to help you entertain?"

"Be my bingo caller." As the words came out of her mouth, Caroline wanted them back. What was she doing? Trying to be normal? How could that happen when his presence had just triggered a terrible flashback? But maybe part of normal was doing what she'd always done—encouraged people to be helpers.

"You're not serious."

This was her chance to back out, but she wouldn't.

She would face her demons. "I am. I know the little old ladies will love you."

"Is this your way of helping me be kind?"

"I think you're capable of doing that on your own, but I can always use a volunteer."

He opened his mouth as if to say something, then closed it just as quickly as he shook his head.

"Remember what you said. 'You can call on me any time to help.'" Caroline gave him an impish smile. "I'm counting on that."

"Guess I opened my mouth and walked right into your trap."

"I wasn't trapping you. I'm merely taking you up on your offer." Caroline suppressed a smile.

Wyatt let out a sigh. "When is bingo?"

"I can make it whenever is convenient for you."

"But what if my convenience isn't convenient for your residents?"

"We'll make it convenient." Caroline gave him a wry smile. "Face it, Wyatt. You're stuck helping me."

"And I can't think of anyone I'd rather be stuck with."

"Since we've got everyone checked in, let's join the others at our table." Jumping up from the table, Caroline hoped her face wasn't turning red. The invitation had been made, and he'd accepted. She was still questioning why she'd invited him to help with bingo. She had to look at it as healing for both of them, not a problem of her own making.

CHAPTER THREE

Wyatt hobbled to keep up with Caroline as she charged toward their assigned table. He had done it again. Said way too much. What was there about her that made him second-guess himself right and left?

Ever since he'd joined the rodeo circuit, women had trailed after him. They tried to impress him. Now he was trying to impress Caroline Keller without much success. She tolerated his presence because Nathan and Melanie had pushed Caroline and him together. He would have to make the best of the evening, despite her resistance.

But hadn't she just invited him to help her at the nursing home? He should take that as a good sign, but maybe her missionary instincts just kicked in as she tried to involve people in her do-good work. Actually she had already succeeded in getting him to do good. Nathan had mentioned how excited Maisey was when she'd learned about the scholarship. That knowledge warmed Wyatt's heart. He wanted to do good. Maybe it would make up for all the bad he'd done when he was a surly kid.

When Wyatt reached the table, he pulled out Caroline's chair, and she looked at him with surprise.

"Thanks." Her surprise morphed into a smile as she settled on her chair. "George and Denise, I hear you're going to be part of the couples' game, along with Melanie and Nathan."

Denise laughed as she patted George's arm. "I don't know how we got roped into this, but we're going to give it our best shot. I hear there's a trophy that goes to the winners."

Caroline nodded. "It's a doozy of a trophy, not one you'd display on your mantel. I'm not sure who made it, but it's pretty cheesy."

A lively discussion about the couples' game ensued, and Wyatt observed Caroline. She had a natural way with people that he envied. While he watched, his mind buzzed with his attraction to the banker's daughter, someone he'd admired from a distance during his school years. Were they on a more equal footing now? He wanted her to know him as something more than the son of the town drunks, who had spent more time in the bars than at home.

Did she think he'd never grown beyond that rotten kid who had taunted her on the way home from school? He had to show her he was different, but he'd gotten off to a dreadful start with his behavior in the nursing home. Thankfully, she didn't know how he'd treated his grandparents while he'd been there. Things were good with them now. They were always willing to forgive, because they loved him. He would be forever grateful for that love.

Wyatt wanted her to know the man behind the rodeo star, but he wasn't sure that was possible. How could he show her when he wasn't sure who he was? His identity had been all tied up in being a rodeo cowboy, and that had been taken away from him. So who was he now? Where was he headed? If he didn't know the answer, there was little chance he could make Caroline see him differently.

As Wyatt pondered his plan of action, Ray Keller hopped onto the stage.

"Good evening, everyone." Ray waved the microphone in the air. "It's good to see you all here tonight. Let's get the evening started with a prayer of thanks for our food."

Wyatt bowed his head along with those around him. After Ray finished praying, he punched a button on a nearby machine. Soft background music floated through the air. Teenagers dressed in white shirts and black pants hurried through the room as they delivered salads to each table.

While Wyatt ate his salad, his thoughts took him back to his first year on the circuit. He'd fallen hard for Shelby Pollard. He didn't know why he was thinking about her tonight. Or maybe he did. The last time he'd worn a suit coat and tie was the last time he'd taken Shelby out to dinner. He'd been in love, but he'd been fooled. Maybe he was just a fool for love. He wasn't in love with Caroline, but here he was entertaining romantic thoughts about her.

Foolish thinking for sure!

"You look lost in thought." Nathan's voice made Wyatt look in the other man's direction.

Wyatt shook his head. "Just thinking about how long

it's been since I've worn this suit jacket. I didn't have much use for it when I was on the circuit."

"I guess you'd look pretty silly wearing a suit coat while riding a bucking horse." Caroline smiled at him. "Your tie would be flying."

With a chuckle, Wyatt glanced at Caroline, the image of a flying red tie tickling his thoughts. That image was better than the dreams he had about flying through the air himself and waking just before he hit the ground. He didn't want to think about the bad dreams that haunted his sleep. He was here with Caroline, so he should be thinking happy thoughts, not remembering all the things that had brought him pain.

"Do you miss the rodeo? How soon before you get to return?" Melanie asked, a sweet smile on her face.

The question made Wyatt stop his fork halfway to his mouth. Yeah, he missed it, but he was never going back unless something changed. Talking about it only reminded him of what he had lost and could never get back.

"Melanie, I guess you haven't heard. Wyatt's injury will keep him from returning to the rodeo." Caroline's gaze flitted between Wyatt and Melanie.

Melanie's brown eyes widened as she placed a hand on her chest. "I'm so sorry. I didn't know. That has to be tough."

Yeah, tough. He should be tough and not let it bother him, but he couldn't shake his desire to return to the rodeo. A broken dream. Could he find a new dream? He was lost in a desert of doubt about where his life was headed. Wyatt finally nodded but didn't say a thing.

Nathan patted Melanie's arm. "Sweetheart, it's a subject Wyatt doesn't want to talk about."

A frown puckered Melanie's brow. "I'm so sorry I mentioned it."

Wyatt placed his fork next to his empty salad plate. "Don't worry about it. It's something I have to get used to, but it's not my favorite subject right now."

"Okay. Let's talk about Caroline's big move." Melanie put on a perky expression.

Wyatt glanced at Caroline as he narrowed his gaze. "You're moving? You just got here."

Caroline chuckled. "I'm just moving out of my parents' house and into the house I'm renting from Nathan."

"Yeah, I'm giving up my bachelor pad to move in with this lovely lady and her two rambunctious sons." Nathan gave Melanie a peck on the cheek. "She makes the best Italian food this side of Italy."

Pink tinged Melanie's cheeks as she gazed at Nathan. "You always say that."

"It's true." Nathan glanced around the table. "You should taste her manicotti."

"Does that mean we're all invited over to your house for dinner after you get back from your honeymoon?" Caroline eyed Nathan.

"Inviting yourself to dinner? Do you think that's good form?" Nathan smirked.

Melanie poked Nathan on the arm. "I think that's a lovely idea. Be looking for an invitation."

Nathan put an arm around Melanie's shoulders. "I was only teasing my sister. We'd be glad to have you all over. The boys will especially like it."

"Then we'll plan on it." Excitement lit up Melanie's face.

"You don't have to include us." Denise glanced around the table. "You young folks should get together."

"You should definitely be included. I love to entertain." Melanie smiled. "And when I make one of my Italian dishes, I make enough to feed a lot of people."

George chuckled. "Well, in that case, we'll have to come. We don't want any food to go to waste."

"It will go to my waist." Denise patted her stomach as she laughed.

George leaned over and kissed his wife on the cheek. "You look marvelous to me, dear."

Denise blushed. "He's so sweet."

Wyatt took in his grandparents' exchange. Why hadn't he ever noticed how much they loved each other? Maybe because he'd been self-absorbed as a kid and even as an adult when he made his biannual trek to Kellersburg while he'd been on the circuit. He'd like to share a love like that with a special woman.

His gaze slid to Caroline, who laughed at something Melanie had said. Caroline fascinated him more than he'd like to admit. Besides being pretty, she'd been willing to give up her cushy life in Kellersburg to help those less fortunate in a foreign country. What did it take to do that? He wanted to find out.

What would it take to capture her interest?

Wyatt shook the question away. He'd asked himself that question too often lately. He didn't need to go there. His life was in turmoil. He shouldn't add a romantic interest to the mix.

"I hear you're going to be part of the entertainment tonight." Caroline's statement brought Wyatt's crazy thoughts to a halt.

Wyatt looked at Nathan. "How does she know about this?"

"It seems that my sweet wife-to-be can't keep a secret, but she doesn't know the whole story." Nathan smiled wryly as he patted Melanie's arm. "So we're good."

Wyatt didn't know how he'd let Nathan rope him into joining his uncle's chorus, but it would probably be fun to see the look on Caroline's face when it took place.

Before anyone else could comment, the servers whipped away the salad plates and replaced them with the entrée.

"You know, even though this is good, Melanie makes it better." Nathan cut a piece of his chicken parmesan.

Melanie smiled at Nathan. "If you keep bragging on me, they'll all be disappointed when they come for dinner."

Nathan shook his head. "Never. You will wow them with your cooking."

"I can hardly wait to see these two lovebirds in the couples' competition," Caroline said.

"We'll only have a chance if all the questions are food related." Melanie gestured toward Denise and George. "I don't know how we can compete against people who have been married for over fifty years."

George chuckled as he shook his head. "You might have a good chance. I think I've forgotten almost everything I know about Denise. My brain just doesn't recall things so well these days. She keeps telling me that my favorite word is *doohickey*, because I can't remember what something is called."

"Just don't call me your doohickey." Denise chuckled.

Everyone at the table laughed, and Wyatt joined in. It felt good to laugh and share this time with his grandparents and the others at the table, especially Caroline. They were surely destined for some kind of connection, but where it would lead was a huge question. Was he brave enough to find out the answer?

As the meal continued, Wyatt sat listening to the conversation buzzing around him. He thought about how he had a lot of amends to make, especially to his grandparents.

"You're awfully quiet. Are you finding the company boring?" Caroline's voice was barely above a whisper as she leaned closer.

Trying to keep his voice as low as hers, he took in her concerned expression. "No. Just have a lot on my mind."

"You're supposed to be enjoying yourself, not saving the world."

He gave her a wry smile. "And how do you know that's what I'm trying to do?"

"You look awfully serious."

"I'm a serious person."

"Hmm. I never thought of you that way."

"So you've been thinking about me?" He smirked.

A pink tinge slowly crept across Caroline's cheeks. She straightened in her chair. "Yes, I've been praying for your successful recovery. The extent of your injuries has caused me to think about you quite a bit."

"You mean it's not my considerable charm that has you thinking about me?"

"Are you fishing for compliments?"

Wyatt grinned. She knew how to flirt. She surprised him, and he liked that. "Maybe."

"Sorry. I'm fresh out."

Wyatt laughed out loud. "That puts me in my place."

Caroline grimaced. "I didn't mean for it to come out like that. That wasn't very nice."

"No offense taken. I kind of like sparring with you, Caroline Keller."

Caroline's cheeks pinkened again as she stared at him. "I should behave myself."

"Wow! Caroline is misbehaving. You've got my interest."

Caroline huffed. "Quit teasing me."

"But it's so fun."

"You win." Caroline let out a sorry chuckle.

"Good. What do I win?"

Caroline gave him an exasperated look. "What do

you want to win?"

"What do I want to win?" Wyatt's smile grew mischievous. "That's a dangerous question, but I'll come up with an answer and let you know."

"Caroline, you're in trouble now." Nathan chuckled.

"Have you been eavesdropping on our conversation?" Caroline shot Nathan an annoyed look.

"Just looking out for my little sister. I wouldn't want some cowboy to come along and take advantage."

Caroline gave her brother an annoyed look. His statement was all too close to the truth of why she hadn't returned to the mission field. But Nathan didn't know anything about that. No one did. She just had to put it out of her mind. "Okay, you two. You've had your fun."

"Not nearly enough. The fun has just begun."

Caroline's frown deepened. "What are you guys up to?"

Nathan winked at Caroline. "Wouldn't you like to know?"

"Yes, I would." Caroline looked at Melanie for help. "Do you know what's going on?"

Melanie shrugged. "Something. All I know is they're singing later."

Caroline sighed. "Okay. I can wait to find out."

Wyatt laughed along with Nathan. "She says that, but I know she's dying of curiosity."

While the two men chuckled, the teens whisked away the dinner plates and served the strawberry shortcake.

Caroline took a big bite. "This is delicious."

"But Melanie makes—"

"It better." Caroline finished the sentence for her brother, and everyone at the table laughed.

While they ate dessert, Ray Keller once again took the stage. "Okay, ladies and gentlemen, in a few minutes we'll have our couples' competition, and after that, we'll get on with the singing. We've got some talented people who are going to entertain us tonight. I want you to welcome our MC for the evening, Seth Finley."

Applause filled the room as Seth took the stage and commandeered the microphone. "Good evening, everyone. I hope you've had your fill of the delicious food and you're ready to cheer on our contestants in the couples' competition."

Again applause filled the room as the couples made their way to the stage and the chairs set up for them. They joked with each other as they took their seats. Wyatt's heart filled with pride as he watched his grandparents. He wished he'd been more attentive during the years he'd been away riding broncs and wrestling steers. They had made a home for him when his parents hadn't cared.

Caroline clapped enthusiastically. "Your grandparents are so cute together."

"They do make a great couple." Wyatt gazed at Caroline and wondered whether he could persuade her to take a chance on him. An excellent thought, but highly unlikely. "So who's going to win? My grandparents or your brother and his bride-to-be?"

"I'm thinking your grandparents."

"Me, too." Wyatt smiled. "Great minds think alike."

"Thank you for recognizing that I have a great mind."

"You're welcome. You do." *Among other lovely attributes.*

The competition started as the men were escorted to one of the Sunday school classrooms, while Seth asked questions of the ladies. After the men returned, they had to answer the same questions. Laughter filled the room over some of the responses from the men that didn't match what their wives had said. Then the ladies were escorted offstage while the men answered questions. Several rounds ensued, with Seth asking the questions and his wife, Elise, keeping score.

"Seth sounds like a professional MC," Wyatt whispered.

"That's because he worked as a cruise director for a number of years. That's where Elise met him."

"*The Love Boat*?"

"Not quite." Caroline leaned closer. "Seth broke Elise's heart, but he realized he still loved her and moved here just to win her back. Just a wonderful love story."

Wyatt thought about the love story he'd like to create with Caroline. His mind was on one track tonight—a track that he feared led to nowhere. And even before it got to nowhere, he was sure she would derail the idea. But he could hope...

When the competition ended, Denise and George held the trophy high while everyone applauded. As they returned to the table, they were all smiles. Nathan and Melanie congratulated their opponents.

Nathan held out the chair for Melanie. "We may not have won, but at least I know I'm not completely ignorant when it comes to knowing my future wife. Just two more weeks. The wedding can't come soon enough."

"It'll be here before you know it." Caroline glanced from Nathan to Melanie.

"And speaking of the wedding, Caroline, you'll need to give Mom, Dad, and Wyatt a ride to the airport," Nathan said.

"I will?"

"Yeah. Wyatt here won't be able to drive for a while." Nathan nodded.

Wyatt gave Caroline an apologetic look. "Yeah. Sorry you're going to be stuck with me."

"I don't mind as long as you don't throw any rocks or call me names."

Wyatt laughed, hoping she was just joking. "I think I can manage that. I've outgrown my rock-throwing and name-calling days."

"Good to hear."

Seth tapped on the microphone to get everyone's attention again. "Okay, folks, we have a treat for you tonight. Carl Keller and his band of merry men will perform a special song. Give a big round of applause for them as they take the stage."

Wyatt followed Nathan and several other men to the stage. Wyatt grabbed a guitar that sat off to the side and pulled the strap over his head. He was looking forward to this little surprise for Caroline. He smiled as Caroline's uncle Carl took the microphone.

Carl looked at his fellow singers. "You guys all ready for this?"

A chorus of yeses filled the air.

"Since we're all ready, we have a special surprise for my niece, Caroline. She's been away on the mission field, and we'd like to welcome her home with our rendition of 'Sweet Caroline.'"

The melodious instrumental introduction to the familiar song sounded through the room. As the men gathered around the two standing microphones, the attendees clapped to the song. Wyatt took in Caroline's reaction, his heart beating in double time to the music. She laughed and cried at the same time as Melanie hugged her.

As the song came to a close, applause erupted. Then Carl stepped to the microphone. "Okay, everyone, we're going to do that chorus one more time and give a resounding welcome home to our own sweet Caroline."

Voices raised the song, and Caroline cried and laughed some more as she waved and voiced her thank-yous as she threw kisses to the crowd. Wyatt wished he were on the receiving end of a real kiss. He didn't know why he kept torturing himself with such thoughts.

When the song ended for the second time, everyone cheered and clapped. Wyatt smiled in her direction, and she smiled back as their gazes met. Her smile took his breath away. He loved that this was truly a surprise and that she appreciated the sentiment behind the song and those who sang it. Her family, her church, and the whole community obviously loved her. Wyatt wanted a part of that.

CHAPTER FOUR

Nathan kissed his bride, and the guests applauded and cheered. With the sun shining down on them, the bride and groom, all smiles, made their way toward the aisle between the chairs set on the sand. A sea breeze swayed the sea oats in a rhythmic dance on the dunes between the flat sand and the old historic inn just yards away. Caroline followed on the arm of her older brother, Marcus.

Marcus glanced down at her. "Now it's your turn."

Caroline tried to laugh. "Don't get any ideas. Single works for me."

Marcus patted her arm. "I've observed a certain cowboy who might have other ideas."

"What are you talking about?"

"Wyatt Bayer has his eye on you for sure."

"Your imagination."

Marcus shook his head. "I've got that guy pegged, but I'm watching him. I don't want him trifling with my little sister's heart."

Caroline gave Marcus an annoyed frown. "Your imagination is running wild. That man has his pick of women. I don't think he's much interested in me, so he won't be doing any trifling."

"Just ask Becca."

"What does your wife know about it?"

"She's got eyes just like I do, and we both see the same thing." Marcus took both of Caroline's arms as he gazed into her eyes. "Don't dismiss his interest. Nathan tells me Wyatt is a good guy."

"We don't have time to talk about it. We have guests to greet." Caroline put a smile on her face that she hoped looked genuine. She didn't want her brothers pushing Wyatt at her. She wasn't ready for any kind of relationship. She wished she were brave enough to let her family know why.

Caroline took her place next to Marcus. She smiled and shook hands and greeted her relatives and family friends, young and old, who had come to share in Nathan and Melanie's day. She even greeted Wyatt, who didn't seem the least bit interested in her as he greeted her in return. One of her younger female cousins appeared to have his ear as they made their way into the historic hotel near the beach.

While the photographer took photos of the wedding party, Caroline chided herself for letting thoughts of Wyatt fill her mind. She should blame it all on Marcus. He'd crammed her mind with possibilities—possibilities that would only lead to heartache. Marcus was right about one thing. She wouldn't let Wyatt trifle with her heart.

After the photos, Nathan and Melanie appeared in the reception area to the sounds of applause and the gurgling of the tiered fountain that sat at the far end of the open space in the center of the first floor. Brightly colored mosaic tiles created designs on the walls and floor. Hanging plants decorated pillars at the edge of the open space where archways led to the rooms on the first floor.

Caroline found her seat next to Marcus at the head table. Her gaze was immediately drawn to where Wyatt sat with her grandma Addie Keller, who had recently lost her husband of nearly sixty years. Caroline's heart hurt when she thought of how she had missed seeing her grandfather one last time. She'd still been in Kenya when she'd received word that he had died. Sadness threatened, but she couldn't be sad on this happy occasion.

But the past year had been one of turmoil and melancholy. Being home with family helped to soothe some of the wounds, but somehow she would have to find a way to tell someone why she wasn't returning to the mission field. She had almost told her friend Ashley, but Caroline didn't want to burden her friend during the happy occasion of her wedding. Besides, it just seemed easier not to talk about it.

Caroline forced herself to think about something else. She didn't need to wallow in her own pity. This was a day to celebrate her brother's happy day. Happiness surrounded her. She should soak up as much as possible and store it away to combat any despondency in her own life. She had a toast to give. She should ponder that.

Marcus leaned closer. "You're looking a little glum. Wishing you were sitting with Wyatt instead of being stuck with your big brother?"

"No, thinking about my toast."

"I'm sure you'll give the best one. You were always good at public speaking."

"This isn't about giving a speech. It's about sharing my heartfelt wishes for Nathan and Melanie."

"See. You've already got the right attitude." Marcus smiled.

"I'd have a better attitude if you'd quit with the matchmaking comments."

Marcus's smile morphed into a grin. "I knew you were thinking about Wyatt. Don't be surprised if Grandma Addie isn't promoting you to him."

Caroline groaned. *Not Grandma, too.* "I think she's wasting her breath."

"Grandma never wastes her breath."

Caroline gave Marcus a wry smile. "I know."

"Good."

Throughout the meal, Caroline tried her best not to let her gaze drift in Wyatt's direction. But time and time again, she found herself looking his way. He laughed at something Grandma Addie said. She would definitely keep him entertained. Was she filling his ear with ideas about her granddaughter? Caroline's thoughts wavered on the idea. An interest in any man would make Caroline confront the recent past she was trying to forget. How long could she keep it bottled up?

As most of the guests finished the meal, the DJ set up his equipment. Not long afterward, the bride and groom had their first dance, followed by the mother-son and father-daughter dances. Melanie danced with her former father-in-law. The duo brought tears to Caroline's eyes. Melanie had told Caroline how her former in-laws had been negative toward her for years. Now love and respect replaced the prior animosity. Melanie's story put hope in Caroline's heart. God could take all the bad stuff and make it good. She prayed that would happen in her life.

Heartfelt laughter and camaraderie encompassed the gathering as Marcus and Caroline gave their toasts. Following the toasts, Nathan and Melanie cut the cake. Then Melanie threw her bouquet and Nathan tossed the garter, which Wyatt caught, a grin on his face.

Caroline watched Wyatt and marveled that he'd managed to catch the garter while leaning on his cane. Maybe it had all been preplanned. Nathan had made sure Wyatt would catch it just as her friend Ashley had made sure Caroline caught the bridal bouquet at Peter and Ashley's wedding. Did it mean anything? Most likely not. Marriage was only on Caroline's mind because she was at her brother's wedding.

Caroline snagged herself a piece of cake and headed back to the table. As she crossed the outer edge of the dance floor, Wyatt stumbled toward her.

"Caroline, how about a dance?"

Caroline stared at Wyatt as he leaned heavily on his cane. "Are you drunk?"

"No, ma'am. Never touch anything with alcohol in it. I don't want to end up like my parents." With a smile tugging at the corners of his mouth, Wyatt eyed her, the garter still in his hand.

"But you look a little unsteady on your feet."

"If I sway or stumble, it's because one of my legs is shorter than the other thanks to my carelessness and a thousand-pound horse."

"Why are you following me?"

"I was trying to get a dance. I've come to collect my prize. After all, at the Valentine banquet you did tell me I'd won."

A little frown creased Caroline's brow. "If I dance with you, will you quit following me?"

He rubbed his chin. "I don't know. Why don't you dance with me and find out."

Caroline's frown deepened. "That doesn't sound like such a good deal to me. Are you sure you're not drunk?"

"If I'm drunk, I'm drunk on you."

Caroline's heart tripped. She took a deep breath and tried not to let his statement affect her. She didn't know how to deal with a man anymore. "What's that supposed to mean?"

"Dance with me and find out."

Caroline studied his handsome face. It would be so easy to fall for this guy and his charm. Why was she so afraid? But she knew the answer to that. She feared her reaction to close contact with a man. "I don't want to dance."

"With me, or you just don't want to dance period?" Sadness radiated from his eyes.

"I just don't want to dance." Caroline regretted questioning his sobriety. He didn't deserve that, but the thought of dancing with him sent shivers up her spine for more than one reason.

"I know we've had our differences in the past, but I want to get to know you and for you to know me now, not how you remember me."

That was fair, but how could she tell him her reasons for wanting to keep her distance? She'd never told anyone. She would be insane to tell him.

"Caroline, you can be honest with me. If you just plain don't like me and don't want me around, I'll butt out of your life."

Caroline's heart thudded with sorrow. She swallowed a lump in her throat as she stared back at him. She wanted to like him, but could she trust him to understand the secret she harbored? He was practically a stranger, and yet he wasn't. She'd known him since they were kids.

Wyatt stepped closer.

Caroline instinctively backed away.

"Caroline." Wyatt's brown eyes studied her.

Caroline swallowed hard again as words stuck in her throat.

"Did someone hurt you?"

The sympathy in Wyatt's expression brought tears to Caroline's eyes. She blinked rapidly to keep them from spilling onto her cheeks. She pressed her lips together as she nodded.

"Would you like to tell me about it?"

Would she? Did she dare? Wyatt was the first person to notice that things weren't quite right with her. No one had questioned her sudden decision to leave the mission field. She had fooled everyone except him. How was that possible when he hadn't seen her in years?

"It's okay if you don't want to. But I want to understand what makes you fearful and sad."

Caroline let out a harsh breath. Her thoughts wrestled in her mind. "I can't talk here. It's too noisy."

"Outside?"

Outside. Alone with Wyatt. Caroline's defenses went into high gear. She couldn't.

Wyatt motioned toward the lobby on the other side of the pillars that created a separation. "There's a bench on the portico. I'll sit at one end, and you can sit at the other end. And we can talk. How does that sound? I have something I'd like to ask you."

Separated by the length of a bench. Surely he could be trusted with a crowd of people just yards away. She had to learn to trust again, but would that ever happen? "Okay."

Wyatt stared at her. "You don't sound so sure."

"I'm not." Caroline stared back, honesty her best friend.

"Okay. I won't pressure you into doing something you don't want to do, but I'd still like to understand." His eyebrows wove in a question above those soulful brown eyes.

Understand. How could he understand, when she didn't? "Promise to listen without judgment?"

"How could I begin to judge when I have so many issues of my own?"

Caroline's pulse skittered. Would he understand all the wrong choices she had made? Maybe. She had to be brave, strong, and open. Without saying a word, she scurried around the dance floor as she headed to the doors that opened onto the portico. She didn't turn around to see if Wyatt had followed. She sat on one end of the bench and waited, her heart pounding.

Wyatt appeared in the doorway, silhouetted against the light inside. He turned her way, but she couldn't read his expression. "When you make up your mind, you don't hesitate. I like that."

"May I sit here?" He stepped into the dim light, his expression still unreadable.

Caroline nodded. "Okay."

Wyatt hobbled to the bench and sat on the other end.

Caroline stared out at the pedestrian walkway that separated the beach from the hotel. Palm fronds rustled in the sea breeze as the waves tickled the sand. A half-moon lit the scene before her. If only the peaceful setting could bring peace to her heart.

"I'm going to sit here until you tell me to leave." Wyatt folded his arms across his torso and stretched his legs out in front of him, his cane settled against the side of the bench.

Caroline wasn't sure where to start or even if she wanted to start at all. She had to be brave. She hadn't been brave before. Now was the time. She licked her lips and watched the water rush to shore in the distance. Her mind rushed with hundreds of thoughts, swirling and swirling like the foaming waves on the beach.

Her voice barely above a whisper, she blurted, "A man I trusted raped me."

***

Wyatt strained to hear Caroline above the sound of the surf. Had he heard her correctly—someone had raped her? His heart hammered, and words wouldn't come. He had to say something. "Wow! I...I don't know what to say, except that I'm terribly sorry that happened to you."

Her head lowered, Caroline twisted her hands in her lap. "It was terrible."

"I can't imagine." Wyatt wanted to reach out and touch her, but he understood her reluctance to seek comfort from him. "Do you want to talk about it? Or is that too hard?"

Caroline said nothing. Maybe that was all she intended to tell him. He sat there, his heart hurting for her as the breeze rustled the palm fronds overhead. What could he say? What could he do? Just listen if she wanted to talk. Helplessness inundated him.

"When did this happen?"

No answer. Her silence made the sound of the waves louder. Finally, she raised her head and looked at him, a haunted, sorrowful look in her eyes. "Right before I left the mission field. That's why I left."

"Then not long ago?"

Taking a shaky breath, she nodded.

"Did you report it?"

Caroline shook her head and put her hands in front of her mouth in a prayerful pose as she closed her eyes.

Wyatt wanted to ask why, but he couldn't put himself in her place.

"I know I should have, but I didn't. I wish I had, but I was in a foreign country with foreign police, and sometimes the police are corrupt. And I had no idea how they would handle such a situation when neither of us are citizens of the country, and often women don't have much standing there. I should've at least said something to my fellow missionaries, but I feared they wouldn't believe me. Why would a respected doctor do something like that?"

Wyatt listened, puckering his brow with concern as the words spilled from her mouth.

Caroline took a deep breath, her head lowered. "He'd come several years to do medical work in the villages. Why should I suspect he would do something like that?"

"So he wasn't a stranger?" Wyatt balled his fist, thoughts of punching something rolling through his thoughts—punching that guy.

Caroline nodded. "We had gone out to a village with a whole group, but we split off, and I accompanied him to another village. After we had finished there, we started back, and that's when..."

"You don't have to go on."

"I just don't know why he did that. I was so gullible. He started kissing me and then got rough and wouldn't stop. There was no one to hear me tell him to stop."

Caroline's voice cracked. "And I don't know why I didn't report it."

"Trauma. You were traumatized."

"Aunt Caroline, Aunt Caroline." Wyatt turned to see Ryan and Andrew, Melanie's two sons, racing onto the portico. The boys stopped in front of Caroline. "You have to come and do the chicken dance with us."

Caroline looked at the two boys as a smile displaced her troubled expression. She stood. "Sure. I wouldn't want to miss the chicken dance."

Wyatt followed behind while Caroline's hard story stamped itself on his brain. Did this mean the end to their conversation and his plans? Probably. He figured she would never agree to go somewhere with him alone. He stood at the edge of the small dance floor and watched Caroline do the chicken dance with her nephews. He ached to make her that happy, but could she overcome what had been done to her? A dozen other questions danced in his mind to the frenetic tune filling the air.

Nathan approached, a wide smile brightening his face. Wyatt looked pointedly at his friend. "You're not doing the chicken dance?"

"No. I'll leave that to my wife and boys. I'm not sure who requested that silly song." Nathan chuckled. "I see you're not joining in either."

Wyatt waved his cane. "I don't want to fall on my face while I'm flapping my imaginary wings."

"Yeah, I see what you mean." Nathan laughed. "Thanks again for finding this place for us. It's great.

Everything has been super."

"Glad to do it." Wyatt's thought wrapped around an idea. Maybe there was a way to take that trip to the ranch he'd planned with Caroline. "Did I hear your parents and the boys are staying here and enjoying the beach while you're on your honeymoon cruise?"

"That's the plan."

"Do you suppose the boys would like to see a cattle ranch?"

Nathan shrugged. "Why do you ask?"

"The guy whose family owns this hotel also has a cattle ranch not too far away, and he's invited me to visit. I'd like to do that, and I thought Ryan and Andrew might like to go with me." Wyatt hesitated. "And I thought Caroline could drive us, since I can't drive."

"Is this a ploy to get close to my sister?"

Weighing his response, Wyatt stared at Nathan. "If it is, do you object?"

Nathan clapped Wyatt on the shoulder. "No, but I'm not sure about Caroline."

"If she agrees, will it be okay with you?"

Nathan shrugged. "You'll have to run this by Melanie and my parents. Caroline can make up her own mind without my permission."

"I would like your approval."

"I think it's Caroline's approval you'll need before mine, but I say go for it."

Relief washed over Wyatt. Now he just had to convince the other parties involved. "Thanks."

"Don't thank me yet." Nathan chuckled. "You may

have to pull out every bit of your persuasive charm."

"Are you telling me you think your sister doesn't like me?" Wyatt narrowed his gaze.

Nathan shook his head. "I didn't say that, but my observations have led me to believe my sister has a mind of her own and isn't easily persuaded."

"So I have my work cut out for me."

Nathan gave Wyatt a wry smile. "You might take some allies with you if you're up to dealing with the likes of an eight- and a nine-year-old boy."

"You mean Ryan and Andrew?"

Nathan nodded. "They seem to have their aunt Caroline dancing to their tune."

"Thanks for the advice." Wyatt saluted as the chicken dance came to an end.

He made his way toward the end of the dance floor, where Caroline was talking with Melanie, Ryan, and Andrew. As Wyatt approached the group, he mentally went through his speech, but he didn't see any way to speak to the boys before he talked to their mother. He would have to persuade the whole group at once.

"Hey, Ryan and Andrew, you guys are good at the chicken dance." Wyatt hoped for an opening.

Andrew rushed up to Wyatt. "Aunt Caroline is good, too."

Wyatt's mouth twitched with a smile as he looked over at Caroline. "You're right."

Caroline returned his smile, and his heart bumped against his rib cage. What would she say to his request? He wouldn't find out unless he asked her. "Hey, boys.

I've got something to ask you and your aunt."

"What"? Ryan and Andrew chorused as they scrambled to stand in front of Wyatt.

Wyatt watched Caroline, who followed, a curious look in her eyes. "I'm trying to collect the prize your aunt owes me."

"What does she owe you?" Ryan asked.

"My choice."

"Okay, I'll dance with you." Her arms crossed, Caroline stood ramrod straight as she stared at him.

Wyatt shook his head. "I've decided I'd rather have something else."

"What?" The word coming out of Caroline's mouth sounded like a cry for help.

Andrew tugged on Wyatt's arm. "You should've danced the chicken dance with her."

"Maybe." Wyatt gave Andrew a wry smile. "Would you like to help me get my prize?"

Andrew nodded, a big smile brightening his freckled face. "Aunt Caroline, you should give him his prize."

Caroline's expression softened as she looked at her younger nephew. "But he hasn't told me what he wants."

Andrew put his hands on his hips and stared up a Wyatt. "Yeah, you got to tell her what you want."

"Okay." Here was his opening. "I've been invited to visit my friend's ranch a couple of hours from here. I've rented a car, and I'd like you to be my driver, since I can't drive. And if it's okay with the boys' parents, they can come, too."

Andrew flew to Caroline's side. "Aunt Caroline, you have to be his driver."

Caroline stared at Wyatt over Andrew's head, a knowing look in her eyes. "I see you know the art of manipulation."

Wyatt lifted one shoulder. "You might say that."

Caroline let out a loud sigh. "We'll have to talk with Melanie and Nathan about this."

Before Caroline could turn around, Andrew and Ryan sprinted toward Melanie and Nathan. As Wyatt approached with Caroline by his side, the boys both talked at once and pointed in his direction.

Nathan smiled at Wyatt. "I see you've told the boys about your plan."

Caroline glanced at Nathan, then back at Wyatt. "So you two have talked about this before?"

"I might have mentioned it," Wyatt said.

Caroline frowned. "My parents may have something to say about this."

"What do *you* have to say?" Wyatt gave her a pointed look.

"Talk to my parents, and then I'll give you an answer." Caroline pointed to where Ginny and John Keller stood.

Wyatt made his way in that direction. Would these VIP citizens of Kellersburg be willing to entrust their daughter and new grandsons to his care? He had no idea where he stood in their eyes. As Wyatt neared the older Kellers, Ryan and Andrew buzzed by. In seconds they were engaged in an animated conversation. Wyatt slowed his step as the boys pointed in his direction for the second time. Were the youngsters pleading his case for him?

With hope in his heart, Wyatt joined the group. "Hi. Are Ryan and Andrew telling you about the invitation I've given them?"

John nodded. "Can you give us more details?"

Wyatt explained his friend's invitation and the need for a driver. "The plan is to spend a couple of days and an overnight. They have plenty of room to accommodate us."

John looked over at his wife, then at Ryan and Andrew. "Is this what you boys want to do rather than spending those two days at the beach?"

"We can do days at the beach when we get back?" Ryan said.

Her gaze focused on Wyatt, Ginny stepped forward as she put her arms around each of the boys who stood on either side of her. "So give me your timeline."

Wyatt let his plans filter through his mind. Would they please Caroline's mother? "I understand that we're having a church service on the beach in the morning, then brunch before we give Nathan and Melanie a big sendoff for their cruise. I planned to leave after that. We'd spend the rest of tomorrow and Monday on the ranch and return that evening, probably late. The boys will have the rest of the week for the beach. Does that work for you?"

Ginny looked down at the boys. "What did your mom say?"

"She said it's up to you cuz you're in charge of us while she's gone." Andrew squinted up at Ginny.

Taking in Andrew's expression, Wyatt held back a smile as he waited with trepidation for Ginny's answer. If he passed this hurdle, would Caroline agree? Surely she couldn't turn down her newly minted nephews.

Ginny took a deep breath. "I give my okay as long as your mom is agreeable."

Andrew raced off to see his mom, Ryan close behind. Wyatt smiled over at Caroline, who stood off to one side with her arms crossed. Did that closed position mean she still wasn't on board? Wyatt turned his attention to Andrew, Ryan, and Melanie.

"Wyatt, do you have your sights set on my daughter?"

John's question made Wyatt turn back. The older man stared at Wyatt. A knot formed in his stomach while his head pounded with the question. *Yes.* He wanted to say yes, but the word stuck in his mouth. Nathan had been in Wyatt's corner, but could the same be said of Caroline's dad?

"If that question is out of line, let me know." John continued to stare.

Wyatt shook the cobwebs from his brain. "It's not, and yes, I'd like to get to know Caroline better. We knew each other when we were in school, but we're grown-ups, not kids anymore. Things are a lot different for us now."

"Don't push her. She needs time to settle in after coming back from the mission field."

Did Caroline's dad suspect that something had happened to her while she'd been gone? Maybe her dad was more perceptive than she'd realized. "Sir, I just want to be her friend for now."

John nodded, his expression indecipherable. "I'll leave it up to her. She knows her own mind, but don't break her heart."

"I don't plan to do that. I want to be her friend, and we'll see where things go from there."

"I'll be watching."

Wyatt forced a smile. "And I'll be on my best behavior with your daughter."

"Good. Don't forget that promise."

"Yes, sir. Have a good evening." Wyatt turned, hoping to get away from the older man's scrutiny.

The conversation with Caroline's dad rolled through his mind as he limped toward Caroline, who stood with Melanie, Nathan, and the boys. Caroline's smiled brightened Wyatt's thoughts.

Did Caroline's father think someone had broken her heart? Maybe that was why he'd told Wyatt not to push. He had to admit, when he'd asked Caroline if someone had hurt her, that was what he'd expected to hear, not a story of cruel violation. Just thinking about it made his heart hurt. For sure, he wouldn't push Caroline. Knowing what had happened to her, he couldn't. She had trusted him enough to tell him the horrific story, so that should give him hope.

CHAPTER FIVE

"Will we get to see alligators?"

Andrew's question brought worry to Caroline's mind as she turned the dark-gray SUV with every imaginable convenience onto the narrow road covered in sand, gravel, and shells. Wyatt had an answer for every question the boys had asked. She waited for him to answer this one.

"Do you want to see one?" Wyatt asked.

"Yeah. That would be so cool." Ryan's voice raised a pitch.

Wyatt chuckled. "You don't want to get too close, but you might get to see one."

"I don't want to get close, but I want to see one." From the backseat, Andrew tapped Caroline on the shoulder. "Aunt Caroline, will you take a picture if we see an alligator?"

"Sure." Caroline hoped they wouldn't encounter any large reptiles, but she didn't want to disappoint the boys.

"Your aunt Caroline doesn't sound too sure about seeing an alligator." Wyatt placed his arm on the console of the SUV as he turned toward the backseat. "Maybe you could take your own picture."

"But I don't have a camera," Andrew said.

"I'll teach you how to use the camera on my phone,"

Wyatt said.

"Really?" Wonder filled Andrew's voice. "My mom won't let me use hers."

Wyatt nodded. "I'm trusting you to take good care of my phone when you use it."

"I will."

"You better watch him close. Sometimes he's clumsy. That's why Mom wouldn't let him use the phone," Ryan said.

"Uh-huh." Andrew defended himself.

"I'll tell Mom you're not telling the truth."

"Am so."

Caroline tried to catch a glimpse of the youngsters in the rearview mirror, but she had to concentrate on the narrow road.

"Hey, guys. If you're going to fight, maybe we should just turn around and take you back." Wyatt glanced over at her, as if seeking her approval. "What do you think, Caroline?"

Now she was on the spot. "It would be a shame to ruin your trip just because two boys can't get along. Maybe we could just leave them in the house while we explore the ranch. I'm sure someone will watch them. What do you think?"

Wyatt nodded. "As I recall, Morgan has a teenage daughter who might babysit you guys."

"We don't need a babysitter," Ryan said. "We won't argue anymore."

"Good. I'll count on that." Wyatt nodded.

"Look at those huge trees. It looks like they're

growing beards." Andrew pointed straight ahead.

"Those are oak trees, and that stuff hanging from them is Spanish moss." Caroline motioned ahead as sunlight filtered through the branches and Spanish moss, giving an eerie feeling to the landscape. "The trees kind of make it feel like we're driving through a tunnel."

"A tunnel with lots of cobwebs." Ryan scrunched up his face.

"We're almost there." Wyatt tapped the built-in GPS system on the dashboard. "It says we have less than a mile to go."

"But I don't see anything but trees and grass. I don't even see any cows or horses. Are you sure this is a ranch?" Ryan asked.

"And where do we stay?" Andrew added.

"You'll see." Wyatt grinned.

"Have you been here before?" Caroline glanced Wyatt's way.

"Once, the year Morgan retired from the rodeo." Wyatt laced his fingers behind his head. "He was my mentor and gave me a lot of good advice. I missed him after he retired. Now he's a real working cowboy, not just a show cowboy."

"Is that what you are, a show cowboy?" Andrew asked.

Wyatt shook his head. "I'm not any kind of cowboy right now."

Caroline heard the sadness in Wyatt's answer. Would being with his old friend make Wyatt's longing for the rodeo even worse?

"What are you going to do if you aren't a cowboy?" Ryan asked.

"That's a good question. It's something I have to figure out, but first this leg needs to get better." Wyatt tapped his right leg. "And that takes time and lots of exercise. You guys want to do exercises with me?"

Caroline couldn't help but chuckle. "I can just see you leading these guys in exercises every morning."

Andrew raised his hand. "I wanna do exercises. I'm good at that kind of stuff."

"Then I'll count on you being my exercise buddy." Wyatt smiled.

"There's a house. It's huge!" The excitement in Ryan's voice was contagious.

Caroline took in the house with siding made of cedar shakes and a wraparound porch that encircled the whole structure. It didn't look much like the stucco-covered houses she was used to along the Florida coast. This house looked more like the low-country houses along the coast of North Carolina. Wyatt hadn't exaggerated when he said they had plenty of accommodations.

Andrew joined in. "Does it have a pool?"

Wyatt nodded. "Yes."

"Do we get to swim?" Andrew asked.

"If you're on your good behavior." Wyatt glanced at the boys in the backseat.

"I'll be extra good," Andrew replied.

"Then you'll get to swim."

Caroline maneuvered the car to a spot where there was no grass. "Should I park here?"

"Sure." Wyatt unbuckled his seat belt. "Let's get our luggage."

Caroline punched the button that opened the SUV hatch. Andrew and Ryan jumped out of the backseat and hurried around to the back. Wyatt moseyed to join them. Caroline took in the camaraderie that had already developed between Wyatt and her nephews. He was a man of many surprises. She didn't want to like him, because she wasn't ready for any kind of relationship with a man, and he had made it clear he was interested in her. Had confiding in him changed his mind?

He'd said he was sorry that had happened to her, but how did he view her now? They hadn't had a chance to discuss it after the boys had interrupted the conversation. It would stand between them like a Plexiglas wall—a clear but ever-present barrier.

"Here's your suitcase." Wyatt held out her black-and-white-plaid roller bag.

"Thanks." Their fingers brushed as Caroline took the case, and her heart tripped. She warned herself again not to like this man—something that would be all too easy. But that was crazy considering her current state of mind. She had to learn to trust again.

"You're welcome." His tentative smile didn't brighten his expression, as if he knew what she was thinking. He turned to Ryan and Andrew. "You guys got your bags?"

The boys nodded as they held up their duffels.

Wyatt closed the hatch, then pointed toward the house. "Follow me."

Before Wyatt reached the steps leading to the wraparound porch, a middle-aged man wearing a light-tan felt cowboy hat, blue jeans, and a long-sleeved chambray shirt came down the steps.

Wyatt quickened his hobble as he extended his hand toward the man. "Morgan, it's good to see you."

The man grasped Wyatt's hand and shook it. "Good to see you getting around, even if it's a little slower than usual."

"A lot slower than usual, but at least I'm not hanging out in a nursing home."

Morgan laughed. "I bet you were charming all the nurses."

"More like scaring the nurses. I wasn't a very good patient."

Caroline took in the exchange and recognized Wyatt's honesty and the fondness between the two men. Wyatt had probably looked upon Morgan as a father figure. Not surprising since his own father hadn't been there for him. They were even dressed alike, or maybe that was just the normal cowboy apparel. Ryan and Andrew fit right in with their jeans and T-shirts. She, on the other hand, hadn't dressed well for this occasion. Florida didn't strike her as the place to be wearing jeans, so she had opted for tan capri pants and a floral print blouse. She'd had to tiptoe across the drive to keep from getting sand in her sandals.

"Who do you have with you?" Morgan's question shook Caroline from her thoughts.

Wyatt turned and smiled at Caroline as he motioned

for her and the boys to join him. "This is my friend Caroline Keller. We've known each other since we were kids. And these two young men are Ryan and Andrew Drake. Caroline's brother Nathan just married their mom. Everyone, this is Morgan Garrity."

"So that must've been the wedding you needed the venue for," Morgan said.

Wyatt nodded. "Thanks for helping us. The place was just right."

"Good to hear." Morgan smiled as he tipped his hat to Caroline. "Welcome. It's good to meet Wyatt's friends. Come on in, and I'll introduce you to my wife and daughter."

Caroline let Morgan grab her roller bag, then followed close behind as he led them into the house. He removed his hat as he stepped inside. The entryway led to a huge open room with a stone fireplace that went from the floor to the vaulted tongue-and-groove pine ceiling. The inside of the house was even more of a surprise than the outside. The western theme didn't say *Florida* in any way. The cozy tan leather couch invited one to take a seat and enjoy the view of the pool and the grove of palm and oak trees in the background, the only thing that let Caroline know she was still in the Sunshine State.

"Is that where we get to swim?" Andrew raced to the French doors that led to the wraparound porch and the lanai beyond.

Wyatt looked over at Morgan. "When I told you had a pool, their excitement about this visit doubled."

"Would you like to take a look?"

"Sure." Andrew's eager response made Morgan chuckle.

"Follow me." Morgan opened the French doors.

Just as he stepped onto the porch, a teenage girl with long dark hair that cascaded past her shoulders and equally dark eyes emerged from the room on the other side of the fireplace. "Hey, Dad, are our guests here?"

"They sure are. Come and meet them. This is my daughter, Isabella, but we call her Bella." As the young woman joined Morgan, he put an arm around her shoulders. "Bella, do you remember Wyatt Bayer?"

A thoughtful expression covered Bella's face. "Sort of. You came to visit when I was much younger. And Dad has some pictures of you from his rodeo days."

Wyatt nodded. "Yeah, your dad was a big influence on my life, and I appreciate his friendship."

"Now let me introduce you to the rest of the gang." Morgan extended his hand. "This is Caroline Keller and her nephews, Ryan and Andrew Drake."

"Hi, everyone." Bella gave a little wave.

"It's nice to meet you, Bella." Caroline smiled, feeling better about her clothes as she observed Bella's tan shorts and a T-shirt emblazoned with a big palm tree.

"We were just about to show these boys the pool." Morgan motioned toward the door that led from the porch to the lanai.

"It's always good for an afternoon or evening swim when the weather's hot." Bella opened the screen door between the porch and the lanai. "We can swim later after we go horseback riding. Dad said I get to lead the tour."

"We'll have to find a couple of good horses for these boys and a cowboy hat for each of them." Morgan joined Bella beside the pool.

"We've got some in the barn they can try." Bella slipped off a sandal and stuck a toe in the pool. "The water's the perfect temperature."

As Bella showed the boys the gas-fired fire pit, surrounded by six comfy-looking chairs covered in a floral pattern with splashes of aqua and gold, Caroline took in the built-in grill and bar that went along the side of the lanai closest to the house. Aqua lounge chairs lined each side of the pool. The place was built for relaxation and fun. What would it be like to live in a place like this?

"What's everyone doing out here?"

Caroline turned at the sound of another female voice. Wearing a brightly colored tunic and navy capri pants, a middle-aged woman who looked like Bella entered the lanai. Morgan strode over and ushered the newcomer toward the group.

"Hey, everyone, I'd like you to meet Alicia, my wife." Pride showed on Morgan's face as he again listed the members of the group without hesitation.

Alicia smiled up at her husband. "Thank you, dear. I want to show all of you where you'll be staying before Morgan and Bella whisk you off somewhere."

An indulgent smile curving his mouth, Morgan

looked at his wife. "We'd better listen to her. She's the one who feeds us."

"Wyatt, I remember you from your early days on the rodeo circuit and your visit with us a few years ago." Alicia nodded.

"Yeah, I was just a dumb kid then. Your husband helped me through some bad decisions I made back then, and I'm grateful for it."

"The rodeo life can be tough when you're away from family for long stretches of time." Morgan gave his wife a loving smile, then turned to Wyatt. "I kind of adopted you because I was missing my own family."

"I traveled with Morgan when he first went on the circuit, but after the kids were born, it was too hard." She motioned toward the house. "But he built me this palace and made us a home."

Wyatt stepped forward. "I hope we're not making too much work for you."

Alicia chuckled as she waved a hand at Wyatt. "This is nothing. I'm prepared to feed big groups all the time. This group is comparatively small. It's no work. You'll meet Juanita later. She's my right-hand woman."

"Let's get those suitcases upstairs, then we'll go for a horseback ride." Morgan led the way back into the house and picked up a couple of suitcases as he headed to the stairs on one side of the large gathering room.

As they reached the second floor, Alicia led them down a hallway, then stopped. "Here's where I'm putting the guys. This used to be our son's room, but he's a senior in college and spends very little time at home anymore. So we added this bunkbed that Ryan and Andrew can use. Wyatt, you get the big bed unless you want to fight the boys for one of the bunks."

Wyatt laughed as he tapped his bad leg. "I'm definitely not fighting for the top bunk."

"I'll take the top," the two boys said in unison.

"Looks like you might have to flip a coin for that unless you can settle it some other way." Wyatt gave the youngsters a wry smile.

Andrew's shoulders sagged as he dropped his duffel onto the floor. "I'll let Ryan choose."

"Thank you, Andrew. That's being a good sport." Morgan tapped the boy on the back. "We like that around here."

Andrew beamed at Morgan's approval, and Caroline wondered how Wyatt felt about sharing a room with two rambunctious boys. He didn't appear to care, maybe because he'd invited them. She glanced down the hall. Where was her room?

"Caroline, your room's right across the hall." Alicia pointed toward the open door.

"Thanks." Caroline stepped into the well-appointed room with the modern canopy bed sporting a white quilted coverlet and brown and white decorator pillows. A filmy light-tan gauze material covered the top and flowed down the back. "This is lovely."

"And this room has its own private bathroom." Alicia looked at the guys. "The men will have to share the bath off the hallway. If you need anything let me know."

"This is great." Wyatt leaned against the doorframe and gazed at Caroline. "Are you ready for that horseback ride?"

"I am." Andrew's voice echoed down the hall.

The adults laughed as everyone congregated at the top of the stairs.

"Guess we'd better get this eager young cowpoke out to the horse barn." Morgan motioned forward.

Ryan and Andrew scrambled down the stairs while Bella hurried to catch up to them.

"After you." Wyatt motioned to Caroline. "I might be a little slow on the stairs."

Caroline gazed at him. "I don't mind waiting."

"But I mind you watching me hobble down the stairs like an old man."

"Okay, I'll go first if you insist, but I don't mind you hobbling. You've come a long way from the man I knew with the walker." Caroline bit her lower lip.

Wyatt shook his head. "I guess you've already seen me walking like an old man. So I've got nothing to hide."

Caroline nodded. "For sure."

"Okay, you two. Are you going to jaw all afternoon or ride horses?" Morgan called up the stairs.

"We're coming." Caroline took the first two steps, then stopped. "I'm just making sure he doesn't fall down the stairs."

Wyatt laughed. "She's such a joker."

"Aunt Caroline is pretty funny," Andrew called up the stairs. "I like having her for my aunt. We've never had an aunt before."

Caroline ran a hand across her brow as she joined the group on the main floor. "Whew! That's good to know, since you're stuck with me. I like having you guys as nephews."

After Wyatt negotiated the last step, he came to stand beside Caroline and winked at the boys. "Do you suppose she could be my honorary aunt?"

Andrew shook his head. "That would be pretty silly. She's not old enough to be your aunt."

Morgan chuckled. "You don't have to be older to be an aunt. Do you know I have an aunt who's the same age as me?"

"You do?" Ryan's voice went up a pitch.

"I do." Morgan nodded. "I'm the oldest child in my family, and my dad is the oldest child in his family. The year I was born my grandparents had another child, my aunt Jackie. So we're the same age."

"Wow!" Andrew's eyes grew wide. "That must be cool."

"I had a lot of amusement when I was young introducing her as my aunt. No one wanted to believe it." Morgan chuckled. "We had a lot of fun growing up together here on the ranch."

"So your parents and grandparents were ranchers here?" Caroline asked.

"This ranch has been in my family for five generations. My great-great-grandparents started this ranch with a little bit of nothing and made it into our own little empire." Pride sounded in Morgan's voice.

Caroline nodded. "That's kind of like the little town we're from in Ohio. My great-great-grandparents settled the town. That's why it's called Kellersburg."

"Yeah, she comes from a line of VIPs in the town," Wyatt said.

"I wouldn't say that." Caroline stared at Wyatt. "There are just lots of Kellers in Kellersburg."

Wyatt shrugged. "I consider you VIP."

Caroline didn't know what to make of Wyatt's assessment. Did it mean he thought she thought she was better than he was? She didn't want him to think just because her ancestors had founded the town they lived in that she had an advantage.

"Sometimes it's not always easy being the descendant of the founders. That's why I did rodeo for a few years. I had to learn this was where I belong." Morgan nodded. "I learned I love ranching and everything it involves."

"I've got to figure out where I belong." Wyatt gazed at Morgan.

"Maybe you belong here, too?" Morgan gazed back. "You ever think about ranching? I can always use another good cowboy."

"I'm not in any shape to think about that. I've still got a lot of rehab ahead of me."

"When you're ready, give me a holler." Morgan clapped Wyatt on the back. "Now let's head to the horse barn and do a little riding while Bella shows off the ranch."

Caroline followed the group out of the house and

down a sandy path. More sand in her sandals. She should have better footwear. She watched Wyatt, who shambled as fast as he could to match Morgan's strides.

Would Wyatt take Morgan up on his offer? Did the thought make her a little sad?

***

Wyatt limped into the horse barn. The smell of leather and hay put him back at the rodeo. His heart hammered. Was he ready to get back on a horse? His leg ached. He'd been trying too hard to keep up with everyone, but he wouldn't give in to the pain, because he wanted to impress Caroline. How could he do that when he wasn't the man he used to be? The one thing he had going for him was not being the kid he used to be.

"Hey, Mr. Wyatt, do you like my hat?" Ryan bounded over as he adjusted the straw cowboy hat on his head.

"You look like a real cowboy in that hat." Wyatt smiled. "Now we have to find you a horse."

"How about my hat?" Wearing a nearly identical hat, Andrew presented himself to Wyatt.

"Looking good." Wyatt stepped closer to one of the stalls. "Let's see what horses Morgan has picked out for you."

"I've got a couple of Tennessee Walking horses here that'll be perfect for these young cowpokes. We'll get them saddled and ready to go." Morgan grabbed a couple of saddles from the nearby tack room as Bella brought out one chestnut horse and one bay horse from the stalls.

"Hey, Wyatt. I've saved this big guy for you. What do you think?" Morgan led a big bay horse from a stall.

"Nice mount."

"This is Champ. I thought you'd like him." Morgan handed Wyatt the reins. "What did you do with your horses after your injury?"

"They're retired on my grandparents' farm."

"So you haven't done any riding since the accident?" Morgan asked.

"Nope." Wyatt sighed. "This will be a test of my rehab."

"You're cleared to ride?"

"Yeah, just no competition." Wyatt tried to keep the bitterness out of his voice. He had to come to terms with a future that meant no more rodeos. "Let's get these horses ready."

After Morgan, Bella, and Wyatt saddled the horses, Morgan helped the boys into the saddles and showed them how to hold the reins and instructed them on how to use them to guide the horses. "You guys ready?"

Andrew didn't look too sure. "I don't know. Will the horse listen to me?"

"As long as you do what Morgan said, and I'll be right here beside you if you need help." Wyatt ran a hand down the horse's neck, then gave it a pat. "You'll do fine."

"I hope he doesn't buck me off." Andrew looked concerned.

"He won't do that. He's one of my best horses for young guys like you," Morgan said. "Bella used to ride him when she was younger. His name is Buster."

"Hi, Buster." Andrew patted the horse's neck, and the horse shook his head, as if to acknowledge the greeting.

Wyatt grabbed a hat for himself and one for Caroline and walked over to where she stood next to her assigned horse. He grinned as he handed her the hat. "You look about as wary as Andrew. Have you not been horseback riding before?"

Caroline took the hat and plunked it on her head. "I haven't ridden a horse since I was in college. You'll have to repeat those instructions Morgan gave the boys."

"Gladly." Wyatt stepped closer. "You need some help getting into the saddle?"

She turned to him, irritation puckering her forehead. "I think I can manage that."

"Great." Wyatt wanted to tell her how cute she looked in the straw hat, but he didn't want to irritate her further. He'd rather stay on her good side.

After Caroline mounted her horse and settled in the saddle, Wyatt took his time explaining how to use the reins to guide the horse. He liked having her rapt attention. Too bad it involved a horse and not him. When he finished, he ambled toward his horse. As he took the reins, he braced himself for the shooting pain that was sure to go up his leg as he put his foot in the stirrup and hoisted himself into the saddle. He smiled to himself. The pain was bearable. Like all the other pains he'd suffered in his life, he would get over it. And looking at Caroline while they rode would certainly help.

The horses fell in line behind Bella's horse. They took a leisurely pace as they followed the sandy road that wound its way through the palm trees swaying overhead in the warm breeze. They went by a small pond with green lily pad–looking vegetation growing at the edges. A small dock jutted into the water.

Morgan pointed to the water. "A big gator lives in that pond."

"Do you think we'll get to see him?" Andrew's voice filled with excitement.

"We can sit here for a moment and watch." Morgan again pointed. "If you look over to the right, he sometimes hangs out near the dock on the other side of the pond. You can see the top of his head."

"I hope we see him." Andrew looked over at Wyatt. "Will you take a picture so I can show my mom?"

Wyatt fished his phone from the pocket of his jeans as he maneuvered his horse closer to Andrew. "Remember how I showed you how to use this?"

"I think so." Andrew took the phone.

"Take a test photo." Wyatt nodded.

Andrew held the phone out in front of him and tapped the circle on the screen. "Like this?"

"Absolutely." Wyatt took the phone. "Let's look at the photo you took."

Wyatt explained to Andrew how to find the photo. Andrew beamed with pride as he looked at the picture he'd taken. Then Bella suggested she take pictures of the group. An impromptu photo session took place next to the pond. Wyatt took the opportunity to get photos of Caroline as she smiled next to her nephews, then one of him and Caroline as their horses stood side by side.

"Look!" Morgan motioned toward the pond.

"The alligator!" Andrew took the phone and snapped a picture of the gator as its spiny back showed just above the water. He took another photo and another. "Do you think he's going to come out of the water?"

Morgan chuckled. "I don't know, but you'd better be careful. A gator can eat a cow, especially a calf. We have to keep an eye on these gators. If we start missing cattle, it's a sure bet a gator is involved. Then we have to call a gator catcher to come get it and cart it someplace where it won't bother our herd."

"Wow!" Andrew's eyes grew wide. "It can eat a whole cow."

"That's right." Morgan nodded. "So it's time to move on. Gators are nothing to mess with. It's best we leave while he's still in the water."

"We're off again." Bella led the procession along one of the canals that provided water for the ranch.

As the horses ambled along, Morgan told the history of the ranch. Pride captured every word as he talked. He pointed out where his grandparents, parents, and siblings lived in the smaller ranch houses dotting the property. They passed by the cow pens and the pastures filled with grazing cattle. "We breed our cattle specifically to endure the hot, humid summers here in Florida. We have an excellent operation, and the whole family works on the ranch, although my grandparents are pretty much retired now."

"We're coming to an orange grove, and you can pick an orange off a tree and eat it if you'd like." Bella stopped at the end of one row of trees and plucked an orange from a branch and held it up. "This will taste better than any orange you've ever bought from a store."

Everyone took a turn picking an orange. Quiet settled as they peeled their oranges. The smell of citrus filled the air. Wyatt watched for Caroline to take her first bite. He knew from his previous visit here that Bella's statement was true. There was nothing like eating an orange fresh off the tree.

Caroline split her peeled orange in half and broke off one section. She put the piece to her mouth and took a nibble. Her face lit up with delight as she took a larger bite. She wasn't just cautious about him. She was cautious about everything. Had her bad experience made her that way, or had she always been the guarded type? He didn't know the answer, but he enjoyed her delighted expression.

"Enjoying that orange?" Wyatt gazed at Caroline.

Startled, she gave him a look he couldn't decipher. "Best orange I've ever had. Bella was right. Why aren't you eating yours?"

Wyatt popped nearly half an orange into his mouth to avoid having to confess that he'd been staring at her, but then she'd probably already guessed that. What other cool moves could he make?

"Don't choke on that." Caroline's mouth curved in a wry smile.

Wyatt managed to swallow without choking. "Yeah, I might've bitten off a little more than I should have, but it's so good."

As Bella started their ride again, Wyatt knew for sure that he'd bitten off more than he could chew when it came to Caroline, because he wasn't sure how to move forward with a woman who had experienced such a horrific encounter. Even though she'd told him, she seemed to be pretending it had never happened. She was humoring him while he was trying to impress her without much progress.

Wyatt didn't know how to negotiate his feelings for Caroline. Maybe it was all bad timing. He didn't know where he was headed, and she had a trauma to work through. He might just have to settle for friendship.

CHAPTER SIX

Sunlight filtering through the clouds near the horizon gave them an iridescent glow as Ryan dove into the pool and swam to the other side. Andrew followed right behind him. The boys cavorted in the pool like two dolphins, jumping and splashing. Caroline enjoyed the boys' antics. She thought about how much joy they had brought to her brother's life. He was a blessed man. Could she find such blessings?

"They're having a good time." Caroline glanced at Wyatt as he leaned back in his chair and stretched out his bad leg.

"They are. They had a good time all day." Wyatt glanced her way. "They certainly took to horseback riding like pros."

"They did. Thanks for inviting them."

"Does that thanks include you?"

Caroline didn't know how to answer that question. Conflicting emotions accompanied her every thought about Wyatt.

"You guys should join the boys in the pool." Bella appeared wearing a royal-blue tank swimsuit and saved Caroline from having to answer Wyatt's question. "I plan to swim."

"Riding a horse for hours didn't help this leg. So

maybe I should take it easy."

Bella shook her head. "Swimming should help that leg."

"I'm only going in if your dad does." Wyatt patted his stomach. "Besides, I'm still full from that delicious dinner your mom served. It's been a long time since I've had chicken burritos that good."

"Mom does keep us well fed." Bella laughed "But you know my dad's not much for swimming. He only put this pool in to indulge us kids. I wouldn't be surprised if he fills it in when I go off to college next year."

"Not if I have anything to say about it." Alicia, wearing a swimsuit similar to Bella's, joined her daughter near the pool's edge. "Come on, you two. You have to join in the fun."

With the hint of chlorine floating through the evening air, Caroline looked over at Wyatt to see his response before she committed to anything. She should go in even if he didn't. She'd been warned to bring her swimsuit.

With a sense of resignation, she stood. "Guess I'll change into my suit."

Wyatt stood at the same time and looked toward the pool. "Before we swim, the boys have to join me in my exercises. I haven't done those today."

"I can do that." Ryan swam to the nearby ladder and climbed out, dripping water onto the pool deck.

"Me, too." Andrew scrambled to follow his brother.

Caroline glanced at Wyatt. "You aren't planning to

exercise in jeans, are you?"

A wry smile curved Wyatt's lips. "No, I'll change into my swim trunks and meet you back here. Last one back is a rotten egg."

"Aunt Caroline, don't let him beat you. He should be the rotten egg," Andrew shouted.

Caroline laughed as she raced to the stairs. She left Wyatt in the dust. Before she started up the stairs, she turned to see him hobbling along. She shouldn't feel sorry for him. He was the one who'd made the challenge. "Looks like you're going to be the rotten egg."

"Not if you keep standing there. I change faster than you do." He grinned.

Caroline took the stairs two at a time. When she reached the top, she turned. Wyatt still stood at the bottom of the staircase. "You still think you can beat me?"

"Of course. Remember the story of the tortoise and the hare? I just might be the tortoise, and as I recall the tortoise won."

Caroline laughed again as she dashed into her room. She slipped into her black-and-white one-piece swimsuit, then threw on her white terrycloth cover-up. When she stepped into the hallway, she wondered about the wisdom of taking advantage of an injured man. But he'd warned her that he was the tortoise and she was the hare. Had he already made his way downstairs?

The water in the pool shimmered with the colors of the setting sun obscured in the clouds. The boys sat on the edge of the pool with their legs dangling in the water while Bella swam laps with her mother. Wyatt wasn't there. So she had beaten him back.

As Caroline opened the screen door that led into the lanai, Wyatt jumped out from behind a cabinet where beach towels were stored. "You're the rotten egg. I told you the tortoise wins."

Taking in Wyatt's black swim trunks splashed with palm trees and coconuts, Caroline widened her eyes. "How did you beat me?"

He grinned. "That's my secret."

"I can tell you, Aunt Caroline." Andrew waved a hand in the air as he hurried toward her.

Wyatt shook his head and put a finger to his mouth. Making a face, Andrew stopped in his tracks.

Caroline put her hands on her hips. "Since I've lost, I think it's only fair that you tell me how you did it. I was at the top of the stairs when you were still at the bottom. You don't change that fast."

Wyatt laughed as he looked at Andrew. "Do you think she's competitive?"

Andrew wrinkled his nose. "What does that mean?"

"It means she likes to win."

"I like to win, too," Andrew said.

Wyatt laughed again. "We all like to win."

"Explain how you won." Caroline wagged a finger at him.

"I might after we exercise." Wyatt waggled his eyebrows.

"All right. Let's exercise." Caroline eyed Wyatt.

"You lead the way."

Wyatt stood on the pool deck and grinned at her. Caroline's heart beat in double time, and she looked away. She didn't want him to know that anything about him affected her. She'd gotten very good at masking her true feelings about everything going on in her life. So she could deal with the emotions Wyatt evoked, too.

Wyatt grabbed his phone and set it on a nearby lounge chair. "I'll use my phone to set a thirty-second timer. I'll demonstrate what you're supposed to do, and then we'll all hold the position for thirty seconds. You need to cup your foot while you do this."

Andrew watched Wyatt stand on one leg. "I can stand on one leg easy."

Wyatt pointed at Andrew. "Remember you have to cup your foot. You might not find it so easy. You can stand close to a chair if you think you'll need to catch your balance."

"I don't need no chair," Andrew bragged.

"We'll see about that." Wyatt laughed.

Wyatt started the timer as the group stood on one leg. They resembled a flock of flamingos. Caroline pressed her lips together to keep from laughing. Thirty seconds was a long time when one was teetering on one leg. Wyatt was right. Cupping the foot made standing on one leg much harder. Andrew waved an arm as he worked to maintain his balance. Finally, the timer went off, and loud sighs floated through the lanai as everyone stood on two feet.

"Mr. Wyatt, you were right. That was harder than it

sounded," Ryan said.

"Now you get to do the same thing with the other leg." Wyatt held up his phone again. "Ready?"

Caroline loved how Wyatt related to Ryan and Andrew. Besides involving them in these exercises, Wyatt had shown the boys how to care for their horses after the ride. He was good with kids, and that just made him that much more likable. How could she reconcile these feelings with her fears?

She couldn't. Not now.

For the next twenty minutes, she tried to concentrate on the exercises, not her conflicting thoughts. Her attitude brightened as Ryan and Andrew joined Wyatt in laughter while he demonstrated the butt tap.

When Wyatt demonstrated an exercise in which he took wide sidesteps, Andrew chortled. "It looks like you're dancing. You should do that one with Aunt Caroline. You wanted to dance with her."

"Yeah, you should do that." Ryan nodded his head.

"It's not really a dance. It's an exercise." Caroline wanted to run from the lanai.

"But you can make it a dance," Andrew said.

The boys chanted, "Dance, dance, dance."

When Wyatt looked at Caroline, she didn't miss the question in his gaze. He understood her hesitation. What could she say? The boys were urging her on, but would she freak if Wyatt put his arm around her waist? She couldn't do something like that in front of everyone. Was she brave enough to try? Her heart raced as she swallowed hard.

Wyatt stood with his arms wide open, the question still in his eyes. "I promise I won't step on your toes."

Caroline held her breath as she took a step closer to Wyatt. Her pulse pounded all over her body. She put her hand in the one he held out to her. She was good. So far. He took her other hand and took a sideways step.

"Stop." Andrew ran up to them. "That's not how you do it."

Wyatt stopped midstep, still holding one of Caroline's hands. She was getting used to the feel of his rough hand against hers. Maybe she could do this. Maybe.

"So show me." Wyatt gave his undivided attention.

"You gotta put your arm around her." Andrew took Wyatt's arm and placed it around Caroline's waist.

"Are you okay?" With his voice barely above a whisper, Wyatt looked at her.

She nodded because she didn't dare speak.

"Aunt Caroline, you have to put your hand on his shoulder." Andrew lifted her arm.

Caroline let out the breath she'd been holding as she rested her hand on Wyatt's shoulder. An unexpected calm came over her. She was going to be all right.

"That's good." Andrew nodded as he stepped back. "Now you can dance with her."

"Are you still good?"

Caroline nodded and took a shaky breath as she found her voice. "I'm good."

Wyatt sidestepped along the side of the pool as the boys clapped and Bella broke into song. When he reached the far end of the pool, he sidestepped back the other way as Caroline followed his lead. After repeating this three times, he stepped back and bowed. "Thank you for the dance, my fair maiden."

"You're welcome, kind sir." A little smile formed on her lips. She'd made it. Maybe this was a first rung to feeling normal again.

"My pleasure." Wyatt's smile warmed her heart. "Now let's swim."

"I thought you weren't going to swim unless Morgan does," Caroline said.

"I changed my mind." Wyatt motioned toward Ryan and Andrew. "These boys were good enough to do exercises with me, so I'll swim."

"Before you swim, you have to tell me how you beat me."

"Can I tell?" Andrew shifted from foot to foot.

"Sure." Wyatt grinned.

"Aunt Caroline, after you went upstairs, he never followed you, but he changed in that little room right over there." Andrew pointed to a narrow door at one end of the porch on the other side of the screen which made up the side of the lanai closest to the house.

Caroline looked Wyatt's way and shook her head, her gazed narrowed. "I should've known you had some trick up your sleeve when you challenged me. There was no way you were getting up and down those stairs that quickly."

Wyatt shrugged. "You have to remember I've been here before."

Before Caroline could respond, Morgan appeared in a pair of gray swim trunks and a towel slung over his shoulders. "Time to swim. I have to help entertain the company."

The adults slipped into the pool along with the boys. The sounds of splashing, dunking, and a lively game of Marco Polo filled the evening air as the sun sank below the horizon. The pool lights illuminated the darkening landscape. Caroline hadn't felt this carefree in months. Could the feeling last?

When it was time for Ryan and Andrew to go to bed, they made little protest. They'd had a busy day, and even these rambunctious boys were tired. Caroline checked on them after they put on their pajamas and brushed their teeth.

She stood in the doorway. "Are you guys all settled?"

"When is Mr. Wyatt coming to bed?" Andrew sat on the edge of the lower bunk.

"I don't know, but I'll tell him to be quiet so he doesn't wake you."

"But maybe I'd like him to wake me."

Ryan laughed. "Nothing will wake Andrew. Mom says a bomb could go off in his room and it wouldn't disturb him."

Andrew punched the pillow at the head of the bed, then looked at Caroline. "Mom always says prayers with us. Will you do that?"

Caroline nodded, realizing that even though these boys had a good time today, they were probably missing their mom. "I sure will."

Ryan jumped down from the top bunk. The threesome held hands as Caroline prayed, thanking God for the beautiful day and the fun activities. She asked for the safety of all of those traveling and asked God to bless their activities tomorrow."

After the prayer, Caroline tucked the boys in. "Good night. See you in the morning."

"Good night," the boys chorused.

As she stepped into the dark hallway, she bumped into something solid, and she let out a yelp. Fear seized her as her heart hammered. Thankfully, she hadn't screamed at the top of her lungs. Wyatt stood there in the dark. The past rushed through her brain like a huge wave crashing onto the beach, inundating her, pulling her under into the place where she didn't want to go, where fear had the upper hand.

"Are you okay?"

Caroline somehow found her voice. "You scared me."

"Didn't mean to do that. I was just listening." Wyatt stepped back. "I think some boys miss their mom."

"That's what I was thinking, too." Pretending everything was normal, Caroline headed toward the stairs as she regained her emotional equilibrium.

"I can relate in some ways. When my parents lost custody of me and I had to live with my grandparents, I missed my mom, even though she wasn't a good mom. So it must be even worse when you have a mom like Melanie."

"That must've been hard."

Caroline wished her response didn't sound so lame, but Wyatt's revelations surprised her. Maybe he felt comfortable sharing with her because she'd shared a traumatic part of her life with him. Who would ever have guessed she and Wyatt would share some of their most guarded feelings with each other?

"It was, but my grandparents have been great. I just wished I'd appreciated them more when I was growing up." His head down, Wyatt gingerly negotiated the first step on the staircase.

"I think we learn to appreciate a lot of things when we grow up." Caroline followed close behind Wyatt as he took one step at a time.

When Wyatt reached the bottom of the stairs, he turned. "Speaking of appreciation, I want to thank you for being my driver."

Feeling less apprehension, Caroline smiled. "You're welcome, and to answer your earlier question, thanks for inviting me."

Wyatt nodded. "Thanks for that. I didn't want you to hate that you'd come."

"How could that be the case? This is a side of Florida I would never have known about except for you. I had no idea there were so many cattle ranches in the state. Florida always said beaches and theme parks."

"A cattle ranch in Florida is truly a unique place." Wyatt chuckled. "I thought Andrew was going to come right out of his saddle when he saw that gator."

Caroline joined in the laughter. "That's something

those boys will talk about forever."

When they entered the lanai, Morgan climbed out of the pool and dried off. "The rest of us are calling it a night, but you two are welcome to stay out here. I lit the fire pit for you, and Alicia left you a few snacks."

"Thanks." Wyatt turned to Caroline. "Are you good with that?"

Caroline nodded, knowing he was asking if she felt comfortable being alone with him.

"And about tomorrow. I hope you're planning to stay for supper, since it's only a two-hour drive back to the hotel," Morgan said.

Wyatt looked at her. "Does that work for you?"

"Whatever you want is fine with me." Caroline's mind wrapped around the truth of that statement. He was winning her over little by little. But was she brave enough to let a man into her life? Everything inside her said it wouldn't be wise, but she didn't want to answer those questions tonight.

"Great! Then we'll plan to leave after supper." Wyatt fetched his phone from a little table near one of the chairs and held it out to her. "Maybe we ought to call your folks and let them know our plans."

"Sure, but I'll do it in the morning. Sometimes my folks go to bed early."

Wyatt glanced at his phone. "This early?"

Caroline laughed. "You never know. My dad falls asleep watching TV almost every night."

"Okay." Wyatt set his phone back on the table.

As Morgan disappeared into the house, Wyatt

motioned for Caroline to take a seat, and he sat on the chair perpendicular to hers. He stretched his bad leg out in front of him and rubbed it. The scars were visible even in the waning light.

"Is your leg bothering you?" Caroline sat forward in her chair.

He gave her a wry smile. "Twinges of pain live with me."

"I'm sorry."

"It's better, much better. I don't have anything to complain about."

Caroline studied Wyatt's face in the flicker of the light coming from the fire pit. Her heart danced like the flames as she remembered the way he had entrusted his phone to Andrew at the pond so he could take a picture of the gator. Wyatt was a kind man, even though he didn't always show it. There was a lot to like about him.

Wyatt piled his plate high, then poured a drink and handed it to Caroline.

"Thanks." Caroline helped herself to some of the goodies on the tray. She popped a piece of cheese into her mouth and savored the unique flavor. Caroline took another bite while the surrounding landscape grew darker. A strange sound erupted from the nearby trees. Caroline squinted into the darkness. "What's that sound?"

"Cicadas. It's a common sound in Florida. They hang out in the trees. It's their mating call." Wyatt motioned toward the grove of trees shadowed in the light from the pool and fire pit.

"They sound like a buzz saw. I've never heard them that loud." Caroline popped a cracker into her mouth.

Suddenly Caroline's heart hammered, and a lump rose in her throat at the thought of being alone with Wyatt. Had the sound of the cicadas triggered an unreasonable fear? Morgan and Alicia were just steps away in the house. Wyatt wasn't going to hurt her. She knew that. She shouldn't be afraid of him, but she had trusted a man before and paid a terrible price. But she couldn't continue to let that one awful incident color her whole life.

Wyatt turned to look at her, his expression obscured in the shadow. "Are you good with staying out here for a while?"

Her heart raced in rhythm with the cicadas' song. "Yeah. It's a nice night."

"But you're not too sure about this."

Caroline swallowed hard. Again he had sensed her insecurity. She should be honest with him. Honesty. That was what she needed. Honesty with Wyatt and with herself. "You're right. I'm not, but I have to get over this…this…whatever it is."

"Trauma. Fear. Uncertainty. I imagine you're feeling all of those things."

How did he know? She wanted to trust him, trust herself, and trust God again. Being with Wyatt made her realize how broken she was. A new job and the upcoming wedding had distracted her from these feelings, except for the bad dreams. She had pushed them aside and moved on with family and friends, whose love helped to blunt the effects of the trauma, but their presence hadn't made her face it or taken it away. How could they have helped when she hadn't told them about it?

She took a shaky breath and stared at the flames. She couldn't explain her feelings.

"It's okay if you want to leave. I'll understand."

Caroline looked up at Wyatt, who had settled in the chair across the fire pit from her, his handsome face illuminated by the firelight. He seemed so kindhearted, but it didn't square with the Wyatt Bayer she had known growing up. Was he really different, or was he putting on a good show? Was she brave enough to find out? "I don't know if you can truly understand."

Wyatt leaned forward, giving her his rapt attention. "True, but I'd like to help in any way I can."

"It's not your problem to worry about."

"But I worry about you."

"Why?"

Wyatt lowered his gaze, as if he were formulating an answer, then looked up. "You said you were praying for my recovery, and I appreciate that. So is it okay for me to care about you and pray for you? I'm healing from physical trauma, and you're healing from emotional and physical trauma. We can heal together."

Caroline shrugged. "I don't know that I'm doing much healing."

"Why do you say that?"

"I've never told anyone about what happened except you." Caroline held her breath as she stared at Wyatt.

"Wow!" Wyatt shook his head. "Why me?"

"Because you're the first person who recognized that something was wrong." Caroline let out a harsh sigh as she placed a hand over her heart. "It just came out. I'd been suppressing my feelings about that horrible incident, and I needed to tell someone."

"I'm humbled and troubled at the same time." Wyatt knit his eyebrows. "You should talk to a counselor or someone. Your parents?"

Caroline shook her head. "I just don't know how to tell them, especially since I didn't report it to anyone. I fear their reaction."

"They love you. They would only have concern for you."

"I know that, but even when someone loves you, they can be disappointed in your actions." Caroline wished she could explain the doubts and fears that had crowded her mind over the last few months. Why had God allowed such a thing to happen? Even though she said she prayed for Wyatt, sometimes she felt as though God didn't hear her prayers. What kind of missionary was she? One who doubted God? Doubted her place? Doubted that she would ever be whole again?

Wyatt moved to the chair closest to her and put his hand on the arm of the chair. "Caroline, tell me what you're thinking, feeling, wishing. I want to listen. I won't judge. I can't. I've made too many of my own ill-advised decisions in the past. I'll just be a sounding board."

Caroline stared at him, her heart pounding. She

swallowed the lump in her throat that kept returning. "I don't know what to say."

"Will you just promise me one thing?"

"What?"

"That you'll talk to someone, someone who can help you get through this."

Taking a deep breath, Caroline nodded but didn't meet his gaze. "Not someone from Kellersburg. Maybe I can talk to a counselor in Cincinnati. I have contacts in several churches there. I'm sure they can recommend a Christian counselor."

"I'll hold you to that."

"Thank you for caring. Thank you for recognizing my need." Tears threatened, but Caroline blinked them away.

His kindness filled her heart, but she couldn't reveal any more of her doubts and fears to him. He would think she was a hypocrite, telling him to be kind when he already was.

After the rape, at first she had prayed that this doctor would realize his sin and repent, but as the weeks went by, she couldn't pray for him. Instead, she began to hate him. Hate what he'd done to her. How could she do good works when her heart was filled with hate? Even though Wyatt was trying to help, being with him brought back her fears. She couldn't tell him that either. What a mess she was.

"Anytime." Wyatt leaned back in his chair. "I care about you, Caroline, and I was hoping we could be more than just friends. That's why I invited you to join me, then I realized you weren't going anywhere with me alone. So I invited the boys so you'd come."

"Thanks for being honest with me. I appreciate that you care, but we can't be more than friends. I'm messed up, and you have an uncertain future that you have to figure out." Caroline wished it were different, but she had to deal with this. Wyatt was right. She had to seek some counseling.

"I said we could heal together."

"We might be able to do that, but we have to heal before we can think about any kind of relationship that goes beyond friendship."

Wyatt laced his fingers behind his head. "Trying to let me down easy?"

"No. Just being realistic."

"I don't like realistic, but you have a point."

"A very valid point." Caroline wanted to talk about something else, anything else. "What's happening tomorrow? More horseback riding?"

"I didn't ask Morgan, but I think he's planning to take us out on his airboat to cruise the canals."

"An airboat?"

"Yeah, you know the kind with the big fanlike thing on the back that propels it."

"You mean like the ones you see people using in the Everglades?"

"Yeah, you've got it. Have you ever been on one?"

Caroline shook her head. "The boys will love that, too."

"What about you?" Wyatt raised his eyebrows.

"I'm sure it'll be fun."

"Again you don't sound very enthused. Is it the company?" Wyatt narrowed his gaze.

"It has nothing to do with you." She shook her head. Maybe she should try to explain, even though she was on the verge of tears again. She willed them away. "Fear is my constant companion. New experiences trigger the fear, but I force myself to plow through them. I've been doing that for weeks."

Wyatt sighed. "Caroline, I wish I could take it all away."

"You can hold me to finding that counselor." Caroline nodded. "That's what you can do."

"And I will. You can count on me."

"Thanks for listening." Caroline stood. "I'm headed upstairs. I'll see you in the morning."

"Sure. Anytime."

Caroline scurried away, not daring to turn around. Maybe she was making progress. She had pushed herself to come on this trip because of the boys. Wyatt had admitted that he'd used them to get her to come. He wanted more of a relationship than she was ready for. Would she ever be ready? Was it fair to him to even rely on his help when he freely declared his intentions toward her? She was no more ready for a relationship than a baby was ready to walk. Maybe this counseling would teach her at least to crawl through her emotional minefield.

When Caroline reached the stairs, instead of going up, she walked to the front door and opened it. She stepped onto the wide front porch and went to the balustrade. She rested her hands on the weathered wood and stared into the night sky. Stars twinkled in the blackness. Too often her fears rose like a monster in the dark. She hated the dark, even though the rape had happened in broad daylight. The incident brought darkness to her soul, a darkness she feared would never go away.

Caroline shivered, and she rubbed her hands up and down her arms. She gazed at the heavens. Could God hear her prayer? Why did doubts crowd out every good thing from her mind? She had family and friends who loved her, and she had leaned on them mightily since she'd come home. But she had to step out from behind their shadow and deal with her dread and anxiety. She wanted to heal and get better. *Dear God, please help me. Guide me to someone who can lead me out of this cesspool I've created in my mind. Help me heal.*

The hum of the cicadas grew louder, as if carrying her prayer heavenward. Wyatt had brought good and bad into her life. The good part—he pushed her to seek help. The bad part—he made her long for love. Real love. Lasting love. Could she have that?

The words from the third chapter of Ecclesiastes rolled through her mind. *A time to be born and a time to die, a time to plant and a time to uproot, a time to kill and a time to heal, a time to tear down and a time to build, a time to weep and a time to laugh, a time to mourn and a time to dance, a time to scatter stones and a time to gather them, a time to embrace and a time to refrain from embracing, a time to search and a time to give up, a time to keep and a time to throw away, a time to tear and a time to mend, a time to be silent and a time to speak, a time to love and a time to hate, a time for war and a time for peace.*

It was her time to heal and mend, then maybe all those other things would fall into place in her life.

CHAPTER SEVEN

As Wyatt rolled his suitcase out of the Cincinnati airport, a cold blast of air captured his breath. Spring would be here in two weeks, but there was snow on the ground in Ohio. Florida and its warm breezes were over a thousand miles away, and Morgan's offer of a job resided there. That sounded pretty good right now. He didn't need to work for a living, but he loved every aspect of ranching. Working on the ranch would give him a purpose.

Wyatt turned to look at Caroline, who talked with her parents. The appeal of a job in Florida didn't match the allure of one Caroline Keller. He wanted to stay here to help her heal and find out whether anything could develop between them. Besides, he had his grandparents to think about. Too many things in Ohio called him not to leave.

"Should we turn around and go back?" Ginny pulled the collar up on her coat.

"Any time you want to retire and spend your winters in Florida, I'm ready, willing, and able." John put an arm around his wife's shoulders.

Ginny sighed. "I'm not ready to give up teaching, and besides, I'd miss my friends in Kellersburg."

John laughed. "Friends are more important than

warm weather."

As they waited for the shuttle to take them to their car, Wyatt took in the exchange between Caroline's parents. They had a loving relationship, just like his grandparents. Could he have that someday? With Caroline? Why did he keep jumping way ahead of reality? Every moment he'd spent with her while they were in Florida only confirmed what his heart had been telling him since she'd walked into his room at the nursing home and told him to be kind. She was a woman worth fighting for.

"What do you think?" Caroline looked at him as she stopped at the curb where they were to get the shuttle.

"About what?"

Caroline waved a gloved hand in the air. "Trading in this cold weather for balmy Florida? After all, you do have a job offer there."

"You know why I can't go back right now." Wyatt gave her a wry smile, wishing he could say out loud that she was the main reason.

"You have to be here for your grandparents."

"And I have to make sure this leg is healed." Wyatt tapped his leg with his cane. "It's a whole lot better after a leisurely week in Florida and those boys making sure I did my exercises. I really don't need this cane anymore, but I'm keeping it close, just in case."

"Good idea. And at least it snowed while we were gone and we don't have to drive home in a snowstorm." Caroline gave herself a hug. "I'll be glad when this cold is over. My blood is still thin from living in Kenya."

Wyatt wished he could give her a hug and whisk her back to Florida, where they could live happily ever after. What a pipe dream! The cold weather had made him abandon his senses. "Remember spring is just around the corner."

Caroline let out a sorry chuckle. "Spring isn't exactly warm until you get to June sometimes, and then it's almost over."

"I'm choosing to put on my optimist hat and believe warm weather is on the way." Wyatt nodded his head toward where Nathan and Melanie stood. "Your brother and his new wife don't seem to mind the cold at all. Their love is keeping them warm."

Smiling, Caroline nodded. "They are happy, and I'm so happy for them. And after swimming at the ranch, Ryan and Andrew are lobbying for a swimming pool."

"How do you know that?"

"I heard them on the plane."

Wyatt laughed. "Nathan might not be happy with me for taking them to the ranch."

Caroline shook her head. "Nathan's so wrapped up in Melanie that those kids just might have their way."

"You could be right." Wyatt glanced at Nathan and Melanie once more. "Here comes the shuttle."

As Wyatt joined the others while they scrambled to get on the shuttle, he took in their camaraderie. What would it be like to be part of the Keller clan? He'd like to find out. He took the seat next to Caroline. He liked being close to her, but he had to remember the secret she harbored, the one that kept her at arm's length. She laughed and talked with her family as the shuttle motored down the road. She was good at hiding her troubles. Was he doing the same?

After they were on the road for the drive back to Kellersburg, Caroline didn't do much talking. She concentrated on the highway lined with snow. Wyatt wondered what she was thinking. He wished she were thinking about him and the time they'd shared. He needed to put his mind on a different track, or he'd be disappointed.

"I'm going to give my grandparents a call and let them know we've landed and should be there in about an hour and a half." Wyatt pulled out his phone and tapped their number.

After Wyatt finished talking, he shoved the phone back into his coat pocket. "I hope you guys can stop in for a few minutes. My grandma has some refreshments for us." Wyatt held his breath. If they accepted the invitation, he'd have more time with Caroline.

"That sounds delightful." Ginny clapped her gloved hands together.

Ginny and John reminisced about the hours they'd spent with Ryan and Andrew on the beach, in the pool, and on the plane ride. They laughed at their antics and expressed their joy over being grandparents. Had his grandparents ever had such joy, or had he been a burden? He hadn't been the easiest child to rear. And there was a difference between being a grandparent who could send the grandchild home and being a grandparent who had constant parental duties.

Wyatt gave himself a mental shake. He should be reliving the week he'd spent with Caroline. An unexpected week, for sure. And now there was another unexpected development. His grandmother had something to show him when he got home—something she didn't want to discuss over the phone. Something told him it wasn't good news.

After their visit to the ranch, they had spent lazy days lounging on the beach near the historic hotel where they'd stayed. Because they'd been reading as they sat side by side on beach chairs at the water's edge, they hadn't spent much time talking. But just being near her made his day. They had shared some time riding waves on bodyboards with Andrew and Ryan. They'd helped the boys build several sandcastles. Those fun activities had made him forget that he had to figure out a plan for his life, one that didn't include the rodeo.

He should remember how he'd convinced Caroline to take a walk on the beach, just the two of them among the other beachgoers. When he'd asked, he'd read the hesitation in her eyes, but she'd said yes. Her agreement was a tiny battle won. They'd talked about their adventures on the ranch, and she'd asked him whether he would eventually take Morgan up on his job offer. Wyatt hadn't known how to answer that question other than to push his lack of a decision off on taking care of his grandparents. He didn't want to scare her off with his thoughts about a relationship with her.

"This coming weekend we're going to help Caroline move. Wyatt, are you in for some work?" Ginny asked.

Wyatt would like nothing better than to have an excuse to spend more time with Caroline. "I'd love to, but I'm not sure I'll be of much use. I can't lift anything heavy."

"We'll find something for you to do." John nodded. "Even if it's holding open doors. She actually doesn't have that much to move. It's more Nathan's stuff we're taking out of his house."

Wyatt chuckled. "Door holding is about my speed. My leg is much better. Being in the warm Florida sun helped."

"But now you're back in the Ohio cold." Ginny made a shivering motion.

"Mom, you shouldn't bug Wyatt to help me move."

Caroline ended her silence with that downer of a statement. Did that mean she didn't want him around? He pushed the negative question away. This wasn't the time for negativity. He couldn't win with that kind of attitude.

"Caroline, it's no bother, and the more I move the more I improve."

"Ryan and Andrew sure got a kick out of helping you with your exercises." John laughed. "Wyatt's right. You have to keep moving, or you don't improve."

Caroline shook her head as she gave him a sideways glance. "I wouldn't want to keep you from getting better. If you want to work, you can help me move. I just didn't want you to feel obligated."

"Helping you is never an obligation. It's a pleasure." Wyatt hoped she knew for certain that was true.

With her gaze trained straight ahead, she nodded. Was she just keeping her eyes on the road, or was she afraid to let him see her response to his statement? He had to watch himself and not take things a step too far with her. She was like a skittish colt. He didn't want to spook her.

As they neared the outskirts of Kellersburg, sadness overtook Wyatt's thoughts. The ride was almost over, and time with Caroline would end after the visit with his grandparents. He'd gotten used to seeing her every day. He would have withdrawal symptoms, at least until he helped her move. Ginny had no idea how much he welcomed the invitation to help her daughter. Next weekend couldn't come soon enough.

Wyatt turned to look at Ginny. "Just let me know what time you're starting the move, and I'll be there."

"Do you need someone to pick you up?" Ginny asked.

Wyatt shook his head. "I'll get one of my grandparents to give me a ride. Hey, if I do well with my PT, maybe she'll release me to drive by then. Or maybe that's wishful thinking."

"It's always good to have a positive outlook." John nodded.

"I'm learning that. Your daughter taught me to look on the bright side the day she walked into my room at the nursing home and told me to be kind." Wyatt glanced at Caroline to see if she had any reaction to his statement. "I needed that attitude adjustment."

John patted Caroline's shoulder. "She's always been

my glass-overflowing girl."

"Thanks, Dad. I got it from you."

Wyatt took in Caroline's forced smile. He knew the pain behind it. He'd gathered from their conversations that she'd been trying to live up to that expectation ever since she'd arrived back in Kellersburg. Something terrible had ripped the optimism from her life. He wanted to be there to help her restore it.

"Caroline, I've got a great idea. You should pick Wyatt up since he's helping you."

Wyatt let relief wash over him when she turned to him with a smile that morphed into a chuckle.

"Dad, you're not being subtle at all. You're as bad as Nathan and Melanie."

"Bad at what?" John held out his hands as he shrugged.

"Don't play dumb. You know you're trying to push Wyatt and me together. We're adults, and we can make our own plans if we wish."

John looked at his wife. "Was I trying to push them together?"

Ginny laughed. "In your not-so-subtle way. You know you were, so don't deny it."

Wyatt wanted to let them know he didn't have a problem with their matchmaking, but he didn't want to embarrass Caroline any further. He didn't miss the pink tinge creeping up her cheeks, and it wasn't from the cold. The interior of the car was warm despite the cold outside. He should probably not say a thing. Responding would only make things worse.

"Dad, give it up." Caroline laughed. "Just to make you happy, I'll be glad to give Wyatt a ride on moving day. In fact, I'll take him out to breakfast."

Wyatt couldn't stop the grin that curved his mouth. "I'm looking forward to that."

"Good. Then it's settled." Caroline tapped the steering wheel as she let out a sigh. "Now it's back to reality and the cold."

In minutes Caroline drove down the lane that led to his grandparents' house. She stopped the car at the end of the walk leading to the front door. Piles of snow lined the lane and the walk. The barnyard and fields were covered in white as far as one could see.

"I'll help you get your bag." John jumped out of the backseat.

"You don't have to do that." Wyatt unbuckled his seat belt.

Caroline chuckled. "You might as well let him help you. He's already got your bag out of the back."

"Thanks for driving me to and from the airport and to the ranch. And thanks for being my friend." Wyatt hoped she understood just what he meant.

"Thank you for understanding." Caroline unbuckled her seat belt.

Wyatt shut the car door. "Now let's see what treats my grandma has for us."

"Look. Your grandma has crocuses pushing up through the snow. I guess spring is on its way." Caroline pointed as she stopped by the steps leading to the front porch that ran the full length of the white clapboard farmhouse.

The crocuses gave Wyatt a picture of his attempt to forge a relationship with Caroline. He'd push through whatever was in his way. "Gram is quite the gardener."

"I know. I remember she used to provide the most beautiful flowers for church when I was a kid. Does she still do that?" Caroline turned to her mother for confirmation.

"She does whenever she has something available from her flower garden." Ginny shook her head. "I do not have a green thumb, so I envy her ability to grow beautiful flowers."

"You're here." The front door opened, and George stood in the doorway. "Come on in."

"Thanks so much for inviting us to stop in." Ginny shook George's hand.

"You're welcome." George nodded as he also shook John's hand. "Wyatt, your grandmother needs you in the kitchen."

"Sure thing." Wyatt shrugged out of his coat and left it on the back of a living room chair as he approached the kitchen.

As he stepped into the cozy room with its dark alder cabinets and the smell of freshly baked cookies swirling through the air, he looked at his grandmother's frown. What had he done wrong to elicit that look? "What's going on?"

"Come with me."

Wyatt followed his grandmother down the hall to the bedroom that served as a guest room and her sewing room. She carefully opened the door, then looked at him with a finger to her mouth. The shades were pulled, and the normally bright room had little light. He peered into the dimness. What was that on the bed?

His grandmother motioned for him to come closer as she stood next to the bed. A child, a little girl, lay under a blanket on the queen-sized bed. A wall of pillows lay on the floral comforter as they surrounded the sleeping child. Her light-brown curls lay across the pillow. What was she doing here?

"Who is she?" Wyatt whispered.

"Your daughter." His grandmother's reply was equally quiet.

"What? That's impossible. I want an explanation." He used every ounce of his willpower not to shout, then pointed to the door.

"And so do I." His grandmother gave him a pointed look as she went into the hallway.

Wyatt joined her, closing the door behind him. "She's not my daughter. Where did she come from?" His words came out in a harsh whisper. He couldn't figure this out. Even though his grandmother had told him she had something to discuss with him when he got back, he'd never imagined this.

His grandmother's blue eyes filled with tears. "A young woman came to the door not long before you called. She had the little girl with her, and the young woman told me she was very ill and couldn't take care of the child. She was rail thin with a strange color to her skin. She said you were the girl's father, and she would be better off with you."

Wyatt felt as if his head would explode. "Did this young woman have a name?"

His grandmother nodded. "Shelby. Shelby Pollard. That's what she told me. She said she used to be your girlfriend."

"Yes, she was my girlfriend, but that was when I first went on the rodeo circuit ten years ago. We haven't dated in years. I haven't seen her in years. She's delusional. There's no way I could be this child's father." *Unless she's a lot older than she appears.* That thought ran through Wyatt's mind.

"If you're not the child's father, why would the young woman say you are?"

Wyatt let out a heavy sigh. "I'm not sure, but she has lots of problems. Substance abuse, for one."

"Then maybe it's a good thing she wants someone else to take care of her little girl." His grandmother's brow wrinkled in concern.

"So Shelby just shows up unannounced and leaves her child here? She's even more unstable than I remember." Wyatt looked heavenward, then back at his grandmother. "What am I supposed to do with this little girl who isn't even mine?"

"I don't know, Wyatt. I just didn't know what to do." Denise laid a hand over her heart. "Shelby told me the little girl is three. She'll turn four in April. Her name's Tasha."

Wyatt shook his head. Tasha had been Shelby's sister's name, the sister who had died in a car accident when they were young. Wyatt didn't understand any of it. "How on earth did Shelby find me? We haven't spoken in years."

"I don't know. I didn't think to ask. I was so shocked that you had a child." Denise frowned.

"But the child isn't mine."

Denise pressed her lips together, as if trying to hold back her emotions. "Maybe John and Ginny can help us figure out what to do."

Wyatt glanced down the hallway toward the living room. Did he want to air his dirty laundry in front of the town's VIPs, especially Caroline? What would she think about his ex-girlfriend dumping a child in his lap, even if said child wasn't his? "Why would you ask them?"

"Because they're smart people."

"You're smart. We can figure this out."

Denise put her hand on his arm. "That's right. We're both smart, but sometimes you have to ask advice from others and then weigh all the options. It doesn't hurt to ask for help."

"Is that what you did when I came to live with you?" Wyatt couldn't help thinking of how his parents had abandoned him, but things had turned out all right in the end.

"Wyatt, we didn't need to ask. You were kin, and we loved you. There was no asking. We were happy to give you a home."

Emotions overwhelmed Wyatt as he stared at his grandmother. He gathered her in his arms and held her tight. "I love you, Gram. Thanks for giving me a home."

Tears once again filled Denise's eyes as she stepped out of Wyatt's embrace. "It was all worth it. You've turned out to be a good man, and I know you'll do what's best for that little girl in there."

"What's going to happen when she wakes up? Does she know her mother won't be here?"

Denise shook her head. "I don't know what Shelby said before she left. I'm sorry I handled things so badly."

"Gram, it's okay." Wyatt put his arm around her shoulders. "I wonder what Shelby would've done if I'd been here. It's almost as if she knew I wouldn't be here. How is that possible?"

Denise looked up at Wyatt. "Let's go talk to the Kellers. Please?"

Wyatt looked at the pleading expression on his grandmother's face. How could he say no? How could he say yes? This whole situation was sure to blow a huge whole in any plans he had about Caroline.

He took a deep breath. "I suppose."

"Oh, one more thing. She just seemed so desperate and so insistent that you are the child's father. I just didn't know what to do."

"So that's why you believed the child was mine?"

"I didn't really believe it, but I didn't know what else to think."

"What did Gramps say?"

"Not much." Denise lowered her gaze. "He just said you'd have to live up to your responsibility."

That sounded like Gramps. He was all about responsibility. Wyatt had learned that early when he'd come to live with them. Now this was like a bad nightmare, worse than the ones where he got bucked off a horse and was flying through the air only to wake up just before he landed. This wasn't a dream. It was real. How could Shelby do such a thing when she knew it was a lie?

"Well, I plan to set the record straight. I'll agree to get advice from the Kellers, but I'll let you do the talking."

"You may have to fill in some of the blanks." Denise looked up at him. "Ready?"

"Not really, but I'll go along with your wishes." Wyatt followed his grandmother into the living room.

"Sorry to keep you waiting." Denise grimaced. "Something happened before you got here, and I had to explain it to him before we talked to you."

"That's okay. George has shared your wonderful cookies with us, as well as tea." Ginny held up her tea cup. "These are marvelous. Do you have a special recipe?"

Wyatt listened to his grandmother explain the secret to her cookies. As far as he was concerned, they could talk about cookies for the rest of the afternoon. Then the conversation morphed into a blow-by-blow of the wedding and time spent at the beach. Ginny showed the photos of the wedding she had on her phone. If they never got around to talking about the child in the other room, he wouldn't mind. But the topic couldn't be avoided forever. So he wished they'd just get it over with. Maybe his grandmother didn't know how to bring up the subject.

"Where's my mommy?"

The conversation came to an abrupt halt as the little girl stood at the edge of the living room. Her dark curls were a tousled mess around her cute face. Shelby in miniature. The child held a battered pink elephant under one arm.

Denise ran over and picked up the child. "Your mommy has gone away for a while, and you're going to stay here with me. Is that okay?"

The little girl's lips quivered as her brown eyes filled with tears. "I want my mommy."

"Hi, Tasha. I'm Wyatt, and I'm a friend of your mother's." Wyatt held his hands out to the child and prayed she'd come to him. "Will you come and see me? I've got something to show you."

Still holding tight to the elephant, the little girl blinked, her expression uncertain, but she reached out her arms. Wyatt took the child from his grandmother. "I've got a big surprise for you in the kitchen. Would you like to see it?"

Tasha nodded but didn't say a word. She clung to Wyatt like her life depended on it. He strode into the kitchen. He'd let his grandmother deal with the fallout. He didn't want to be around to see Caroline's reaction to this unexpected problem.

Wyatt stopped at the kitchen counter, where chocolate chip cookies sat on the cooling rack. He held one out to Tasha. "These are really good. Would you like one?"

She nodded and took the cookie with her free hand. She held it for a moment, then took a small bite. Her face lit up. "It's good."

Wyatt breathed a sigh of relief. The cookie would satisfy her for a few minutes. While Tasha munched on the cookie, he could hear the rise and fall of his grandmother's voice, then his grandfather's. He couldn't exactly hear what they said, but Tasha's appearance was surely the topic of conversation. John said something, then Ginny chimed in. Still, he didn't hear the words, only the voices. Caroline said nothing. What was she thinking?

"More cookie."

The statement brought his attention back to Tasha, who looked at him with expectation, messy chocolate surrounding her mouth and painting her fingers. He probably had chocolate on his blue shirt. He hoped there wasn't any on the elephant. Though he supposed it would wash along with his shirt, but would all this mess come out in the proverbial wash?

"Before you have another cookie, let me show you something."

"Okay." Her expression told him he had earned her trust with a cookie.

He set her on the floor. "Let's wipe that chocolate off your mouth and fingers."

After ripping a piece of paper towel off the holder, he wet it. Then he gently wiped away the offending brown goop. She smiled at him when he finished, and his heart melted. Was it because she looked like her mother, or just because she was such a cute little thing? Either way, the reaction was unexpected.

"All clean now." She held up her fingers and gave him a cheesy grin.

He picked her up and held her close. Did Shelby choose him because she knew he had a soft heart? Why did she want to give up her child? But he feared he knew the answer. She was using again. At least she had the sense to know she shouldn't subject her child to that lifestyle.

"Yes, you're all clean." He wished her mother was. As he headed for the laundry room, he balanced her in his arms. "Do you like kittens?"

Tasha's blank expression made him think she didn't know what a kitten was. That made him sad. This whole scenario made him sad. It reminded him of the day he'd been left here on the farm, never to see his parents again. He'd cried himself to sleep many nights in the beginning, and he'd been terrible to his grandparents. But they'd loved him through it all, loved him enough to give him the foundation he'd needed to become the man he was today, one they could be proud of, even with the mistakes he'd made along the way.

His relationship with Shelby was one of those mistakes. Now he was paying for it in a way he'd never expected.

When Wyatt reached the laundry room door, he set Tasha down. "Now I'm going to open this door, and inside are some kitties. They're nice, but you have to be gentle. Don't squeeze. Just pet them."

Tasha nodded her head, but uncertainty filled her eyes.

Wyatt slowly opened the door. High-pitched meowing came from every corner as the four little balls of fur hurried toward them, while the mother cat lay on the bed. Tasha cried and raised her arms for him to pick her up. He scooped her into his arms just as the kittens rubbed up against his legs.

After quickly closing the door, Wyatt patted her back as she whimpered. "It's okay, Tasha. They won't hurt you."

The child clung to him and buried her face on his shoulder. Had this bright idea backfired? He thought for sure fuzzy kittens would be just the thing for her to love. He tried to pry her lose from the death grip she had on him, but she only clung tighter.

He rubbed her back. "Tasha, honey, please let me set you right here. The kittens can't reach you up here." He moved toward the washer and set her there. He stayed still until she finally relinquished her hold on him. He looked at her as he pointed to her. "You stay right there, and I'll show you a kitten."

Tasha sat there wide eyed while Wyatt scooped a gray tabby from the floor. The kitten squirmed in his hand but soon settled as he petted it on the head.

"See. The kitten won't hurt you." Wyatt continued to pet the kitten while Tasha watched with fascination. He stepped closer and brought the kitten within Tasha's reach. "Would you like to pet it?"

Tasha shrunk back, but curiosity filled her eyes. The

kitten purred, and the sound filled the laundry room. He remembered Gram saying one of the kittens had the loudest purr. This must be the one.

"What's that noise?" Tasha shrunk back more.

"The kitten is purring. He kind of sounds like he has a motor inside him." Wyatt held the kitten up to his ear. "He's loud."

"Can I hear?"

A breakthrough. Wyatt held the kitten closer to Tasha. "Would you like to touch him?"

Tasha held her body back even as she reached out to touch the kitten. She rubbed a finger down the kitten's back.

"He's soft, isn't he?"

Tasha nodded, then looked around. "What's that big one?"

"The mama cat. These are her babies."

Tasha's little face puckered up, and tears rolled down her cheeks. "Where's my mommy?"

Wyatt wanted to cry himself. He was back to square one. Tasha was worried about her mother. Why had he mentioned the word *mama*? What had made him think this would work?

He let out a heavy sigh. He couldn't lie to the kid. Her mother probably wasn't coming back. She was sick, but was that a good enough explanation for the child? "Tasha…"

Before he could finish his sentence, Denise stuck her head around the door. "Are you okay in here?"

Wyatt let out a sorry chuckle. "I'm not sure."

"You need to bring Tasha out to the living room. Everyone wants to talk to you."

Did that everyone include Caroline? How could he face her? But it had to be done. He picked Tasha up and followed his grandmother to the living room.

When he entered the room, John, Ginny, and Caroline sat there with expectation in their expressions. "Hi, everyone. This is Tasha. I guess Gram has filled you in on how she came to be here."

Ginny nodded. "How do you feel about that?"

Wyatt took a deep breath, then looked at his grandmother. "Do you think she should be here for this discussion?"

"That's a good point." Denise looked over at Tasha. "Hey, sweet girl, would you like another cookie?"

"Yes."

Tasha's smile and enthusiastic response made Wyatt chuckle.

"I guess you'd better get that girl a cookie, and maybe you can do a better job of introducing her to the kittens than I did." Wyatt handed Tasha to his grandmother. "Guess you can see through the walls since you knew I'd already given Tasha a cookie."

"I'm just a pretty good guesser." Carrying Tasha, Denise trotted off to the kitchen.

Wyatt looked over the occupants of the living room. Caroline sat there, her expression blank. He wanted to say the right thing to answer Ginny's question, but he wasn't sure how he felt. This whole thing didn't seem real.

"I understand that Tasha's mother convinced your grandmother that you're the little girl's father, but you say you're not, right?" Ginny looked at him for confirmation.

"That's right." Wyatt gazed at her. Did she believe him? "I dated her mother, but that was years ago. Too long ago for me to be Tasha's father."

"She seems to relate to you. She wasn't afraid to go to you. That's a good sign." Ginny raised her eyes in a questioning gaze.

"I suppose that's good." Wyatt didn't know what Ginny was getting at. Was this a roundabout way to find out if he planned to take this child in as his own? "I think she likes anyone who can give her a cookie."

"Do you have any idea where the little girl's mother is?" John asked.

Wyatt shook his head. "The last time I saw Shelby was probably five or six years ago at a rodeo event. She was a barrel racer."

"So you don't have any idea why she would say you're the father of her child?" John asked.

Wyatt wished he knew. It might make this inquisition a little easier. Maybe now John wasn't so eager to push him and Caroline together. "Shelby had substance abuse problems, and she had too many boyfriends."

"So she drew your name out of a hat?" Leaning forward in his chair, John eyed Wyatt.

"John." Ginny's look could have pinned her husband to the wall. "Be kind."

There was that phrase again. *Be kind*. What was the kindest thing he could do with Tasha? Wyatt didn't know. He stared at John. "What's your advice? What would you do if you were in my shoes?"

Looking contrite, John leaned back and crossed his arms over his midsection. "I apologize for that remark. You've asked a fair question. There's no easy answer."

"I'm pretty sure Shelby's using opioids again." Wyatt shook his head. "She just can't kick the habit. In and out of rehab. I can't believe she had a child. And maybe her thought was to give Tasha a stable home. I don't know what was in her head. I wish I'd been here to talk to her."

"Is there any way you can find her?" Ginny peered at Wyatt.

"I could contact some of my old rodeo buddies. Maybe they would know." Wyatt shrugged. "I know her family's from Kentucky, but she didn't have much use for them. They weren't keen on her rodeo ambitions."

"So in the meantime, what are your thoughts about Tasha?" Ginny asked.

Wyatt stared out the front window at the snow-covered landscape as if he'd find an answer there. Ginny and John had done all the talking. Caroline hadn't said a thing. She must think he was a pretty messed-up guy if an old girlfriend had dumped her child on him.

"That little girl needs a stable home, but I'm not sure I can provide one, and I certainly can't expect my grandparents, who have already reared me, to take care of another child, especially one who isn't related to them in any way."

"You can't abandon her. If you don't take her, she'll be put in foster care. Before you think of doing that, you have to talk to Melanie." Caroline's statement broke the silence and shocked Wyatt.

"Why talk to Melanie?" Wyatt stared at Caroline.

"She grew up in foster care," Caroline and Ginny said at the same time.

"And what will she tell me?" Wyatt looked back and forth between mother and daughter. At least Caroline had finally said something.

"I'll leave that to her, but please talk to her." Ginny nodded.

Wyatt sighed. "I honestly don't have an answer for this."

"You'll need time to think this over before you make a decision." Ginny pressed her lips together in a grim line.

Ginny's scrutiny made Wyatt's stomach curdle. "I agree. I can't make any snap decisions."

Caroline held her hands in a prayerful pose. "And, please, please, please talk to Melanie before you decide what to do."

"Okay, I'll do that." Wyatt would do anything for Caroline. He wished he knew what she thought. Maybe he'd have a chance to talk with her at that breakfast she'd promised him, if that was still on.

"Good." Caroline smiled.

Wyatt's grandfather, who had remained silent during this discussion, stood and looked around the room. "And we should make this a matter of prayer."

John also stood. "Agreed, and we should do it now."

"I'll get your grandmother." George hurried to the kitchen and returned a moment later with Denise and Tasha in tow. "Okay. Now that we're all here, I'll pray, if that's okay with everyone."

Tasha ran up to Wyatt and held up her hands, the pink elephant dangling from one. "I want up."

Wyatt looked down, and his chest felt as if an elephant were sitting on it. "Up you go."

She giggled as she wrapped her arms around his neck. Two elephants were sitting on his chest now.

John surveyed the group. "I'd also like to pray."

There was a murmur of agreement as everyone stood.

"Do you mind if we form a circle and hold hands?" George held out a hand to Denise, and she took his hand.

Tasha clung to Wyatt, and he couldn't take anyone's hand. He'd like to take Caroline's hand though. "I'll just stand in the circle since I'm holding Tasha."

"Your grandmother and I can put our arms around your waist as you stand in the circle." Caroline stepped closer.

"Okay." Denise stepped nearer Wyatt on his other side.

Having Caroline so close made Wyatt hold Tasha tighter. He didn't want Caroline's nearness to distract him and forget his hold on the little girl. As his grandfather prayed, Wyatt closed his eyes and fought hard to concentrate on the words of the prayer rather than Caroline.

"Our heavenly Father, thank You for hearing our prayers. Thank You for family and friends to love us and help us share our burdens. Thank You for Wyatt and the fine man he has become. We pray today that You'll give him wisdom concerning little Tasha. We pray for the best for her and for help for her mother. Let us rely on You to guide us. Amen."

John prayed a similar prayer. After he finished, Caroline's arm tightened around his waist. Wyatt swallowed hard as his pulse raced.

Caroline's soft voice sounded through the quiet room. "Dear Lord, please help Wyatt know what direction to take. We ask that you guide us all in the name of Your son, Jesus. Amen."

"Amen." The voices sending out an affirmation ended the prayer time.

Caroline stepped away as his grandmother gave him a hug. Wyatt took Caroline's willingness to stand close to him as a good sign. She was in his corner, and he wanted to be in hers. What would Tasha's presence do for that wish?

The little girl laid her head on his shoulder. Was all this togetherness giving him the nudge to take in this child? He couldn't answer that today. No rushed decisions. He should locate Shelby first. He needed to know where her head was at. He needed answers. But what if he didn't find any?

CHAPTER EIGHT

Two days after the return from Florida, Caroline poked her head around the doorframe to her mother's home office. She had finally drummed up enough nerve to talk to her mom about what had happened before she'd left the mission field. This wouldn't be easy, but it had to be done.

"Mom, I'd like to talk to you about something."

Always neat and clean, the office was a picture of her mother. How would her mother take the news of the rape? Caroline didn't really want to discuss it, but Wyatt was right. She needed to do this, and his response to having Tasha dumped in his lap made Caroline realize she had to face up to her problem also. Reaching out for help was the answer, and her mother was that help.

Ginny swiveled in her chair and looked Caroline's way. "Sure. Come in and have a seat. What's on your mind?"

Caroline sat in the love seat near the window that looked out on the quiet street in front of her parents' house. She looked at the shelves full of books. The eclectic collection had offered hours of reading for the whole family. During her school years, she had often used some of these books for references. Her mother's office was like her own private library.

"Are you here to talk about Wyatt?"

A little frown creasing her brow, Caroline jerked her gaze away from the books and toward her mother. "No."

"Then what?" Curiosity highlighted her mother's expression.

Caroline let out a sigh. "This is hard for me to talk about, but I need to tell you. It's about something that happened a few weeks before I left Kenya."

"Please go ahead. I'm listening."

Ginny's kind pleading eased Caroline's mind, but still the words wouldn't come. She lowered her gaze and shook her head. "I just don't know where to begin. It's all so horrible."

Ginny joined Caroline on the love seat and put an arm around her shoulders and pulled her close. "Tell me what's troubling you. Just spit it out."

Caroline stared at her lap. Why had it been easier to tell Wyatt rather than her own mother? Caroline guessed telling Wyatt wouldn't ruin a relationship, but she feared her mother would think less of her, because she hadn't reported the rape. Her peaceful life had been torn apart that day. Peace still eluded her because she had shoved all the hurt and pain down inside, but that strategy hadn't made her forget. Instead, guilt over not reporting it and not getting help gnawed at her. She wanted to get help so maybe there was a chance she could love a man—and maybe that man was Wyatt. She had seen his kinder, gentler side—something she had never expected. He had sensed her troubled spirit when no one else had. He'd seen through the facade she had presented to family and friends. He cared about her and wanted her to get better.

On the verge of tears, Caroline took a shaky breath. She could do this. Her mother would understand. At least, that was Caroline's prayer.

"Caroline, you're worrying me. Please tell me what's wrong."

The concern in her mother's voice prompted Caroline to look up. "This isn't a pretty story. It's awful, and I'm sorry I didn't do the right thing."

With her mother's arm around her shoulders, Caroline haltingly told her mother the same story she'd told Wyatt. After Caroline finished, her mother wrapped both arms around Caroline and held her close. The warmth of her mother's arms gave Caroline peace for the moment.

"I'm so sorry that happened to you." Ginny held Caroline at arm's length. "I don't know what I would've done if I'd been in your place. I'm so glad you told me."

Caroline blinked back tears. "Me, too. I wanted to tell you so I can get some counseling. I thought you might know someone, but not here in town."

Ginny nodded. "I understand that. Let me do some checking around. I'm sure I can find someone in Cincinnati."

"I was planning to check there, but I've been away for so long that I didn't know where to start. I appreciate your help."

Ginny sat back in the love seat and eyed Caroline. "Now can I ask about Wyatt? Does your telling me have something to do with him? How do you feel about him?"

"You mean, what do I think about Tasha?"

"No." Ginny smiled. "About Wyatt. Even though your dad was obviously trying to push you two together, I sensed a reluctance on your part, even though Wyatt doesn't seem the least bit reluctant. You did spend a good bit of time together in Florida."

"I know, and he hasn't hesitated to tell me of his interest, but in the state I'm in, I can't think of having a relationship with a man."

"But it's because of him you're wanting to get help, right?"

Caroline nodded, marveling at her mother's perceptiveness. "He's the one who told me I should see a counselor and tell you what happened to me. If it weren't for him, I'd probably still be keeping this all to myself."

Ginny eyed Caroline. "So you've told Wyatt about this?"

"I know it seems strange that I had such a hard time telling you but I just blurted it out to him." Caroline shrugged.

"There must've been a good reason."

Caroline thought back to that night. "Yeah. He wanted to dance during the reception, and I couldn't bring myself to be in a man's arms. The thought terrified me."

Ginny wrinkled her brow. "So if he frightened you, why would you tell him?"

"Because he looked right at me and asked if

someone had hurt me." Caroline remembered that moment as if Wyatt were standing right here in the room and saying it all over again. "He hardly knows me now, but he sensed that I was deeply troubled. He said he wasn't going to leave until I told him what was bothering me. So I did. It was almost a relief to actually tell someone."

Ginny gathered Caroline in her arms again. "I'm sorry I didn't see it. I was just so glad to have you back home again that I missed the signals."

"It's okay, Mom." Caroline squeezed her mother tight. "I just want to heal."

Ginny held Caroline at arm's length. "And I'll do whatever I can to help you do that."

"I know you will."

"Are you still planning to take Wyatt to breakfast on Saturday?"

"Yeah, if he still wants to go." Caroline shrugged. "He might feel like he has to stay with Tasha."

"You have to talk to him."

Caroline laughed. "Mom, are you trying to push us together?"

Ginny laughed in return. "Of course I am."

"What do you think about this deal with Tasha?"

"She's a cute little thing, but I understand a bachelor not wanting to take on the responsibility of a child that isn't his." Ginny nodded. "I think it's wise for him to think it over carefully."

"You like him."

Ginny chuckled. "Of course I like him. If I didn't, I

certainly wouldn't be pushing you together. The question is, do *you* like him?"

Caroline let the question roll through her mind. Of course she liked him, but what did that mean? She'd never felt connected to any man the way she felt connected to Wyatt. "I do. A lot, but that brings up whether I can have a relationship with him that goes beyond friendship. We're at the friendship stage now, and I don't know if I can ever get beyond that."

"Does he understand?"

The conversation Caroline had had with Wyatt by the pool at the ranch swam through her thoughts. Wyatt said he understood, but how long was he willing to wait for her to heal before he gave up and moved on? What if he took that job in Florida? And what about Tasha? How would she affect his thoughts on a relationship? So many questions and no answers. "He says he does. He's the one who encouraged me to tell you and get help. He says he prays for me."

Ginny patted Caroline's arm. "He sounds like a keeper to me."

"Yeah, but how long will he be willing to wait for me to heal?"

"If he cares about you, he'll wait as long as it takes."

Caroline put a fist to her mouth and closed her eyes. Could she pray he would hang on long enough for her to overcome the trauma? Or was that being selfish? She didn't know anymore. Was her trust in her fellow man too broken to fix? She prayed it wasn't. She wanted to get better. That was half the battle.

Caroline looked into her mother's sympathetic eyes. Love resided there. "I hope you're right, because I don't think this will be a quick process."

"I'll speed the process up as much as I can by contacting some people I know today."

"Thanks, Mom. I love you."

"And I love you, too." Ginny hugged Caroline, then stood. "Now I've got to get busy making those phone calls."

Caroline remained on the love seat while her mother went to her desk. Caroline grabbed a Bible from a book shelf and let it fall open. Her eyes were drawn to an underlined verse in Jeremiah 17. *Heal me, Lord, and I will be healed; save me and I will be saved, for you are the one I praise.*

That was what she was looking for. Healing. *Dear Lord, give me Your strength to heal my broken places. Amen.*

***

Sun glinted off the hood of Caroline's gray subcompact car as she drove down the lane leading to the Bayers' house. Warmer weather had come to Kellersburg, and the recent snow had melted, leaving behind muddy fields. The warmer temperatures gave a hint of spring and even warmed Caroline's heart—or maybe that was thoughts of Wyatt.

When she'd called to confirm their breakfast, Wyatt had agreed to join her without hesitation. Even though the original invitation had been issued on the trip home from the airport only a week ago, it seemed like ages ago rather than a few days. Had she missed seeing him every day? Yes. There was no denying it, but the time apart had given her time to think about how to deal with her growing attraction for him. Absence made the heart grow fonder.

But what would transpire if he tried to hold her hand again? Would she whither at a hug or completely lose it if he tried to kiss her? At this point, he wouldn't try any of those things, but if their relationship grew, someday he'd want those things. She didn't know how she'd handle those circumstances. She had made it through a crazy dance that had lasted all of two minutes, but that was different because they'd had an audience. Freaking out in front of them would have required an explanation, so she'd held it together. She was still holding it together.

As she drew nearer to the house, she spied Wyatt waiting on the front porch. He waved and headed her way as she brought the car to a stop. He didn't have his cane, and he looked normal in his jeans, boots, and brown suede jacket. Hopefully, that meant good progress with his rehab.

Wyatt moseyed toward her car, only the hint of a limp in his step. He opened the passenger door. "Hi. You're right on time."

Caroline smiled, her heart doing a little tap dance. "You'll learn I'm usually very punctual."

He grinned as he slid onto the seat and buckled his

seat belt. "I think I kind of knew that already."

"How's Tasha?"

"Not happy I'm going away." Wyatt sighed.

"She's attached to you already. How does that make you feel?"

"Like the choice has been made for me, and I'm not sure that is good."

Caroline nodded. "True. Have you talked to Melanie?"

"Not yet. I thought maybe there would be time today." He glanced her way. "What do you think?"

"I think you have to make time or it will never happen."

"I didn't know how to approach her."

Caroline chuckled. "She doesn't bite."

"I'm serious." Wyatt narrowed his gaze. "How do you ask someone whether they liked growing up in foster care?"

"Okay, I get your point. I'll help you."

"Thanks." Wyatt gave her a wry smile. "While we eat, I've got something to show you."

"What?"

"You'll see it after we order our food."

Caroline let out an exasperated sigh. "Why can't you tell me now?"

"Because it's something you have to read, and I don't want you reading while you're driving." Wyatt chuckled. "And I think I just learned something else about you."

"What?"

"You're impatient."

"I am not."

Wyatt's chuckle turned into a full-blown laugh. "Oh yes you are."

"I'll just have to show you how patient I can be." Caroline joined his laughter, but her thoughts jumped to how Wyatt had to be patient with her, not the other way around. "I hope you're more patient than I am."

"I understand, and I like that you trust me enough now to be alone with me. I think that's progress." He gave her a sideways glance. "Or maybe I shouldn't have reminded you."

Caroline took a deep breath and gripped the steering wheel tighter. "It's a good reminder. I consider this a baby step toward getting better."

"And I'm still praying."

"Me, too." Caroline gave him a glance, then turned her gaze back to the road. "I told my mom, and she has found me a counselor."

"I'm glad to hear that." Relief sounded in Wyatt's voice. "In Cincinnati?"

Caroline nodded. "I have my first session next week."

"Will that interfere with your job?"

"No. I'm taking Tuesday mornings off. Speaking of my job. You are going to help me with bingo, right?"

"You were serious when you asked me to help with bingo?"

"Absolutely. The little old ladies at the nursing home will love you."

Wyatt laughed. "Should I wear my cowboy hat?"

"Maybe for your introduction, but I think the ladies will want you to take it off to be polite."

Wyatt shook his head. "I actually don't plan to wear my cowboy hat. I was only teasing."

"Ryan and Andrew got a kick out of wearing cowboy hats when we were at the ranch."

"I know. Do you think they'd like to have their own?"

"You can ask Melanie when you talk to her."

Caroline found a parking spot in front of the café owned by one of her relatives. It was a favorite for the after-church crowd on Sundays. Saturdays brought in locals from all over town.

"We're here." Caroline turned off the engine and grabbed her purse.

Wyatt hopped out of the car. He hurried to the door and held it open as she approached.

"You must be hungry."

He grinned. "I am. I remember when I first came to live with my grandparents, Gramps took me here once for lunch and let me pick whatever I wanted."

"What did you get?"

"Nothing fancy. A burger, fries, and a big chocolate milkshake." Wyatt had a faraway look in his eyes. "That was a treat. We didn't eat out much."

"So what do you like to eat for breakfast?"

Wyatt shrugged as the hostess led them to a booth with dark faux-leather seats. "I'll have a look at the menu before I decide."

"You mean Nathan never brought his number one client here for breakfast?" Caroline slipped into the booth and set her purse beside her, then shrugged out of her jacket.

Wyatt eyed her as he slid onto the bench seat across from her. "And how do you know that I'm Nathan's number one client?"

"You must be. He invited you to his wedding. I didn't see any other clients there."

"We usually ate at the country club when we met."

"Yes, of course. That makes sense for the number one client."

Wyatt continued to eye her. "He's more like an older brother to me. He's given me a lot of good advice over the years. Nathan and Morgan are the two men besides my grandfather that I look up to. Nathan helped me get my financial footing. Morgan took me to cowboy church and gave me a spiritual footing. And Gramps filled my head with wise advice that, unfortunately, I didn't take until I grew up and realized what a wise man he is."

"You're blessed to have those men in your life." Caroline wished she hadn't made light of Nathan's relationship with Wyatt. That relationship was obviously very important to him. She'd had no idea that while she'd been gone that her brother and her old nemesis had forged a bond. "I'm glad you look up to Nathan. I think he sees you as a friend more than a client."

"I'm beginning to realize that." Wyatt lowered his gaze as he picked up the menu.

While they perused the breakfast choices, the

mysterious thing that Wyatt wanted her to read dominated her thoughts. Finally she laid her menu aside.

Wyatt looked up. "You know what you want?"

"Yeah, an omelet with mushrooms, bacon, and spinach. What about you?"

"The Big Breakfast."

"I guess you are hungry." Caroline chuckled.

"I've worked up an appetite chasing after an almost four-year-old."

"You sound like an old man already."

Wyatt set his menu on the table. "You have to remember I'm working with a handicap."

"Oh, okay." Caroline nodded. "So what do you want me to read?"

Wyatt held up a finger. "We have to order first."

As if on cue, the waitress appeared. As soon as the young woman left, Caroline eyed Wyatt. "Okay, now's the time."

Wyatt let out a harsh breath. "First there are a few things I have to tell you."

"More excuses to put it off?"

"No. I need to give you some background before you read it." Wyatt leaned forward. "I want to tell you about Shelby."

"Tasha's mom?"

"Yes." Wyatt sighed again. "I don't know whether you knew that after high school I took a rodeo scholarship to a small college out west."

"I vaguely remember that."

Wyatt gave her a wry smile. "I guess I wasn't

exactly on your radar in high school."

Caroline shrugged. There was no way she would admit that even though they didn't run in the same circles, he had always intrigued her. "We did have different friends."

"Anyway, I quit college after the first year and joined the rodeo circuit. At that point in my life I didn't see much sense in books, when I could be earning money doing all the things I was doing for free."

"And you did very well."

Wyatt chuckled. "Not so well in the beginning, but it takes time. So I met Shelby that first year. We started dating, and she was my first love. She was pretty, funny, and full of laughter. I fell hard for her, and she stole my heart. She was a barrel racer and a good one. She won a lot of competitions, but she also suffered a bad injury about six months after we started dating."

"An injury like yours?"

"Not as bad, but bad enough. Dealing with that injury is what got her hooked on opioids, and she just couldn't kick that habit. Those horrible drugs led her down a path of destruction." Misery painted Wyatt's face.

Caroline placed a hand over her heart. "I'm so sorry."

"I didn't know she'd gotten addicted to the painkillers. She was good at hiding it, at least from me. Morgan warned me that Shelby was trouble, but I didn't listen to him. I didn't listen until I came home one day and found her in bed with another cowboy, a guy who was supplying her drug habit."

Caroline let out a little cry, then covered her mouth. "So sorry about that, too."

Wyatt took a deep breath. "That was a wake-up call for me. She broke my heart in more ways than one. In the beginning I tried to help her, but she betrayed our love because she couldn't get off the painkillers. I hated seeing her go down that treacherous path. It was a terrible reminder of my parents' problems."

"That must've been hard."

"Shelby and I went our separate ways, but I'd run into her every once in a while at an event. Sometimes she was clean, and other times I could tell she was using again. It broke my heart." Sadness filled Wyatt's eyes. "I lost contact with her, and I had no idea she'd had a child."

Caroline listened to the story with a heavy heart. So Wyatt must have been living with Shelby, but Caroline wasn't going to ask. "And all this explanation is leading up to what?"

Wyatt reached into his jacket pocket and brought out some folded papers. "Gram found this tucked away in Tasha's suitcase yesterday. I want you to read it."

Caroline took the papers and unfolded them. It was a letter from Shelby addressed to Wyatt. Neat handwriting covered the pages. The neat handwriting of the woman Wyatt had loved. Did he still, or had he gotten over his first love? Caroline read the letter.

Dear Wyatt,

You're probably surprised to hear from me and that I have a daughter. I've kept up with your career and know you've done well for yourself. I was sorry to hear about your injury, but I understand you're making good progress in your recovery. I wish I could say the same for myself.

I talked to the lady at the rehab place you went to. She said you'd been discharged. So I figured you were with your grandparents. I'm glad I guessed right. At first I thought I'd talk to you, but when I called and found out you were out of town, I decided it was better this way. I'm sorry I had to lie and tell your grandparents that Tasha is yours, but I was afraid they wouldn't take her if I didn't.

Please forgive me for hurting you. You were the best thing that ever happened to me, and I threw it all away. I've messed up my life, and I can't climb out of the hole I've dug for myself. I don't want Tasha to suffer because of me. I love my little girl, and the best thing I can think of for her is to be with you. I know that's a lot to ask after the way I treated you, but if you ever loved me, please love my daughter.

Please take care of my little girl. She deserves someone better than me, and that someone is you. Don't let my parents have her. They probably wouldn't want her, just like they didn't want me. They were never the same after my sister died. She was the star, and I couldn't compete. I was the one who should have died instead of my sister.

I don't see myself being around for long. My health is really bad. The drugs I waited too long to quit have taken their toll. I'm dying, and I don't know how much longer I have in this life. I've put a copy of my will in with this letter, and I've named you as Tasha's guardian. I hope you can find it in your heart to take care of her.
Love,
Shelby

Before Caroline could comment, the waitress delivered their food and then hurried off to wait on another table.

"Let's give thanks for our food, and then you can tell me what you think." Wyatt unrolled his flatware from inside a napkin, then bowed his head. "Lord, thank You for this day You've given us. Thank You that Caroline gets a new home today. Bless her in it. Thanks for this food, and be with Shelby wherever she is, and help me make the right decision concerning Tasha. I pray in the name of Jesus. Amen."

Caroline looked up. "Thank you for the prayer."

"You're welcome." Wyatt picked up his fork and took a bite of his eggs and then slathered jelly on his biscuits.

"So what do you think?"

Caroline set her fork on her plate. "She admits you aren't Tasha's father."

"Yeah, that's a relief because I'm not sure Gramps believed my denial, even though Gram did."

"I think he knew you were telling the truth."

"Did you?" Wyatt took a big swig of his coffee.

Caroline wasn't sure she should admit when she'd first learned of the child's existence that she'd believed he might be the father. "I was shocked with the whole situation, but when you said you weren't Tasha's father, I didn't doubt your word."

Wyatt stared at her. "But you had a momentary doubt."

"Okay. When Tasha suddenly appeared and you whisked her away, I wondered what was going on. Why would a woman leave her child with you?" Caroline sighed. "But I eventually believed you, and now that I've read her letter, I understand her motivation."

Wyatt gave her a wry smile. "Thanks for being honest with me."

"I'll always try to do that." Caroline nodded. "What are you planning to do?"

"Maybe I need to talk to a lawyer." Wyatt pulled another paper from his pocket. "This is her will. It looks all legal, notarized and everything."

Caroline took the paper and studied it while she continued to eat. "It says she's leaving everything to Tasha in a trust. A lawyer could certainly give you advice and tell you what your responsibilities are as a guardian."

"A trust. That's odd, since I doubt she has much. Seems the most important thing is Tasha." Concern painting his features, Wyatt picked up a piece of bacon. "I don't know what to do. I have to find her."

As she took the wrapper off her muffin, Caroline's heart plummeted. Did he still love Shelby? Caroline couldn't ask. He was concerned about Shelby, and her daughter was with him. He should try to find her.

"You mentioned talking to some of your rodeo friends. Did you do that?"

Wyatt nodded. "Shelby hasn't been around the circuit for a couple of years. One guy did tell me he thought she might be working as a stable assistant at a horse farm in northern Kentucky. Anyway, not far from here."

"So that's how she was able to visit your grandparents, because she's somewhere nearby."

"Yeah, that's what I figured. I did a search for horse ranches in that area." Wyatt pulled another paper from his pocket. "I've got a list right here. I was hoping you'd help me search by calling these places. We could divide the list in half."

Caroline hated that she didn't want to do this for Wyatt. The selfish part of her wanted to keep him to herself. She didn't want to help him search for an old girlfriend. But she wasn't ready to pursue a relationship with Wyatt until she sorted out the effects of the rape. If she and Wyatt were meant to be, this search would have no influence on any future relationship they might have.

"Sure. You're helping me move, so I can help you do this."

"But you're not sure."

Wyatt's scrutiny unnerved Caroline, and she wondered if he could read her body language. He picked up things that no one else did. "Maybe I'm a little jealous that you're looking for an old girlfriend."

Wyatt grinned. "That's interesting. I didn't know you cared that much."

Heat crept up Caroline's cheeks, and she couldn't look at him. "I know that's terrible to say when I said we could only be friends."

"Caroline, look at me."

She looked up. "Don't tease me."

Wyatt shook his head. "I'm not teasing. I'm going to be honest with you. Your feelings make me think we're headed for more than friendship, and you know I'm not opposed to that idea."

"I know, and I don't want to lead you on and then…"

"I understand where our relationship is now, and if I step over the line, feel free to let me know. If I ever make you uncomfortable, tell me. I want to do this right." Wyatt bit into another piece of bacon.

"Thank you for that." Caroline nodded. "I want to get this right, too."

"If I take Tasha in, there will be all kinds of questions. People will question who her father is. A doctor will want to know her medical history. Shelby didn't give me that information. I'm not sure I know how to handle this. I'm not her father."

"Would you consider adopting her?"

"Wow! That's a lot to think about. I'm not even sure about the guardianship thing."

"I know it's a lot to digest, but as her guardian, won't you be like a father in her eyes?" Caroline took another bite of her omelet.

"I keep thinking of how she'll feel when she's old enough to know her mother abandoned her. I know that feeling."

"I think you should give her a home." Caroline looked at him. "You're the perfect person to do that because of your own experience. Maybe that's why Shelby chose you."

"Seriously?"

"Did she know about your background?"

"She did. We had some serious heart-to-heart talks. Now that I think back on them, I should've seen how troubled she was. That letter tells you so much. She had survivor's guilt, and it sounds like her parents didn't help."

"I think she picked you because she knew you'd understand." Caroline nodded. "She knew you'd be the best person to take care of her little girl. You seemed to have a connection to her right from the moment you held out your arms to her. She went without hesitation."

"That's because I gave her a cookie."

"But she didn't know that's what you were about to

do." Caroline smiled. "She likes you."

Wyatt let out a halfhearted laugh. "She does, but I need lots of prayer to make the right decision."

"People are praying for you. It's an important decision." Caroline took a bite of her omelet.

"And I'm grateful, but I have to be honest—how do I know when I get an answer?"

Caroline shook her head. "Good question. For me it's when everything falls into place."

"Does it?"

Caroline shrugged. "I'm going to tell you something that I haven't told anyone else."

Wyatt smiled. "You seem to like to tell me stuff like that. Makes me think I'm a good sounding board. I like that you trust me enough to confide in me."

Heat rose in her cheeks again. He must think all she could do was blush. "The day I walked into your room in the nursing home, and you started complaining about the food and your rehab, I felt this kinship with you. You were hurting, and so was I. But I hadn't been brave enough to tell anyone. You were letting everyone know."

Wyatt gave her a crooked smile. "Yeah, I wasn't very pleasant to deal with. You put me in my place by telling me to be kind."

"I did? I figured you weren't interested in listening to me."

"That's where you're wrong. Caroline Keller was always someone I wanted to listen to."

Surprise inundated Caroline's thoughts. "And what

exactly do you mean by that?"

"You know what I used to call you?"

"What?"

"Perfect Caroline Keller. Perfect grades. Perfect hair. Perfect face. Perfect family. Perfect everything."

Caroline couldn't believe what she was hearing. Wyatt thought she was perfect. "I'm not perfect. Far from it. That's what I'm trying to tell you. Ever since that terrible day, I've had trouble with my relationship with God. I don't understand why He allowed that horrible thing to happen to me. I don't know why evil people prosper."

Wyatt rubbed his forehead. "Me neither. Why do evil people prey on the vulnerable? Shelby wouldn't be so messed up if it weren't for people who would gladly supply her with the drugs that are killing her."

There it was again. Shelby. Wyatt was thinking about her. Caroline didn't want to feel envy, but it sat in her mind like a spoiled egg, stinking up her thoughts. She had to work on a better attitude. After all, she had to live up to Wyatt's thoughts, or at least try.

Caroline picked up her phone. "We still have a half hour before we're supposed to meet everyone at my parents' house. We could make some of those phone calls now."

"We can divide the numbers in half. I'll start at the beginning, you start at the end, and we'll meet in the middle." Wyatt grabbed his phone and put the paper with the numbers on the table as he smiled at her. "You're the nicest person I know."

"Really? You're going to give me a big head with all these compliments." Caroline lowered her gaze, heat creeping up her cheeks again. And meeting in the middle painted a picture of their growing relationship. Was it snowballing too fast, faster than she could handle?

"Never too many compliments." Wyatt tapped in a number on his phone.

Caroline did the same, wanting so badly to be all those things Wyatt said of her but fearing she couldn't measure up. Her life right now looked that way at every turn as she tried to live up to the expectations of her family, the community, and now Wyatt. Perfection. No one could accomplish that.

After twenty minutes, they had exhausted the list without success. Either the calls went to voicemail and they had left a message, or Shelby didn't or never had worked at the place.

"Sorry we didn't have better results." Caroline put her phone in her purse.

"Maybe we'll get a call back on some of those where we left a message."

"Only if Shelby worked there." Caroline picked up her coat and slid out of the booth.

Wyatt joined her. "Yeah, I wouldn't expect a call back if they've never heard of her."

"Let's head over to my parents' place."

"Sure." Wyatt helped her with her coat. "We've got to get you moved."

"It's more like getting Nathan moved. I don't have that much stuff."

"Whatever. I'm happy to help two of my favorite people."

As Caroline drove down the quiet streets of Kellersburg toward her parents' house, she let the morning's events roll through her mind. Maybe she was getting better, better on her own. After all, she'd driven from the Bayer farm with Wyatt, just the two of them, and she hadn't had a panic attack. But that was troublesome thinking. She needed help because those horrid dreams haunted her sleep too many nights.

She might be getting better, but she needed help from a professional. She wanted to do that because her heart longed for true love, and she had learned that there was more to Wyatt Bayer than she had ever imagined. He made her smile. He challenged her. And he made her feel things she thought she'd never feel again. She wanted to believe things could work out between them, but caution was her best friend for now.

CHAPTER NINE

T he sunny weather made a perfect day for moving. Wyatt traipsed up the front walk behind Caroline.

She was a fine woman to look at in her skinny jeans and long-sleeved knit top that hung around her hips. He didn't want to stare, but he had a hard time keeping his gaze on something other than Caroline.

Just because she'd taken him to breakfast didn't mean a thing. Just because she'd admitted his talking about Shelby made her a little jealous didn't mean a thing. Just because he couldn't stop thinking about her didn't mean a thing. If only he could pound those points into his head.

Caroline had insisted on paying for breakfast, and he'd decided not to argue because he didn't think it would get him anywhere. Headstrong didn't begin to describe her. Thankfully, that hadn't kept her from taking his advice to get help. He wanted her to get better.

But was he falling into the same old trap? He'd tried to help his mom. Even as a ten-year-old, he had begged his mom to get help. He'd tried to hide her liquor, even poured some down the sink. That had only earned him a whipping.

He'd tried to help Shelby, standing by her even after

she'd betrayed him with another man. He'd helped her get into rehab only to have her fail to stay clean. He hadn't successfully helped his mom or Shelby. Would things turn out differently with Caroline? He feared to hope. Trying to fix people didn't work. They had to want to get better. They had to rely on God. He should, too.

"Hey, are you sure you're up for this. You're lagging behind." Caroline stood on the wide front porch of her parents' home. The old foursquare house had been built at the turn of the twentieth century, making it more than one hundred years old. But the place showed the care of its owners, owners whose ancestors had founded this town.

"I'm just enjoying the view."

"The view?" Caroline put her hands on her hips.

"Yeah. You."

That familiar blush colored her cheeks. "Are you passing out more compliments?"

Wyatt took it as a good sign that his compliments made her blush. He'd been seeing that blush all morning. "Sure. I like doing that, especially when the recipient is you."

"I don't know if I can handle all these compliments." Caroline laughed, and the sound made his heart beat faster.

"Are you two ready to get to work?" Nathan appeared in the doorway and saved Wyatt from having to make a response. He just wanted to enjoy the day and spend time with the woman who was becoming more important to him each day.

"Ready. What do you want us to do?" Caroline asked.

"I see you've got a lot of your stuff boxed up and ready to go." Nathan motioned toward the stairway that made a right turn at the landing halfway up. "You can start by bringing the boxes down and loading them in your car and the back of my SUV."

"Got it." Wyatt gave a little salute as he followed Caroline up the stairs. Curiosity over Caroline's childhood home colored his thoughts. What would it have been like to grow up in such a grand house?

After they reached the top of the stairs, Caroline turned to look at him. "Things are a bit chaotic up here. There are boxes everywhere and not much space to walk."

"I wasn't expecting anything much different. Moving is always chaotic." Wyatt wondered if she was nervous about having him here. "Tell me what you want me to do."

She stepped into the room and motioned toward a stack of boxes in the corner of the pale-green room. "You can take as many of those boxes as you think you can handle down to my car."

"Okay. I can manage these." Wyatt looked over the room as he picked up two boxes, one stacked on the other.

He traipsed across the room and took in the mattresses and bed frame, which lay up against one wall. He tried to imagine what the room might have looked like before it had been dismantled. He wanted to know more about Caroline, and her room might have given him more information. Maybe her new abode would enlighten him, but her things lay hidden.

After an hour of moving boxes, Wyatt joined Caroline in her car as they headed over to Nathan's place. "What about your furniture?"

"Nathan's gone to get the truck he rented to move his stuff over to Melanie's place. I guess I should start calling it Nathan and Melanie's." Caroline shrugged as she glanced Wyatt's way. "After that we'll move my furniture. Nathan's leaving some of his stuff for me."

"That's nice."

"It only makes sense, because Melanie has a house full of furniture already, and I don't have much since I haven't lived here for six years." Caroline chuckled. "He's using the stuff he's moving over there to make his man cave in the basement."

"Nathan and the boys should enjoy it."

Caroline chuckled again. "Ryan and Andrew already have big plans. I'm not sure Nathan is prepared for those boys, but it's going to be fun to watch."

Wyatt sat silently for the rest of the drive to Caroline's new place as his thoughts filled with how he'd handle taking care of Tasha, if that's what came out of his unexpected situation. Just like Nathan, Wyatt wondered if he was prepared for all the changes that Tasha would bring to his life. He wondered whether he'd get a chance to talk to Melanie, with all the moving. What insight did she have? Would it help him make a decision about the little girl? He needed guidance, and he wasn't sure how God would make things clear to him.

When they arrived at Nathan's, he had just pulled the rented truck up to the curb. Caroline grabbed a couple of boxes, and Wyatt did the same. He followed her up the walk toward the wide steps that led to the front porch, spanning the entire front of the bungalow. The white balustrade stood in sharp contrast to the blue shake shingles siding. In Wyatt's opinion, the house fit Caroline more than Nathan. He could definitely see her living here.

He'd done a lot of following today, and he was still enjoying the view. Caroline Keller punched all the right buttons with him. He wanted to fit into her life just as this house did. Was he reaching too far, wishing for too much?

As Wyatt and Caroline stepped onto the porch, Nathan joined them. "Seth and Lukas are already here. They're getting ready to move my living room furniture."

Caroline stepped into the foyer and looked at Nathan. "Is there anything special you'd like for us to do?"

Nathan glanced around. "As soon as they get this couch out to the truck, you can bring in the rest of your boxes."

"You've got everything out of the kitchen?" Caroline looked toward the back of the house. "The stuff in these boxes goes in the kitchen."

Nathan nodded. "Melanie came over this week and cleaned it up for you. It's ready for your stuff."

"Where is she?" Caroline asked.

"She and the boys will be here in a little bit with my car and the rest of your boxes. She dropped me off at the rental place and then stopped by the house so the boys could get the basement ready for my invasion."

Caroline laughed as she glanced at Wyatt. "I told you they were excited about the man cave."

"It's not a man cave." Nathan scowled. "It's our game room."

"Okay. Your game room." Caroline smiled.

"Go put your stuff away." Nathan then looked at Wyatt. "Don't let her give you a hard time. She's not easy to deal with."

"I'm not going to stand here and take this." Caroline marched toward the kitchen.

Wyatt stood there, not sure if she was unhappy or not.

Nathan laughed out loud. "Wyatt, if you plan to hang around with this family, you'd better get used to the kidding."

"So she's not mad at you?" Wyatt eyed Nathan.

Nathan laughed again. "No. She's just pretending to be miffed."

"You might have to clue me in from time to time."

"Whenever you need advice, don't hesitate to ask."

"Okay." Wyatt headed for the kitchen. He still had a lot to learn about Caroline, and he intended to spend as much time as possible doing so.

"You can set that box on the table." Caroline looked at him as he entered the kitchen, which was off the living room toward the back of the house.

"The table stays?"

"For right now. Eventually it'll go, but we've got time to empty these boxes before they come for the table."

"What do you want me to do with the contents of the box?" Wyatt opened the flaps and looked inside.

"Take everything out and put the stuff on the counter." Caroline turned her attention to her own box.

As Wyatt took the plates and glasses out, he wondered why Caroline had these items when she'd been living out of the country for years. Did he dare ask? "You have a nice set of dishes here."

Caroline gave him a tentative smile. "Yeah, I've got just about everything I need to set up a house. Thanks to Grandma Addie."

"She gave you this stuff?"

Caroline nodded. "She followed a tradition of my ancestors who founded Kellersburg. It's not done much anymore, but as soon as one of her granddaughters was born, she started a hope chest for them. My girl cousins and I all have one thanks to Grandma Addie."

"Do you have an actual chest?"

"Yes." Caroline busied herself as she took more things out of her box and put them on the counter, almost as if she didn't want to talk about it.

"Will you be moving it here?"

Caroline stopped what she was doing and looked at

him. "Yes, but I'm afraid it's a reminder of the hope I will never have."

Wyatt's heart plummeted. Did that mean she thought she'd never overcome the trauma of the rape? Maybe it was just too soon for her to have hope. She hadn't attended even one counseling session. He didn't know how to deal with her despair. He wanted to deny her statement, but wisdom dictated he shouldn't. Was he attracted to another woman who was lost in a sea of discouragement? First Shelby and now Caroline.

"I don't believe you don't have any hope."

Caroline let out a heavy sigh. "I know I should believe that, too, but I don't want you to put too much hope in thinking I'll get better, because I don't feel better now."

Was he putting too much pressure on her with his desire for something beyond friendship? She had to give herself time to deal with her feelings and heal, and he had to give her space. But she had invited him to breakfast, and he'd thought things were going well. "What's changed since we ate together this morning?"

"Hey, you two, we're headed over to the house with this load. Then we'll pick up your furniture and be back here with that. We'll be out of your way so you can bring in the rest of those boxes." Nathan gave a wave as he headed back through the living room.

Wyatt read the panic in Caroline's eyes as she watched her brother leave. "Are you uneasy being alone here with me? If you are, I can go."

Caroline shook her head. "How are you going to

leave? I drove you here."

"I could call Gramps, and he'll come and get me."

"That's not necessary. Melanie and the boys should be here soon." Caroline shook her head again as she shrugged. "You asked what's changed since breakfast. I'm not sure. I'm sorry I keep saying the same things over and over again, but I don't want you to expect something from me and not get it. I'm still broken, and I'm not sure I can fix what's wrong."

Wow! She was feeling pressure, maybe of her own making. "I'm not expecting anything. I care about you, and I want you to be able to deal with the trauma you've been through. I want you to be able to move forward and live a happy life. If that can include me, I'd like that, but if not, I'll still be happy for your progress. And you have to rely on God to help you do that."

Caroline stared at him, tears welling. She blinked, and a tear rolled down one cheek. He used every ounce of his willpower not to reach over and wipe it away.

She wiped away the tear and tried to smile. "I had no idea what a good guy you are. And you reminded me of the things I know about God, but right now I'm doubting. I wish that wasn't so."

"Hey, Mr. Wyatt."

Wyatt turned at the sound of a boy's voice. "Andrew. Did you bring the rest of your aunt Caroline's boxes?"

Andrew pointed toward the front of the house. "Yeah. Mom's coming."

"Did you get everything set up in your game room?"

Andrew made a pouty face. "We had to leave because they didn't want us in the way when they were moving in the furniture."

"Andrew. That's not true." Melanie appeared carrying a box. "We needed to deliver these boxes. Where do you want them?"

Caroline stepped forward, a bright smile replacing the earlier tears. "There should be a label somewhere on the box."

Melanie looked it over. "Yeah, bedroom."

As Melanie moved through the kitchen to the bedroom at the back of the house, followed by the boys, Caroline looked at Wyatt. "Are you going to talk to Melanie?"

"I'm not sure how to start the conversation." Wyatt sighed. "I can't just say, 'How was it growing up in foster care?'"

"Well, you could, but I see your point." Caroline gave him a serious look. "Would you like me to start the conversation?"

Wyatt shrugged. "Shouldn't I start my own?"

"Yeah, but you let me know if I can help."

"Sure." Wyatt weighed his options as the boys raced back through the empty living room. Did Melanie's sons know about her time in foster care? He didn't want to bring up something she didn't want known.

After everyone had made several trips back and forth from the vehicles to the house, every box had been delivered to the appropriate room.

"Thanks for delivering my stuff." Caroline hugged

Melanie.

"You're welcome. Sorry I can't stay to help you unpack, but I have to get back home to help Nathan."

"I understand." Caroline's gaze flitted between Melanie and Wyatt. "But before you go, I want to show the boys something upstairs."

"Okay, just send them out to the car when you're done." Melanie looked at Ryan and Andrew. "You do what your aunt Caroline says."

"We will," the boys said.

Caroline nodded at Wyatt as she took the boys up the stairs. Wyatt joined Melanie as she went out the front door. "Melanie, do you have a minute while Caroline is talking to Ryan and Andrew?"

Melanie stopped on the front porch and turned to him. "Sure. What do you want?"

"Did you hear about Tasha?"

"Is that the little girl someone left with you?"

Wyatt nodded. "Caroline and Ginny said I should talk to you about foster care."

Melanie placed a hand over her heart. "You're not considering turning her over to child services are you?"

"I don't know what I'm doing." Wyatt didn't miss the horror that crossed Melanie's features. "I just thought I'd see what you had to say."

"This is what I know." She looked him squarely in the eye. "Do not let that child go into foster care. It's a terrible way to grow up."

"Okay, but I'm not sure I'm equipped to take care of a three-almost-four-year-old girl." Wyatt shrugged. "I never had a sister, so I know nothing about girls."

"We'll do whatever we can to help you. Foster care can be good for kids who are eventually reunited with their parents or get adopted, but if a child is like I was, you just get shuffled from one home to another and never feel like you belong anywhere. Then I aged out of the program and was left to fend for myself. Don't let that happen to Tasha." Melanie grabbed the top of the balustrade as she looked out on the yard. "If you just can't handle the responsibilities, then Nathan and I will take her."

"I have to be honest. I don't know what I'm going to do." Wyatt wondered if God was using Melanie to give him an answer. Maybe all his doubts stemmed from not being sure he had what it took to be a parent, because that was exactly what he'd be if he became Tasha's guardian.

"Maybe this is unsolicited advice, but I would find Tasha's mother and ask her to sign away her parental rights so you can adopt the little girl. She needs a stable home."

"I'm not sure where to find her mother, and I intend to talk to a lawyer so I can determine what I should do. I have an appointment with one on Tuesday next week."

Melanie turned to look at him. "Please, please let me know if you decide you can't be her guardian. I won't let that child go into foster care."

Wyatt nodded, feeling the weight of the decision he had to make. "I will."

"What does Caroline think?"

"She mentioned adoption, too."

"Great minds think alike." Melanie smiled. "Are you and Caroline dating?"

Wyatt let out a heavy sigh. "We're just friends. We've known each other since elementary school."

Melanie stared at him. "I thought there might be more between you two, since you took her, as well as the boys, to that ranch."

Wyatt refused to mention his wishes concerning Caroline. "I needed a driver. I'm still not released for driving yet."

"Oh, I see." Melanie cocked her head as she stared at him. "So the obvious matchmaking isn't working?"

Wyatt surmised that he wasn't hiding his feelings for Caroline, but he couldn't explain why their relationship would stay in the friends category for the time being. "The matchmaking is obvious, but we'd like to keep the friend status for now."

"For now? Does that mean there might be more than friends in the future?"

Wyatt let out a helpless chuckle. "Is this the way things are going to be?"

"I'm afraid so. It seems the Kellers are determined to marry off every single person they know. I've been a victim of their matchmaking, and I wouldn't have it any other way. You should try it."

"He should try what?" Caroline stepped onto the porch, the boys right behind her.

"My manicotti. You guys are invited over for dinner this coming Friday night. I'll see you around five, okay?" Melanie grinned at Wyatt.

Wyatt gave Melanie an indulgent smile, then looked over at Caroline. Before she had a chance to answer, Ryan and Andrew were tugging on each of her arms. Wyatt knew what was coming before the words even left their mouths.

"Aunt Caroline, you have to come. Mom makes the best manicotti in the whole wide world." Andrew let his arms fly wide.

"Yeah, Aunt Caroline. You haven't had a chance to eat my mom's cooking. She's the best. And you have to bring Mr. Wyatt 'cause he can't drive." Ryan turned to Wyatt. "I hope they let you drive soon."

Wyatt smiled at Ryan, then let his gaze slide to Caroline. "I think Ms. Caroline is hoping that, too."

"But she likes being nice to you, doesn't she?" Andrew nodded his head.

"I think she does?" Wyatt smiled wryly at Caroline.

"Good then we'll see you Friday night for dinner, and bring your grandparents and Tasha, too. She'll have fun playing with the boys."

"Then I think Ms. Caroline doesn't have to drive me. My grandparents can do that."

Andrew put his hands on his hips. "However you get there, make sure you come. You don't want to miss my mom's manicotti."

"Seems your manicotti gets rave reviews." Wyatt looked at Melanie.

"I hope it lives up to all the hype, and you can check out Nathan's man cave." Melanie chuckled.

"I look forward to it."

"Is there something I can bring?" Caroline asked.

"No, no. Just yourselves." Melanie pointed toward the SUV. "Boys, it's time to head home. Nathan will be wondering what's been keeping us."

Melanie waved as the threesome headed to her SUV. Wyatt waved in return. He stood there for a few moments as he watched them drive away. What was Caroline thinking? When he turned around, would he see that panic in her eyes again? He wanted to help her finish unpacking, but he didn't want her to feel uncomfortable being alone with him.

He spun, hoping against hope that she would accept his help. "What did you show the boys?"

"There's a secret compartment off one of the bedrooms upstairs with a safe in the floor. I thought the boys would get a kick out of seeing it."

Caroline's timid smile eased some of Wyatt's worry. "And what do you do with a secret compartment?"

"Hide my valuables in there." Caroline shook her head. "Trouble is, I don't have any."

Wyatt chuckled. "Then someone will have to buy you valuables you can put in it, or you might have some important papers you could keep there."

"That's an idea, but I'm not sure I even have important papers."

"What did Nathan do with it?"

Caroline shrugged. "I don't know. I never asked him."

"How did you know about the secret compartment?"

"This house used to belong to our uncle Carl. He showed it to my brothers and me when we were kids."

"What did he keep there?"

Caroline cocked her head and scrunched up her face. "He had some old coins in a pouch. I recall that much."

"They must've been worth something."

"I suppose."

"I'd like to help you finish here, but that's up to you." Wyatt held his breath as he waited for her answer.

She nodded. "Yeah. You can do that."

Before Wyatt could respond, the ringtone from his phone echoed through the empty room. He pulled the phone from his pocket. A call from Kentucky. He swiped the screen. "Wyatt Bayer. May I help you?"

"Yes, sir. This is Lisa Harper from Harper Farm. I believe you called and left a message asking for Shelby Pollard."

"Yes, I did. Does she work there?"

"She did." The woman paused. "May I ask why you're inquiring about her?"

Wyatt wondered what Shelby had said to these people. Did they know about her opioid problem? Is that why she didn't work for them anymore? "Ma'am, while I was out of town, Shelby left her daughter with my grandparents, who live near Kellersburg, Ohio, along with a document naming me as the child's guardian. It's imperative that I talk to her."

"So you have Tasha?"

"Yes, ma'am."

"That's good news. I was worried about that child,

because Shelby was very secretive on the whereabouts of her little girl. All she would say is that Tasha was safe."

Wyatt wondered if that secrecy had to do with her parents. "Can you just tell me how I can reach Shelby?"

"Are you Tasha's father?"

"No, ma'am. That's why I need to talk to Shelby."

"If you want to talk to her, you may not have much time. She's in hospice care. Liver failure."

The stark reality punched Wyatt in the gut. Too young to die. "Where is she?"

"I can give you the address of the hospice facility."

"Let me get a paper and pencil." Wyatt looked at Caroline as he lowered the phone. "I've found Shelby, and I need something to write on."

"I think I have something in my purse." Caroline hurried toward the kitchen and returned with a pen and a scrap of paper.

Wyatt wrote down the address, then thanked Lisa and ended the call. He folded the paper and put it in the pocket of his jeans, his mind trying to absorb the sobering fact that Shelby was dying and he had her daughter.

"Where is she?"

Caroline's question brought his thoughts back to her. "In hospice care near Cynthiana, Kentucky, a couple of hours from here. I've got to see her before she dies. I hate to leave you in the middle of your unpacking."

"Wyatt, you've done enough for me already. Do what you have to do. And I'm sorry the news isn't good."

"Thanks, but not totally unexpected. She could've died from an overdose long ago, but instead the drugs have taken a toll on her liver." Wyatt pressed his lips together. "I need to go today because I don't know how much time she has left. I'll see if Gramps can drive me."

Caroline shook her head. "I have all day to work on unpacking. You don't need to call him. I'll drive you there."

"Really?"

Caroline nodded. "I have a full tank of gas."

"I'm not asking about your gas." Wyatt narrowed his gaze. "You're not afraid to be alone with me?"

"I'm alone with you now."

"I don't want you to do something that will make you uncomfortable."

"I wouldn't have volunteered if I didn't want to do this." Caroline took a deep breath. "I need to learn to trust again and be brave. You've made me want to do that."

Wyatt wished he could hug her, but he wouldn't. She'd taken a big step, and he didn't want to ruin it. "That makes me smile."

She gave him a shy smile. "Do you need to go back to your grandparents' place before we leave?"

"No, but I was wondering about Tasha. Would she want to see her mom?"

Caroline shook her head. "That's a hard one. A dying parent. I'm not sure Tasha would understand, and it might make it harder for her to be separated from her mother again."

Wyatt let out a harsh breath. "That's what I was thinking, too. Tasha has settled in at my grandparents. She especially adores Gramps, and I think having her around puts a spring in his step."

"You could get Shelby to make a video for Tasha that she can watch when she's old enough to understand better."

"Thanks for that suggestion. You are a wise woman."

"Thanks. Shall we get on the road? We can go through the drive-thru at the Dairy Barn and eat lunch on the road."

Wyatt wished he could tell Caroline how much he cared about her. She was amazing, and he hated what had happened to her. He prayed right there that she would find the peace she deserved. And maybe today's trip was the start of her recovery.

CHAPTER TEN

The Ohio River sparkled in the sun as Caroline drove across the bridge toward Maysville, Kentucky.

Wyatt had been relatively quiet on the hour's drive between Kellersburg and Maysville, which brought them to the halfway point on their journey, according to the GPS on Caroline's phone.

She glanced at Wyatt. Was he thinking about Shelby? Of course he was. Caroline wondered whether she dared to ask if this information concerning Shelby had prompted him to make a decision about Tasha.

With Wyatt's expression of wonder about her willingness to be his chauffer rolling through her thoughts, she hoped she wasn't planting false expectations about her in his heart. Again she wished she could explain her mixed-up emotions, even to herself. He seemed not to be bothered by her erratic decisions. What were these feelings that made her want to please him?

He'd been quiet so far on the ride. In the beginning they'd been eating after their stop at the Dairy Barn, which had limited conversation. But now his silence gave Caroline too much time to speculate, and the two-lane road lined with trees just beginning to bud and an occasional farm did little to take her mind away from

Wyatt. Her thoughts ran rampant with troublesome scenarios.

"Did the person you talked to give you any idea how much time Shelby has left?" Caroline gripped the steering wheel tighter.

Wyatt shrugged, his face grim. "Not really, other than her time is limited. If I wanted to talk to her that I shouldn't hesitate. Knowing what I know about her drug problem, it's a wonder she hasn't overdosed by now. Such a waste of a life. It makes me sick."

"I'm sorry I brought it up."

Wyatt let out a halfhearted laugh. "You asking that question didn't bring it to mind. It's been on my mind ever since Tasha showed up. What am I going to do with a little girl?"

"So you plan to be her guardian?"

A muscle worked in Wyatt's jaw as he stared straight ahead. He rubbed a hand along the back of his neck. "It's a lot of responsibility. Am I cut out to be a dad?"

"As much as any other dad."

"Most dads plan on being a dad months before that actually happens."

"True, but at least you don't have to go through the bottles and diapers stage."

Wyatt turned her way and chuckled. "Thanks for pointing out the upside."

"Glad to be of help."

"I keep wondering whether Shelby has ever talked to her parents. She said she didn't want Tasha to go to her parents What if they would try to take custody of Tasha?"

"If she's estranged from her parents, do they even know she has a child?"

Wyatt shook his head. "That's a good question. I'll have to ask Shelby. It's better to know what I'm facing."

"Would you fight for Tasha when you're not sure if you want to be her guardian?"

"Another good question. I think the answer is becoming clearer and clearer. I'm going to be that little girl's guardian."

Caroline smiled. "I'm glad you've made that decision. You won't regret it."

"I still have to talk to a lawyer and find out how this all works."

"Did my dad recommend one?"

"He did."

"That's good."

Soon the landscape gave way to rolling hills and a winding road lined by more farms, some with old tobacco barns. Eventually the scenery included the familiar white fences of a horse farm that enclosed fields where thoroughbreds grazed with contentment. The graceful animals made Caroline wonder about Wyatt and the horse that had caused his injury.

"Beautiful animals, aren't they?" Caroline glanced at Wyatt, then back at the road ahead. "I hope you don't mind my asking about the horse that caused your injury."

Wyatt let out a sorry chuckle. "Mean horse. A bronc

that not only bucked me off but stomped on me, too."

"So why did the doc say you couldn't go back to the rodeo?"

"You have to bring up a sore subject?" He frowned as he looked her way.

Caroline shrugged. "I just want to know what you're thinking about the situation now that you're doing better."

"Yeah, well, maybe I can walk, but I still can't drive."

"But you rode a horse down in Florida."

"I did." Wyatt gave her a wry smile. "Felt good. Felt like I was at home in a saddle, but it's not the same as competition. The adrenaline rush of conquering a horse with an eight-second ride that sometimes feels more like eight hours."

"So if you're able to ride a horse, why do they say you shouldn't compete again?"

"Because I'm held together with a lot of hardware. You know how they had to screen me at the airport because the screws keeping me from falling apart set off the metal detectors." Wyatt pinned her with a grim stare. "I could go back to riding broncs and roping calves, but if I have another accident, they might not be able to put me back together again. Do I want to chance that?"

"Do you?"

"When the doc first told me my rodeo days were over, I refused to believe it. I told myself I'd show them they were wrong. They couldn't keep me from doing what I wanted to do. I was angry, and poor little Maisey and the other workers at the nursing home got the brunt of my anger. Even you."

Caroline chuckled. "I won't argue with you on that. So you're saying you've changed your thinking?"

"By the end of my rehab at the nursing home, I had come to realize the docs were probably right. I was better off without a return to rodeo life. Then a whole lot of things happened to confirm that thought."

"What are those?"

"One, Morgan's job offer—being needed and a place to go."

"I wondered whether you've been thinking more about that offer." Caroline's heart sank at the thought of Wyatt leaving for Florida. Maybe she wasn't as important to him as he'd led her to believe. But then she was a mess herself, and there was no telling how long it would take for her to feel normal, if ever.

"Yeah, I've been thinking about it. Also I can't forget my grandparents. Besides, now there's Tasha and everything having her involves. And last but not least, there's you. I don't want to leave you behind."

Caroline's heart sang. "I appreciate your including me, but you don't want to miss out on a good opportunity."

"I've talked to Morgan since I've been back and filled him in on everything that has happened. He said a job will be waiting for me whenever I'm ready."

"That's good." If only she really believed that.

Happiness was short lived when she thought about the uncertainty of being whole and unbroken again. She

204 · *MERRILLEE WHREN*

wanted to warn him not to put his hopes on something that might not happen. But she should look on the bright side. She'd been brave enough to make this trip today. Wyatt was a trustworthy man, but hadn't she thought the same thing about her attacker, a respected doctor? She couldn't be wrong again.

Why were her thoughts so disjointed, jumping from trust to wariness in a matter of seconds? What would he think if he knew she had pepper spray in her purse?

"Yeah, Morgan's a great guy, and he understands I have a lot of decisions to make."

"What do you suppose will happen when you see Shelby?" Caroline hoped her change of subject wouldn't bother Wyatt.

"I wish I knew." Wyatt grimaced. "I'm not sure I'm ready to see her on her deathbed. What if we don't get there in time?"

"Then I would say God meant it to be that way." Caroline wondered if she even believed what she'd just said, when she questioned the things that had happened in her own life.

Wyatt gave her a sideways glance. "Do you actually believe that?"

Caroline didn't dare look his way. He had the most amazing way of knowing her thoughts and reading her reactions. "I want to believe everything that happens somehow comes out for good because God's hand is in it somewhere, but sometimes it's hard to see."

"Thank you for being honest with me."

"With you I feel like I can say what I'm thinking

without having you judge me for it." Maybe that was why she found herself trusting Wyatt. He didn't judge.

Wyatt shook his head. "I think I've said this before, but I can't judge anyone, because I've made my share of wrongheaded decisions."

"Don't sell yourself short. You're doing a lot of fine things."

Wyatt let out a halfhearted laugh. "That's because I've been dragged into them without much enthusiasm. Stuff just fell into my lap, and I'm trying to deal with it the best I know how."

"But at least you're dealing with it."

"We both have things to deal with."

The voice on the GPS signaled a change in their route as they neared Cynthiana, saving Caroline from further discussion. She wasn't sure she was dealing with anything. Her life seemed like a swirling mass of expectations that threatened to pull her under. She was just keeping herself from sinking. Relying on God should be her go-to strategy, but God seemed out of reach at times. Some missionary she was. Was her life just one big facade? Was Wyatt the only person who saw through it?

"We're almost there. Help me make sure I see the street I need and don't miss any turns."

"Will do."

The GPS guided them into the parking lot of the hospice facility. Caroline parked the car and turned off the engine. She sat there for a moment in the quiet with Wyatt. He didn't make a move.

"Are you going in?"

He fingered the brim of the familiar cowboy hat on his lap. "I don't know if I can do this."

"Would you like to pray about it?"

He looked at her, his face painted with misery. "What do I pray for?"

"How about wisdom to say the right things?"

Wyatt sighed. "That sounds good, because I'll need plenty of that."

"Would you like me to say a prayer?"

Wyatt nodded and bowed his head.

Caroline did the same. "Dear Lord, thank You for the safety of our journey today. Thank You for allowing us to find Shelby. Please be with Wyatt as he talks to her. Give him the words to say and wisdom for this meeting. Amen."

Wyatt looked up, still fingering his cowboy hat. "Thanks. I guess this is it."

"God go with you."

"I wish I could take you with me, but I know I have to do this by myself, with God's help. Keep praying." Wyatt nodded as he opened the door and set his hat on the seat. "I'll just leave this here with you."

"I'll take good care of it." Caroline wished she could make everything wonderful about this trip, but she had no idea what he faced.

He gave her one last look as he turned toward the redbrick building that resembled the nursing home in Kellersburg. He strode with purpose in his step but hesitated before he opened the door, almost as if he had stopped to say another prayer.

As Wyatt disappeared inside, Caroline bowed her head and prayed again for a good outcome. What was it like to stare death in the face? Even on the mission field, she hadn't encountered death. Her grandpa Keller had died while she was away, and she never had to see him suffer. That was the only good thing about not seeing him again before he died. She could always remember him as a robust and fun-loving man who loved to tell a joke.

Wyatt wouldn't encounter a healthy young woman but one who was slowly dying. *Lord, please help Wyatt get through this. Bring to mind just what he should do and say. Please bring peace to both Wyatt and Shelby. Amen.*

Even as she prayed though, she struggled to know whether God was listening. How had she fallen so far away from feeling God's nearness? She knew the answer, and she couldn't shake it.

Doubts circled her mind like buzzards over roadkill. She pushed away the doubts. She could trust God because she had seen how He had worked in so many lives through the years. Letting doubts win wasn't in God's plan. Even the smallest faith could move mountains. Her faith didn't rely on feelings. Her faith stood on knowing God was there even when He didn't seem near at all.

Wyatt would come through this. She would come through this. She wanted to believe God would work all of this for good.

***

Wyatt stood in the entryway and looked around. The place reminded him of the nursing home from the outside, and the inside did nothing to change his thoughts. He approached the reception desk.

"Could you tell me where I can find Shelby Pollard?" Wyatt wished he hadn't left his hat in the car. The hat would have given him something to hang on to. But shouldn't he be hanging on to God?

"Sir, she's in room one fifteen." The woman pointed to his right. "It's three doors down that hallway on the right."

"Thank you."

Wyatt headed in that direction, his legs feeling as unstable as those of a newborn foal. He tilted his head upward. *God, give me strength*. The silent prayer running through his mind, he read the numbers on the doors.

One fifteen. He stopped and released a harsh breath. While he stood there summoning his courage, voices floated from the room into the hallway.

"Shelby, you need to have a will," a male voice said.

"I have one, and it's none of your business, since you aren't named in it."

"Shelby, listen to reason." This time a female voice responded.

"I don't have to listen to you. You haven't cared about me my whole life, but now that I'm dying you suddenly care. You've been absentee parents ever since your daughter, my sister, Tasha died." Shelby's voice came across as weak but still determined.

Dread filled Wyatt's mind. Should he go in and rescue Shelby from her parents? Would he interfere where he wasn't wanted? What would this mean for Tasha and his planned guardianship of the child?

Wyatt mustered all of his resolve and stepped into the room. "Hi, Shelby."

"Wyatt!" Shelby tried to sit forward as she lay on a raised hospital bed, covers up to her chin. "What are you doing here?"

"I heard you were in hospice, and I had to see you."

Shelby's parents turned and stared at him. Her father towered over the bed, a large man, well over six feet tall with a thick head of graying hair. The resemblance between Shelby and her mother was remarkable. At least the Shelby he remembered. This Shelby was a shell of the young woman he used to know. Her once beautiful chestnut hair that hung around her shoulders in luxurious waves, now lay flat and lifeless around her head. The sallow color of her skin stretched over protruding cheekbones told of her liver disease. The panic in her eyes told him her parents didn't know about her daughter.

"And how do you know our daughter?" The man took a step toward Wyatt.

"We used to be on the rodeo circuit together." Not willing to let the man intimidate him, Wyatt stared and wondered if offering to shake the man's hand was in order.

"Dad, Mom, this is Wyatt Bayer." Shelby's voice sounded barely above a whisper now. "Wyatt, meet Joyce and David Pollard, my parents."

"Hello, ma'am, sir." Wyatt offered his hand to the man.

With clear reluctance, David shook Wyatt's hand. "It's nice that you're here to visit, but we're having a family meeting. Could you come back later?"

Wyatt glanced at Shelby, who gave him an almost imperceptible nod. "Sure. What time should I come back?"

"In about an hour." The words rushed from Shelby's mouth, as if she didn't want her parents to give an answer.

"Okay, I'll be back in an hour." Wyatt forced a smile as he looked at David and Joyce. "Good to meet you."

"I'm sure." David turned away, dismissing Wyatt.

Wyatt hoped his suspicion that Shelby's parents didn't know about Tasha held true. After just this brief meeting with these people, Wyatt understood why Shelby wanted nothing to do with her parents. Their harsh, demanding countenance served as a warning to him.

Wyatt traipsed to the entrance and looked through the glass door to where Caroline sat in the car, her head bowed. Was she praying? He needed it. Letting out a harsh breath, he hurried to the car. He opened the door and slid onto the seat.

Caroline jerked her head in his direction. "Back so

soon? Does that mean Shelby—"

"No, she's still alive, but her parents are with her."

"Oh, how is that going?" Caroline wrinkled her brow.

"Not good."

"Do they know about Tasha?"

Wyatt shrugged. "I don't think so, but I can't be sure. Her expression when she saw me made me think she was trying to signal me not to say anything. But since I know from her letter that she doesn't want them to know, I'm thinking they don't."

"Why do you say things weren't going well?"

"They were badgering her about a will, and she told them she had one and it wasn't any of their business because they weren't named in it." Wyatt shook his head. "Do you suppose that means she actually has something to give to Tasha in that trust?"

"Must be."

"If that's the case, it's certainly important that I see a lawyer." Wyatt rubbed the back of his neck. "I don't know what we can do for an hour to kill time, but Shelby told me to come back in an hour."

"Do you think the parents will be gone by then? After all, Shelby is dying?"

"I don't see them standing around waiting for her to die. It's all very weird. I've never dealt with anything like this." Wyatt shook his head. "And the conversation didn't sound congenial. You'd think they would be more compassionate. I just don't get it."

"That does sound bad." Caroline sighed. "What do

you plan to do?"

"Go back in an hour, if that's okay with you." Wyatt wondered whether Caroline had any reservations about spending more time alone with him.

"We could look for a coffee shop."

"That works for me. I'll see if I can find one." After a short search on his phone, he said, "There's one just down the road. I'll get directions from the site."

Caroline started the car. "Tell me which way to go."

Wyatt tapped his phone. "Got the directions right here. Take a right out of the parking lot."

In minutes they stepped into the small coffee shop on the main road through town. The smell of baked goods and coffee filled the air. They found seats at an unoccupied dark-wood table next to a window. The place was almost empty, with one other couple sitting at a corner table.

"What do you want? I'm buying." Wyatt set his cowboy hat on the table.

Caroline glanced around. "Is that their menu on the chalkboard behind the counter?"

"Looks like it."

Caroline let out a small laugh. "I don't know why I'm asking. I don't like those fancy coffee drinks. I'll just take a cup of plain black coffee."

Wyatt smiled. "Me, too. Want anything to go with that coffee?"

Caroline looked over at the chalkboard again. "I really shouldn't, but how about one of those chocolate chip cookies? Maybe not. They're awfully big."

"But I'm sure they're awfully good. We can split one."

Caroline bit her lower lip as she appeared to weigh his proposal. "Sure."

Wyatt stood and hung his jacket on the back of the chair. "I'll order."

"Thanks." Caroline shrugged out of her jacket but left it around her shoulders.

As Wyatt walked to the counter, his heart ached for Shelby, but at the same time, he cherished this time with Caroline. Never in his wildest dreams had he thought he would have any kind of relationship with Caroline Keller. He had always seen her as out of his reach. But here she was spending the day with him. It was a tentative relationship at best, but it was one. That was what counted.

After Wyatt paid for their order, he brought it to the table.

"Thanks." Caroline took the coffee cup he offered.

Wyatt didn't miss the spark that passed between them as their fingers brushed. Caroline looked away immediately. What didn't she want him to see? Panic in her eyes or maybe a connection to him she wasn't ready for?

He offered her the cookie encased in a wrapper with an open top. "You can split it."

Smiling, she took it, careful not to touch him this time. "You know you're getting the bigger piece."

"I won't argue with that."

Caroline split the cookie into two pieces and set each

on a napkin. She shoved his across the table. "Enjoy."

Wyatt bit into the cookie. "This is good. You shouldn't have given me the bigger piece."

"That's okay. I have to admit to doing a little stress eating, and it's beginning to make my clothes tight. I don't need that. I can't afford a new wardrobe."

She looked perfect to him. He liked the way she filled out her clothes, but he was sure he shouldn't say so out loud. "You look great to me."

"Thanks, but I don't want the unnecessary calories to get out of hand." Caroline nibbled on the cookie, then took a drink of her coffee as she gazed out the window.

Wyatt wondered whether she regretted saying anything about the stress eating. Was she worried about something that wasn't actually a problem? Was she struggling much more than he realized? Was she holding it together for family and friends but falling apart inside? How could he help? If only he knew how to handle all this stuff? Caroline. Shelby. Tasha.

She turned her attention away from what was outside and looked at him. "I'm sorry I mentioned my problems. You're dealing with enough stuff."

"That's what friends are for. To help each other through *the stuff*." Wyatt made air quotation marks with his fingers.

Caroline eyed him. "Thanks for being my friend. It's been a long time since I've had a friend who wasn't a work colleague. So forgive me if I'm not good at being a friend."

Wyatt shook his head. "I don't know why you say

that. You're very good at being a friend. You took time out of your day to drive me to Kentucky. I'd call that friendship."

"See. I don't even know when I'm being a good friend." Caroline let out a hesitant laugh. "I do know that I've been praying for you."

"And that's another reason why you're a good friend."

"I'm better about praying for someone else's problems rather than my own."

"Then we should pray for each other." Without thinking, Wyatt held up a hand for a high five, then worried that she would be reluctant to touch him.

"Good idea." She quickly slapped the palm of his hand, then tucked her hands in her lap.

Wyatt took another bite of the cookie and wished he hadn't made her uncomfortable. He washed the cookie down with a big swig of coffee and wished he could wash away all of their problems as well. But shouldn't he be relying on God? Wasn't that what praying was all about?

He'd come a long way from the rookie bronc rider who'd fallen hard for Shelby and done a lot of things he regretted. Morgan had come along and urged Wyatt to attend cowboy church, and he'd done so reluctantly. That attendance had brought him full circle to the principles his grandparents had tried to instill in him but that he'd determined were useless. But when Shelby had betrayed him, he'd found comfort in the God Morgan had brought into Wyatt's life. He would be forever grateful for that.

"You look worried."

Caroline's statement put an end to his woolgathering. "I was just thinking how my life has made a full circle from the faith my grandparents tried to share with me but that I rejected. I'm glad God didn't give up on me. And I'm wondering whether Shelby…"

"Shelby has turned to God."

"Yeah. How do you ask that question of a person?"

"You just ask."

"I guess you're right." Wyatt shook his head. "I don't know that I'm very good at that kind of thing."

"It can be an uncomfortable question to ask, but it needs to be done if we want to share the love of God." Caroline glanced at her phone. "Should we head back?"

Wyatt took a deep breath. Was he ready? He'd come here on a mission, and he had to follow through. "Sure."

During the drive back to the hospice center, Wyatt prayed for courage to say what he had to say to Shelby, and he prayed that her parents would be gone.

After Caroline pulled her car into a parking space near the door, she looked over at him. "Do you want to pray again before you go in?"

Wyatt nodded. "I was praying while you drove over here."

Caroline smiled. "We should both say a prayer."

"Okay. You first."

Caroline bowed her head. "God, our heavenly Father, thank You that You hear our prayers. Again we ask that You be with Wyatt. Please remind him of the words You would have him say to Shelby. We pray for the success of this meeting. Please give Shelby a receptive heart. Amen."

"Amen." Wyatt glanced at Caroline as she looked up. "Thanks."

"My turn." Wyatt bowed his head. "Thank You, Lord, for Caroline and her devotion to You. Thank You that she is my friend. Lord, I'm asking that You give me wisdom to say the things Shelby needs to hear. You know Shelby's heart. Please be with me. Amen."

Caroline looked over at him and nodded. "You're well armed with prayer."

"I'll have to remind myself of that with every word I say." Wyatt opened the car door and strode to the entrance. He wished Caroline could have given him a hug for good measure, but this wasn't about his relationship with her. This was about Shelby and what was best for her and Tasha.

CHAPTER ELEVEN

The door to Shelby's room stood open. Wyatt prayed again to say the right things to her. He approached with caution as he listened for voices. Silence greeted him. He peeked around the doorframe. She lay back on the raised bed, her eyes closed. No parents in sight.

Wyatt moved warily into the room. "Shelby?"

Her eyes fluttered open. "Wyatt, you came back."

"Sure." He gave her a lopsided smile. "You should know I would."

A little smile curved her lips. "I thought maybe my parents had scared you away."

He stepped closer to the bed. "You should know better than that. You think a couple of quarrelsome parents would keep me away?"

Shelby closed her eyes again, eyes that held the look of one under the influence of sedation. "Thanks for coming. I don't have much energy."

Wyatt knew her sedation was to relieve the pain of someone dying from a dreadful disease, but he couldn't overlook the irony of her being sedated because she had spent too many years sedating herself rather than facing life. "I had to talk to you about Tasha."

"How's Tasha?" Shelby opened her eyes.

"She's doing better each day." Wyatt wouldn't sugarcoat the circumstances surrounding the child. "She misses you and asks for you, but my grandpa and her have a special bond. He reads to her every day."

"What do you tell her about me?"

"I've told her you're very sick and can't take care of her now." Wyatt shook his head. "I'm not sure she understands."

Tears trickled down Shelby's cheeks. She quickly wiped them away. "It was so hard to leave her, but I had to take a chance on you—that you'd take her in. I had to keep her from my parents. Thanks for not giving away my secret."

"What do you think will happen when they find out about Tasha?" That prospect worried Wyatt more than he wanted Shelby to know.

"I'm hoping they don't."

Wyatt thought it sad that the little girl wouldn't know her grandparents, even if they weren't the best. He thought about his own grandparents, who had given him so much. "Are you sure?"

Shelby nodded. "They would just try to ruin her life like they did mine."

"Why me?"

"You mean why did I pick you to be Tasha's guardian?"

"Yeah. We haven't seen each other in years."

"I know the kind way you treated me, even when I didn't deserve it. I knew I could count on you. And I remembered your faith. I want that for Tasha."

"What about you? Do you want that for yourself?" Wyatt held his breath as he waited for her answer.

"I have it. Thanks to the people at Harper Farm. They shared their faith with me, just like you did, and I didn't reject it this time. I'm sorry I threw your faith back in your face all those years ago. If I had accepted it then, maybe I wouldn't be where I am now."

Wyatt sat in the chair next to the bed and took Shelby's thin hand in his. "You don't know how happy that makes me. I've been praying about it ever since I came back from my trip and learned about Tasha."

"The Harpers are truly wonderful people."

"Wouldn't they take Tasha?" Wyatt hoped that question wouldn't upset Shelby.

Shelby shook her head. "They're in their late sixties, and their kids are going to take over the farm. They plan to travel and enjoy a retirement. They didn't need a three-year-old, even though they had volunteered to take her. I knew that wouldn't be fair to them or their kids."

Wyatt leaned forward. "So how are you feeling?"

"Tired. Weak. Ready to leave this life. That's why I wanted things settled for Tasha."

Wyatt's heart ached at her response. So young to have given up on life, but she had treated her body badly, and she was paying a steep price. "I wish you'd talked to me before you just up and left your child with me."

Shelby lowered her head, not meeting his gaze. "Are you saying you won't take care of her?"

Wyatt reached over and lifted her chin. Tears welled

in her eyes. He didn't want to hurt her. She had once meant a great deal to him. He wanted to be honest with her.

"Shelby, I'll take care of Tasha. I plan to explore adopting her, not just be her guardian, but that doesn't mean I wouldn't have liked some kind of warning. You could've talked to me. It might have made for a better transition for Tasha."

"You'd adopt her?" Shelby pressed her lips together as more tears welled in her eyes.

Wyatt nodded. "I plan to look into it."

"I hope you do. You could give her a permanent family." Shelby blinked, and the tears streamed down her face. "I was planning to talk to you, but then I let fear take over because I was afraid you'd turn me away."

"Yeah, you hurt me when you walked away, loving the drugs more than me, but I wouldn't have turned you away." Wyatt squeezed her hand. "I still care about you. That's why I had to find you."

"How did you find me?"

"Through some old rodeo buddies who told me you were working somewhere in Kentucky on a horse farm. I made a few calls, and Lisa Harper returned my call."

Shelby smiled. "Lisa is a jewel among women. Two years ago she hired me and helped me stay clean. I quit the drugs when I was pregnant with Tasha, but it was hard, so hard not to go back, and I relapsed. But I had to stay clean for my little girl, so I tried again. That's when Lisa found me and shared the gospel with me. But then I found out I was dying. It wasn't fair, and I just wanted to sink back into that hole, but Lisa wouldn't give up on me."

"What about Tasha's father? Is he in the picture?"

Shelby hung her head again. "Can't say who the father is."

"Can't or won't?"

"Can't." A painful expression crossed Shelby's face. "Too many guys. So messed up on drugs that I have no memories of where I was or what I did. I really messed up my life. I can't let that happen to my little girl. Please give her a good life."

"I'll try. I'll do my best."

"Do you have someone in your life?"

"You mean like a love interest?"

Shelby nodded. "I knew you hadn't gotten married. I just wondered if you have a girlfriend, someone who might eventually be Mrs. Wyatt."

The image of Caroline praying in her car drifted through Wyatt's mind. He didn't know how to characterize their relationship or whether he should even mention Caroline to Shelby. Wyatt shrugged. "I have a friend, but she's only a friend."

The corner of Shelby's mouth lifted in a tiny smile. "That's what they always say. Will it eventually lead to something more?"

Smiling, Wyatt shook his head. "Don't have an answer to that one, but she drove me here today because I'm not released to drive yet."

"She's here?" Shelby's quiet voice raised a pitch.

"Waiting in the car."

"Why would you make her wait in the car?" Shelby frowned.

"Because she knew the two of us had things to talk about that didn't include her."

"I want to include her. I want to meet her."

"You do?"

"Yeah, I'm thinking she could someday be your wife and Tasha's mom. I want to know who might be in Tasha's life."

Wyatt laughed a little as he shook his head. "You're really getting way ahead of where things are with us."

"That's okay. I still want to meet her." Shelby nodded. "What's her name?"

"Caroline. Caroline Keller. She used to be a missionary."

Shelby laid her head back on the bed, her smile broadening. "The cowboy and the missionary. That has a nice ring. Please go get her."

How could he turn down a dying woman's wish? He made his way outside and found Caroline walking around the parking lot as she talked on her cell phone. He waved to get her attention.

Caroline walked toward him. She finished her conversation and pocketed her phone. "I was just talking to Nathan. They have everything moved."

"That's good news."

"All done?"

"No. Shelby wants to meet you."

Caroline's eyes widened. "How does she know I'm here?"

"I told her you drove me."

"But why would she want to meet me?" A puzzled expression crept across Caroline's pretty features.

Wyatt wasn't sure he should say why, but if he didn't, Shelby might. "She wants to meet the woman who has captured my interest."

"Okay."

Caroline's amused tone and her smile relieved Wyatt's worry as they moseyed toward the entrance.

"So I've captured your interest?"

"I think you already knew that."

Caroline's laughter filled the air. "You are very hard not to like."

"That's good to hear."

Wyatt wanted to put his arm around her shoulders in the worst way, but he pushed the urge away. She needed her space, and he would give it to her as long as she needed it.

"I don't know that I'm very good with dying people. I haven't experienced that." Caroline let out a sigh as they turned down the hallway. "I was thinking about that earlier when I was praying. My grandfather died while I was away, and I never had to see him suffer. No one else I'm close to has died. I often wonder how Melanie survived the death of her first husband."

"She's strong and trusts in the Lord."

Caroline shook her head. "I'm not so strong."

Wyatt stopped just outside Shelby's door. "You're stronger than you know."

"Keep telling me that."

"I will." Wyatt indicated she should go in. "Just so you know, Shelby has become a Christian. That makes talking to her so much easier. She's prepared to meet the Lord when her time comes."

Caroline smiled. "Thanks for sharing that good news. It will make things easier."

Wyatt took a deep breath. "Well, this is it."

Caroline's smile disappeared, replaced with a look of uncertainty. "You go first."

"Okay." Again Wyatt had to restrain himself from taking Caroline's hand as he entered the room. "I'm back, and I have Caroline with me."

Shelby struggled to sit more upright in the bed. "Hi, Caroline. Thanks for coming to meet me."

"Thanks for inviting me."

An uncomfortable silence filled the room, and the wariness in Caroline's eyes didn't match her words. Wyatt tried to put himself in her shoes. What would it be like to talk to an old boyfriend of Caroline's who was on his death bed? Awkward for sure.

Wyatt wanted to comfort Caroline. At least hold her hand while she stood there, but he couldn't do that. His brain told him to go slow, give her time, but his heart wanted more than friendship. His heart wanted love.

"You're welcome." Shelby fingered the edge of the blanket that lay across the bed.

Caroline stepped closer to the bed. "I'm glad to meet Tasha's mom."

"So you've met my little girl?"

Caroline nodded. "I was there when Wyatt returned

home to discover you'd left her with his grandparents. We had just come back from my brother's wedding in Florida."

Silence returned. Wyatt shifted his weight from one foot to another, wishing he knew how to continue the conversation. Caroline still had that apprehensive expression. This had been a bad idea if there ever was one.

"Would you like me to pray for you?" Caroline asked.

Shelby nodded. "That would be wonderful. Should we join hands?"

"Okay." Caroline took Shelby's outstretched hand, then looked over at him.

Wyatt didn't miss the effort it took for Caroline to offer him her hand across the bed. He took it and held it as loosely as he could. His heart sank as her hand trembled in his. When she bowed her head, he took her cue and bowed his.

"Dear heavenly Father, we praise You for Your goodness and mercy. We thank You for the opportunity to pray. Today we bring Shelby before You. Please be with her and comfort her. We know You have the power to heal, and You know what is best for Shelby. Bless her and guide her in whatever days You have remaining for her. We pray in the name of our Savior, Jesus. Amen."

"Amen." Wyatt squeezed Shelby's hand and then realized Caroline was squeezing his. He'd take it as a good sign.

"Thanks." Shelby's quiet voice penetrated the fog of

Wyatt's thoughts. "Now I'd like to pray for you guys."

"I'd like that." Caroline took Shelby's hand again and held out her other one to Wyatt.

Wyatt gladly took her hand. This time she actually gripped his hand. He shouldn't be analyzing this. He should be thinking about prayer, but he couldn't help himself as he bowed his head.

"Thank You, Lord, for bringing Wyatt and Caroline here today. Thank You that Wyatt is willing to care for Tasha, and thank You that Caroline is such a good friend to Wyatt. Please be with my little girl and help her to grow up to know You and the peace You bring. Please give Wyatt wisdom as he gives her a home. Bless Wyatt and Caroline as they serve You. Amen."

Again Caroline squeezed Wyatt's hand as Shelby ended her prayer. Wyatt glanced at Caroline. She was wiping tears from her cheeks.

Caroline looked at Shelby. "Thank you. That was a wonderful prayer. It made me cry."

Wyatt recognized Caroline's tender heart, and his ached that she had been through trauma she didn't deserve. *Lord God, please make her whole again.* The prayer came unbidden to his mind.

Caroline glanced between Shelby and him. "Did you have her make the video for Tasha?"

Wyatt pressed fingers to his forehead. "Haven't gotten around to that."

"What's she talking about?" Shelby asked.

Wyatt pulled his phone from his pocket. "I think it would be a good thing for you to record a video message to Tasha—not that she will see it anytime soon, but one she can look at when she's old enough to understand what it means to die."

Shelby frowned. "What do I say?"

"Just tell her how you feel. Talk to her about her future and what you hope for her." Wyatt held out the phone. "I have it set so all you have to do is press the red dot and start talking."

Caroline stepped closer to the bed. "I could make some graphics and use some music to make it kind of like a movie trailer, if you want. That's up to you."

Shelby took the phone and stared at it. "I have to think about this for a minute. Maybe I should write some things down so I don't forget to say them. There's paper and pen in there."

Wyatt rummaged in the drawer of the bedside stand and held out a pen and paper to Shelby. "Here you go."

"Thanks." Shelby sat there for several minutes without writing a thing. Finally she looked up at Wyatt. "My head's a little fuzzy. Do you really think this is a good idea?"

"I do." Wyatt thought about his own parents and how he'd love to know that they loved him. He remembered his mom tucking him in bed at night before the alcohol took over her life. She had loved him, and he wished he could hear her say it. "Tasha will be able to hear you over and over again tell her that you love her."

Shelby nodded. "I can do that."

"Maybe we should just leave you alone for a few minutes so you can say what you want to say without an audience." Wyatt stared at Shelby.

"Yeah, maybe that would work." Shelby's mouth curved upward in the hint of a smile. "I won't feel so self-conscious then."

Wyatt nodded. "Okay. We'll wait out in the hall."

"Before you go, Caroline, could you brush my hair? I want to look halfway decent when I do this." Shelby shook her head. "I just saw myself on the phone screen, and it's not a pretty sight. I have a major case of bed head."

Caroline drew closer. "Where will I find a brush?"

Shelby pointed to the drawer where Wyatt had found the paper and pen. "Right in there."

After Caroline finished brushing Shelby's hair, she let Shelby examine herself on the phone screen.

Shelby nodded. "Thanks. That's a little better."

"You're welcome. Now we'll let you have some privacy." Caroline hurried from the room.

Wyatt followed close behind. He leaned against the wall and shoved down the hurts from the past that this situation had resurrected into the far corner of his mind. He looked over at Caroline, who also leaned against the wall. She hadn't said a thing. What was she thinking? He didn't know, but he saw the two of them clearly.

Two broken people trying to overcome the past.

Could they actually have a relationship that worked? He hoped with God's help they could, because no matter how hard he tried, he couldn't push away the feelings he had for her. He couldn't stop thinking about her. Her smile, her laughter, her kind heart.

Caroline finally broke the silence. "You're doing a good thing, you know. A really good thing."

"Thanks, but it hurts my heart to look at Shelby, because I remember the vibrant woman she used to be. Substance abuse has ruined the lives of too many people in my life."

"I know. It's a troublesome thing, but you can be glad Shelby has found the Lord and that she sought you out to take care of Tasha." Caroline looked at him. "Thankfully, some people find their way out of substance abuse before it takes their lives. Lukas and my uncle Ray are prime examples."

"Julianne's husband, Lukas, and your uncle Ray? Wow! I had no idea."

"Yeah, alcoholics. Julianne told me they started a support group at church."

"That's a good thing." Wyatt knew such a group would only help those who really wanted help. His grandparents had tried and tried over the years to reach his dad and mom, but they had never wanted help.

"Do you have any idea where your parents are or how they're doing?" Caroline asked.

"I don't. I quit thinking about them for years. It hurt too much, so I just put them out of my mind." Wyatt held his hands out. "But all of this has filled my thoughts with them. How do I deal with that?"

"Would you like to find them?"

Wyatt shrugged. "I don't know. I wouldn't want to find them in a bad place, and that's where I fear I would find them."

"But aren't you glad you found Shelby?"

"Part of me is for Tasha's sake, and part of me isn't. I didn't want to find her like this."

"But aren't you glad you know she's found her way to God and that someday you'll see her again in heaven?"

"That's the only good part."

Caroline smiled at him. "You should go in and see how she's doing, and I'll head out to the car."

"Don't you think you should say goodbye?" Without thinking, Wyatt took hold of Caroline's arm as she headed for the entrance.

Caroline turned, her eyes filled with alarm.

Wyatt immediately dropped his hand and raised his arms as if someone were robbing him. "I'm so sorry. I didn't mean to frighten you."

Caroline briefly closed her eyes, her hand over her heart and her lips slightly parted. "It...it's okay. I know you didn't mean any harm."

Wyatt shook his head. "I have to remember."

"Really. It's okay."

"But I have to be better at remembering not to make you uncomfortable."

"Wyatt, you've done so much. Don't beat yourself up over this." Caroline took a deep breath. "I have to get better, and I know you're trying to help me. Just keep praying and be patient with me."

"I will." Wyatt raised his eyebrows. "So will you say goodbye to Shelby?"

"I should." Caroline nodded as she turned back.

Wyatt followed Caroline into the room and stood near the doorway while she went over to the bed. Shelby looked up from the phone.

"Hey, Shelby, I just came in to say goodbye and best wishes. I'm going to let you talk to Wyatt. Just let him know if you want me to do any editing to your video. It'll be something Tasha cherishes."

Shelby tried to smile. "I hope you're right. I wish I could say goodbye to her in person, but I just didn't figure a little girl who isn't quite four years old would understand what is happening to me. I want her to remember me before it's too hard to smile."

Caroline nodded. "It's a tough call, but I think you're doing the right thing. Now I'll leave you and Wyatt to finish your conversation."

"Thanks for meeting me, and take care of Wyatt."

Wyatt laughed. "Believe me—she will."

Shelby gave a little wave as Caroline slipped out of the room. Then Shelby turned her attention to him. "She's a keeper. Don't let her get away."

"My intentions exactly." Wyatt wished it were that easy. "So did you get your video done?"

"I think so." Shelby handed him the phone. "What do you think?"

Wyatt poked at the screen, and the video played. He listened intently to the rise and fall of Shelby's voice and tried to imagine Tasha watching this. He paused the video and looked at Shelby. "She'll treasure this."

"Do you think it needs editing?"

Shelby's expectation touched Wyatt's heart. "I think

it's just about perfect, but I can have Caroline look at it if you'd like. Some soft background music might add to it, but I'm not sure."

"I don't mind if Caroline sees it. She can do what she thinks is best." Shelby held up a paper. "Besides the video, I wrote out a letter, too."

"Do you want me to read it?"

Shelby nodded. "Just to make sure I didn't leave out a word or misspell something. My mind is fuzzy from the medications they give me for the pain."

Wyatt read over the letter as he held back his emotions. A dying mother's wish tore at his heart. Shelby should be here to see her little girl grow up, but that wouldn't happen unless God performed a miracle. Wyatt wasn't sure he had enough faith to believe in miracles, but he believed in the miracle of salvation. Shelby had found that, and at least that comforted his heart.

After Wyatt finished reading, he looked up. "Another treasure for your daughter. I'll try to do my best to give her a good home. I see a lawyer on Tuesday."

"Then you should probably have the stuff that's in the big envelope in the drawer."

"What's in there?" Wyatt opened the door and found the envelope under a Bible and a paperback novel. He held up the envelope. "This?"

Shelby nodded. "It's all the paperwork that goes with the trust for Tasha."

"Do you want me to look at it?"

Again Shelby nodded.

Wyatt pulled on the papers from the envelope and glanced at them. When Shelby said trust, she meant trust. He couldn't believe what he was seeing. He glanced up. "This all belongs to Tasha?"

"Yes, and you're the trustee and in charge of the money. She'll inherit it when she's twenty-five."

Wyatt sat on the nearby chair. "Nearly two million dollars?"

"It's from the trust I got from my grandparents when I was eighteen. Thankfully, I didn't blow through it all, just a little over half of it."

"Is that what your parents were badgering you about when I arrived?"

"So you heard that?"

"Some of it." Wyatt nodded. "So if you had this kind of money, why did you travel across the country competing in barrel racing?"

"Because I loved it. I loved the freedom. I loved horses. I loved the competition." Shelby's eyebrows puckered. "Even though I didn't have to work, after I stopped racing, I went to work at Harper Farm. I wanted to be useful. I wanted a purpose and something to keep me from sliding back into my old ways."

Wyatt stood and reached for Shelby's hand. He could relate to her in so many ways about the freedom and competition. "I can't tell you how happy I am that you didn't go back down the wrong path. I'm glad you found me."

"And I'm glad I found you."

"I have a financial advisor. Is it okay for me to get his advice in managing Tasha's trust? He's Caroline's brother, and he helps me manage my money."

"You'll be the trustee, so you can make whatever decisions you want. There's a provision for a monthly allowance so you can buy whatever Tasha needs."

Wyatt wondered about the wisdom of questioning Shelby's actions, but he needed answers. "Why wouldn't you give me this information before? What if you'd died before I found you? How was I going to know about this other than the fact that you mentioned it in the letter you left in Tasha's suitcase? I was figuring she had what was in her suitcase and you had little more than that."

Shelby pulled the blanket up around her as she stared toward the window. "I didn't want anyone to know until I was gone because I thought they'd treat me and Tasha different if they knew."

"But you're telling me now."

"Yeah, that's because I now know you plan to take care of Tasha." Shelby bit her lower lip, then took a shaky breath. "The lawyer who drew up the will and the trust would have contacted you. I mean, he still will do that after I'm gone. So he has all this information. This is just my copy."

Wyatt frowned. "So you weren't sure you could trust me to know this?"

Shelby gripped the blanket tighter. "I don't know, but I do know money corrupts. I should never have gotten that money so young. I was foolish and ruined my life. It's always been a source of contention with my parents."

Wyatt knit his brow. "How so?"

Shelby sighed. "My mom came from big money. Her parents, my grandparents who set up my trust, got a lot of their money from manufacturing. They also owned a lot of land and sold it at a very good price. They were unhappy that my mother didn't marry the man they wanted her to marry and pretty much cut her out of the will by setting up the trust for me and my sister. But she died in that car accident, and I got what would have been hers in addition to my own."

"Wow! Do you think your parents will contest your will?"

Misery painted Shelby's face. "I don't want you to be dragged into something like that."

"Maybe you need to tell them about Tasha. After all, they are her grandparents."

"But they might try to take her from you, and I don't want them to raise her."

"I understand that, but—"

"No. I don't want them anywhere near Tasha."

Wyatt realized Shelby wasn't going to change her mind, so he might as well drop the subject. "Have you made provisions for a funeral?"

Shelby nodded. "Lisa will have a memorial at the farm. I'm being cremated, and I want my ashes spread on the farm."

"Does Lisa visit?"

"Yeah, whenever she can."

"Please have her contact me about the memorial. I'd like to come." The conversation made Wyatt uneasy, but he needed to say these things.

"Okay." Shelby nodded but didn't meet his gaze. Wyatt sensed she might not tell Lisa. He would have to make sure to contact Lisa himself.

Wyatt rubbed the back of his neck as he looked down on Shelby. "I need to head back home now. I'm glad I got to talk to you and sort things out."

"Me, too. Thanks for finding me and for all you're doing."

"Let me pray for you again before I go."

"Sure." Shelby bowed her head as Wyatt took her hand.

Wyatt prayed a simple prayer for Shelby's well-being. He prayed silently for her to make the right decisions about her parents and Tasha. After he ended the prayer, he squeezed Shelby's hand. "Well, this is it. Goodbye until we meet again. Someday in heaven."

Shelby nodded, her eyes brimming with tears. Wyatt leaned over and hugged her, then left quickly before he cried himself. His thoughts overflowed with emotions of every stripe. He had big responsibilities and big decisions to make. He prayed that God would guide him to do the right things.

By the time he reached the car, Wyatt had his emotions under control. He didn't want to cry in front of Caroline. He didn't know why. He was sure she would understand, but he guessed it was the manly thing—keep the emotions in check. Don't cry.

Swallowing the huge lump in his throat, Wyatt opened the car door and picked up his hat. As he slipped onto the passenger seat, he clutched the envelope with the trust papers in his other hand.

Caroline glanced at him as she started the car. "How did it go?"

"Tough."

"You want to talk about it?"

Wyatt sighed. "I'm not sure. Right now I'm pretty raw inside. Let me just digest it all. Then I might want to talk."

"Sure. It's a tough situation all the way around, but thanks for encouraging me to meet Shelby."

Wyatt nodded. He feared he might not hold it together if he opened his mouth. He eventually would share everything with Caroline. She would understand better than almost anyone. She'd been through something horrific, and it had taken her time to talk about it.

More than anything he wished he could stand in the circle of Caroline's arms and they could get solace from each other.

CHAPTER TWELVE

The smell of garlic and tomato sauce filled Melanie's kitchen as Caroline helped Ryan and Andrew set the table. She had come over as soon as she'd gotten off work to help Melanie get ready for the manicotti dinner with Wyatt and his grandparents. She'd taken special care to wear her favorite cotton teal sweater and black ankle pants to work so she didn't have to change. After growing up with two brothers, it was nice to have a sister—someone to talk to about anything.

As Caroline put the last piece of flatware in its appropriate spot, she looked over at Ryan. "Where did you guys learn to set the table?"

"Grandma Drake." Ryan wrinkled his nose. "She was always teaching us stuff like that when we stayed with her."

"Good thing she did. Now you're good helpers," Melanie called from the kitchen.

"Grandmas are good for teaching you stuff like that." Caroline smiled at Ryan's obvious disdain for setting the table.

"Yeah, I suppose." Ryan glanced toward the kitchen. "Mom, can Andrew and I go play in the basement now?"

"Yes, you may. Just don't mess with anything that's

not yours." Melanie's voice rose above the cheers from her sons as they raced away.

Caroline chuckled as she joined Melanie, who wore an apron over her red sweater that went so well with her dark hair and eyes. "Is there anything else I can help you with?"

Melanie shook her head. "It's all done. You really didn't need to come here early to help."

"I did because I want to talk to you about something." Caroline wanted this conversation to go well. It was part of her therapy to tell her rape story to a trusted friend who would understand.

"What do you want to talk about?" Melanie gestured toward the stools situated along one edge of the kitchen island. "We can sit here if you'd like."

"This would be good." Caroline glanced toward the door leading to the basement. "You don't think the boys will return anytime soon, do you? Because they shouldn't hear what I have to say."

Worry stole into Melanie's eyes. "I don't think so, but if we need to go somewhere more private, we can do that."

"This is good as long as they stay in the basement."

"I'm pretty sure they're playing with one of their video games, bowling or baseball. They could do that for hours if I let them. So I don't think you have to worry about them coming up anytime soon."

Caroline twisted her hands in her lap. "I haven't told many people this, but I thought I could tell you."

Melanie licked her lips. "Tell me what?"

"Right before I left the mission field, I was raped."

Melanie placed a hand over her heart, her eyes growing wide. "Oh, I'm so sorry. So that's why you left so abruptly."

Caroline nodded. "I wanted to get away as soon as possible. Then I had to go to Georgia for Ashley's wedding. She's a good friend from my mission school days. I managed to make it through that. I was pressing everything down inside to keep from falling apart. I couldn't bring myself to tell anyone. I tried to pretend it never happened."

"How terrible!" Melanie pressed her lips together, then let out a long sigh. "Do you want to tell me more about it, or did you just want me to know?"

Caroline took a deep breath. "I want to tell you what happened. I had my first therapy session this week, and it's led me to tell you this. Each time I tell the story, it helps me process it and hopefully helps me deal with it."

"I'll be glad to listen. I'm sure it's hard to talk about."

"It is." Caroline blinked back the tears that threatened. She took a calming breath. "Besides my therapist, you're the fourth person to know about this."

"Have you told Nathan?"

Caroline shook her head. "I have to work up to that one."

"He'd understand."

"I know, but he's my brother, and for me it's been harder to tell my family than anyone else. Wyatt had to convince me to tell my parents."

"Wyatt? You've told Wyatt?"

"Yeah. Surprising, I know." Caroline gave a little shrug. "I didn't plan to tell him, but it all came to a head when he wanted to dance with me at your wedding reception."

"That's why you told him?"

Caroline nodded again. "Yeah, because I couldn't bring myself to be held in a man's arms. The thought of it terrified me. I knew it was illogical, but the fear was there. I thought he should know why."

"I can't imagine what you've been through, but I know it has to be hard to trust people and let others in."

Caroline let a smile work its way across her lips. "I know you've mentioned how trust was an issue for you after your experience in foster care."

"True, but your experience goes way beyond any trust issues I've had." Standing, Melanie reached out to Caroline. "Would you feel uncomfortable if I hugged you?"

Caroline shook her head as she stood. She clung to Melanie and felt the warmth and love of her sister-in-law's embrace. Caroline drank in the feeling of a hug that brought security rather than hurt.

With a shaky breath Caroline stepped out of Melanie's arms. "Thank you. I needed that."

"Whenever you need a hug, just call on me." Melanie smiled.

"I'll remember that." Caroline shook her head. "This whole thing makes me a little weird. Sometimes I just can't stand to have people close, not just men. I tell myself to be brave."

"Like driving Wyatt to Kentucky?"

Caroline laughed. "Yeah. Surprised myself with that one."

"How did that go?"

"It was fine. Since he understands, it's easier, but even though I know he wouldn't hurt me, sometimes I'm still wary being with him." Caroline shook her head. "I know that sounds crazy since I volunteered to drive him, but he needed to go."

"No, not crazy at all. You've been through something horrific, and it takes time to heal."

"That's what I keep telling myself, but it reminds me of when I was a kid and wasn't looking as I ran through the living room. I hit the corner of the piano bench that was sticking out. It killed my knee, and it hurt for quite a while even though I hadn't broken anything. For years every time I went by that piano bench, I would cringe. So now I'm cringing for a whole different reason."

"You have every right to feel that way." Melanie peered at Caroline. "Just let me know if I ever do anything to make you recoil."

"I have to work on not letting things bother me, but I've just started that journey." Caroline crossed her arms over her torso. "It's kind of like giving myself a reassuring hug."

"And now that I know, I'll pray for you, and I hope you'll eventually tell Nathan. He'll want to pray for you, too."

"Thanks, but I really do have to find the courage to

tell him."

Melanie smiled. "I'm glad you felt comfortable enough to tell me."

"It's nice to have a sister."

"It is. I love being part of your family." Melanie smiled again. "Now is it all right to ask about you and Wyatt before he gets here?"

"It was a hard trip for Wyatt. I think it took a lot out of him emotionally. I'm eager to hear what transpired with the lawyer he talked to this week." Caroline couldn't reveal the private conversation she'd had with Wyatt on the way home from Kentucky. She'd sensed that Wyatt had fought to hold himself together as he'd told her about Shelby's will and Tasha's trust.

Melanie chuckled. "Thanks for giving me that information, but I really want to know what your feelings are for Wyatt."

"Oh." Caroline bit her bottom lip, then shrugged. "It's complicated."

"Isn't it always? You've got a whole lot of relatives who are trying to push the two of you together."

Caroline nodded. "I've seen that. I like him now that I've spent time with him and gotten to know the grown-up Wyatt. I didn't like him much when he was a kid because he was such a bratty little boy and teased me terribly when we were in elementary school. Then I didn't have much contact with him after he went to live with his grandparents until high school. Then he teased me again, but not in the same way. He used to call me 'Miss Goody-Goody.' I tried to ignore him. He just seemed like trouble."

Melanie laughed. "I can just see him doing that."

"You can?"

"Yeah, he has that impish twinkle in his eyes."

"Really?"

Melanie nodded. "But maybe he looks at you differently now because he's grown up and cares about you in a whole new way."

Caroline sighed. "He's told me he's interested in a relationship, but he knows I can't even think about that now."

"So where does that leave you?"

"Wishing I was better. Wishing I didn't have this irrational fear. Wishing I could be normal again." Caroline held back her tears as she tried to put on a happy face.

"Me, too. I wish all of those things for you, and I'll pray every day that you'll get there."

"Thanks." Caroline knew wishing wouldn't make it happen. She had to rely on God, but sometimes He still seemed far away.

Melanie pointed toward the kitchen clock. "Everyone should be here in a few minutes. I'd better get the manicotti in the oven and put the antipasto on the counter.

"Can I help?"

Before Melanie could answer, the doorbell rang. "You can get the door while I get the antipasto. That must be Wyatt and his grandparents."

"I'll let them in." Caroline smoothed her hair and

tugged on her sweater as she headed to the door.

She hadn't seen Wyatt since Monday, when he'd come to the nursing home to help with bingo. He'd brought Tasha with him, and she'd been a hit with the residents as she pulled the bingo balls from the cage and handed them to Wyatt. He'd read them off with crazy puns and jokes. She had to admit she was eager to see him.

Her pulse beating in double time, Caroline opened the door. Wyatt stood there, a smile on his face and his cowboy hat in his hand. Tasha stood beside him, clinging to his leg. For a moment Caroline felt like hugging him. Was that another good sign? "Hi. Come on in."

"Hi yourself." Wyatt stepped aside as he ushered Tasha and his grandparents into the house, then stepped in behind them. "It smells good in here, and I'm looking forward to that manicotti."

"We all are." Caroline laughed, her heart filled with joy over seeing Wyatt.

"I missed seeing you when I was at the nursing home for my PT on Thursday. Were you hiding out from me?" Wyatt said.

Caroline shrugged. "I don't know why you didn't see me. I was there."

"Well, I missed you. I had news to share."

His intense look gave her a fluttery feeling in the pit of her stomach. "Sorry I missed you. What's your news?"

"I feel like I'm sixteen again. I've been cleared to

drive!" Wyatt grinned.

Caroline's face broke into a smile. "So you drove tonight?"

"I sure did, and would you believe that Gram didn't backseat drive once?" Wyatt put an arm around his grandmother's shoulders, then looked back at Caroline. "Now you don't have to be my chauffeur.

"Maybe I liked being your chauffeur." Caroline would miss that duty. Wyatt's presence in her life was something she was becoming used to. That was good, wasn't it?

"He's such a tease." Denise patted Wyatt's arm.

"Welcome, everyone." Melanie hurried in from the kitchen. "I'm so glad you're here."

"Thanks for inviting us." Denise glanced around. "You have a lovely home."

"Thanks." Melanie pointed toward the kitchen island. "I've got some antipasto over there. You can help yourselves and let me know what you'd like to drink."

As Melanie took the drink orders, Nathan rushed in from the garage and gave Melanie a hug and kiss. "So sorry to be a little late."

Melanie smiled. "I wouldn't expect anything else from you."

Nathan shook his head as he surveyed the group. "She has me pegged. No one can tease me about keeping banker's hours."

Melanie pointed toward the basement. "Tell the boys to come up and greet our guests."

As Nathan headed toward the basement door, Tasha

tugged on Caroline's pant leg. "Missy Caroline, see what I brought you."

Caroline looked down at the dark-haired child whose eyes brimmed with excitement as she held out a paper. "What do you have here?"

"I drew a picture for you."

Caroline took the paper and studied it, then hunkered down beside Tasha. "Tell me about your picture."

"That's you." Tasha pointed to a stick figure with brownish hair.

"Who is this?" Caroline touched the stick figure with the short black hair.

"That's My Wyatt."

"And who is this?" Caroline tapped the stick figure with the long dark hair.

"That's my mommy." Tasha looked up at Caroline. "She's sick. That's why she didn't come with us tonight."

"May I keep this picture?" Caroline's heart melted.

Tasha nodded. "I already gave Gram and Gramps the pictures I drew for them."

"I bet they liked your pictures. I really like the one you gave me. Thank you." Caroline hugged the little girl, and it felt good and right when Tasha hugged her back.

"Tasha, I want you to meet my boys. Ryan and Andrew, come meet Tasha." Melanie ushered the boys forward.

Caroline stood back and watched as Melanie made the introductions and Ryan and Andrew agreed to entertain Tasha. They were sweet boys. She'd known that from the first time she'd met them and knew why her brother had been so excited to be their dad. She also recognized that they had good instincts about people, and they loved Wyatt. So many reasons to like him gathered in her thoughts.

"Looks like Tasha's in good hands."

Caroline's heart skipped a beat as she turned to find Wyatt standing next to her as he held a small plate filled with some of Melanie's antipasto goodies. "You know she is."

Wyatt held up his plate. "You should get some."

"I'll wait for the main course."

"Not hungry?"

"Just waiting for the main course. I don't want to ruin my appetite." Caroline wasn't going to tell him that his presence tied her stomach into knots. He charmed her and filled her with trepidation all at the same time. Now the fear wasn't about being alone with a man but about the feelings she was developing for this man— feelings that left her unsettled.

Wyatt lifted his plate. "But this is supposed to enhance your appetite."

Caroline laughed. "It might enhance yours, but not mine."

"Each to his own." He popped an olive into his mouth and gave her a wink. "Did you get your furniture?"

"I did. You want to come over next Friday and check it out?"

Wyatt grinned. "Is this a dinner invitation or just an invitation to see your furniture?"

Every nerve in Caroline's body raced with energy. Had she just invited Wyatt over to her house without thinking? Yes, she had. Now what? *Be brave and move forward with your life.* "Sure. I'm not much of a cook, but you can take your chances."

"I could always help you cook. I'm not bad in the kitchen. We can collaborate on the menu. Deal?" He extended his hand.

"Deal." Caroline stared at his outstretched hand. He wouldn't be offended if she didn't shake it, but she smiled and placed her hand in his.

It was just a handshake, but it was so much more to Caroline. The touch of his hand made her heart flutter, not in a fearful way but in a way that held a promise of better things to come. This was a step forward, a step she needed to take.

Melanie rang a little bell that she had picked up from the counter. "Okay, everyone, we're about ready to eat. Let's gather in the dining room."

Wyatt leaned closer to Caroline as they headed that way. "The dinner bell. My taste buds are on alert."

"You are entertaining." Caroline eyed him.

"Thank you. I'm glad I can be of service." He bowed slightly, a lopsided smile curving his mouth.

As the group gathered in the dining room, Tasha sidled up next to Wyatt, and he hugged her to his side. Caroline wondered if the little girl's presence made him think of Shelby. The child did resemble her mother.

Caroline couldn't purge her mind of Shelby's image or the sadness in Wyatt's expression after they'd left the hospice center. The two images were tattooed in her thoughts.

"We're so happy everyone could join us tonight for some of my wife's marvelous manicotti. We're serving buffet style. Melanie will tell you which seat is yours, and you can grab your plate." Nathan put an arm around Melanie's shoulders. "Let's give thanks for the food."

After the prayer, Melanie showed each of them where to sit. Caroline wasn't surprised when she found herself sitting beside Wyatt, with Tasha on his other side on a booster seat. As they went through the line, Wyatt helped Tasha fill her plate, then his own.

While they ate, Nathan mentioned how busy they were at the bank, and Melanie asked Caroline how things were going at the nursing home. Wyatt again expressed his joy over being released to drive. Caroline noticed that Denise and George said very little, except how much they enjoyed having Tasha, but they didn't say anything about what they were doing on the farm. Then the boys took over the conversation as they talked about the upcoming youth baseball.

"Aren't you guys playing basketball now?" Caroline asked.

"Yeah, but we like baseball better," Ryan said.

"Why is that?" Caroline raised her eyebrows.

"Because the weather is warmer and we get to be outdoors. And I need to be taller to be good at basketball." Andrew made a face.

"One of these days you'll be taller, and then I'm sure you'll love basketball just as much as baseball." Wyatt's gaze went from Andrew to Ryan.

"Maybe." Ryan narrowed his gaze. "But Nathan likes baseball best, and so do we."

Nathan laughed. "He's right. Baseball is my sport."

As the meal ended, Melanie instructed the boys to play a game with Tasha. While the boys grabbed Candyland from the basement and took it to the family room, the adults cleared the table and put the dishes in the dishwasher. They accomplished the task in a matter of minutes, then settled in the living room.

Caroline found herself sandwiched between Wyatt and Melanie on the beige couch with the wide rolled arms. Caroline breathed a sigh of relief when panic didn't set in because of Wyatt's close proximity. Things were getting better. She prayed that trend would continue.

Nathan sat forward in the beige-and-blue club chair. "Wyatt, how did things go during your appointment with the lawyer on Tuesday?"

"Very well. He contacted the attorney who drew up Shelby's will and Tasha's trust. Everything's in order, and he started the paperwork for me to officially be Tasha's guardian and eventually adopt her. That process should take a few months, depending on court dates."

That meant Wyatt wasn't going anywhere until the adoption was completed. What did this timeline mean for that job in Florida? Did that mean he would choose to stay here permanently?

Wyatt looked at her, then glanced around the room. "I'd like some feedback on something I'm planning to do."

A murmur of encouragement filtered through the room as everyone focused on Wyatt. Caroline wondered if this had anything to do with the questions that had been swirling through her mind.

"You all know Tasha's mother, Shelby, is in hospice, and I could receive word any time that she is gone. I plan to attend her memorial service, and I want to take Tasha with me."

"Do you think that's a good idea?" Melanie asked.

Wyatt shrugged. "I'm not sure. That's why I'm seeking everyone's advice. I've done a little research about kids attending funerals for their parents. Some psychologists say that kids who don't go to their parent's funeral feel cheated later in life. They feel like they never got to say goodbye or have closure. I don't want Tasha to feel that way. She may be too young to completely understand, and maybe she won't even remember going, but I don't want her to feel cheated out of saying goodbye."

Caroline turned to look at Wyatt. "That makes sense to me, but what about Shelby's parents? Won't they be at the memorial?"

"That's another issue to deal with. They will most likely be there. If I take Tasha, they'll likely discover her existence, which Shelby didn't want." Wyatt wrinkled his brow. "But I think Tasha will also feel cheated not knowing her grandparents."

"So you'd go against Shelby's wishes?" Caroline stared at Wyatt.

"I think I have to." Wyatt let out a heavy sigh. "I tried to convince Shelby that she should tell her parents about Tasha."

"Then you've pretty much made up your mind about the whole thing?" Denise asked.

Wyatt shook his head as he released a harsh breath. "I guess I have. I just wanted to say it out loud to someone and see if there were any major objections."

"What if they want to try to take Tasha from you? Have you considered that?" Denise eyed Wyatt.

"Yes, but if Tasha were your grandchild, wouldn't you want to know?" Wyatt returned his grandmother's stare.

Denise nodded. "I would, but I worry you might have a custody battle on your hands, and that won't do anyone any good."

Nathan stood and held out his hands. "Let's join hands and pray about it."

The rest of the group stood, and Wyatt glanced at Caroline as he held out his hand to her. She read the question in his eyes and immediately took his hand. The warmth of his calloused hand made her heart do a little flip-flop and gave her a sense of peace, not anxiety.

While Nathan prayed, Caroline marveled at the way her apprehension was dissipating day by day. She was making more progress than she'd even dreamed of at this point. She forced herself to concentrate on the prayer, not the presence of the wonderful man standing beside her.

After the prayer, Wyatt thanked everyone for standing with him. "Please continue to pray for me and Tasha."

"Now that we've prayed, I'm taking orders for my Italian cream cake. Who wants some?" Melanie asked.

The room erupted with a chorus of "me." Melanie laughed as she headed to the kitchen. "You can all follow me."

The group paraded into the kitchen. The adults called the kids, and they gathered around the dining room table again while Nathan helped Melanie serve the cake.

"This is the bestest cake ever," Tasha proclaimed. "Do I get two pieces?"

Laughter filled the air, and Wyatt patted the top of Tasha's head. "One piece will have to do."

"I can send a piece home with you, if you'd like." Melanie peered at Wyatt for approval.

"That sounds like a good idea." Wyatt looked down at Tasha. "Then you can have a piece tomorrow."

Tasha nodded as she took another bite of her cake. Caroline loved how Wyatt related to that little girl. Caroline prayed that God would grant Wyatt smooth sailing through this adoption process and that Shelby's parents wouldn't cause a problem.

The thought of being part of Wyatt and Tasha's life niggled at the corner of Caroline's thoughts. Did she dare hope for that outcome? Her fears were fading, and life looked happy again. She should hold on to the positive and leave the negative behind. Wyatt was all part of the good things in her life, and she wanted it to stay that way.

***

The following Friday, Tasha carried her battered pink elephant in one hand and a bouquet of daffodils in the other as she skipped up the walk that led to Caroline's house. A rainbow of tulips filled the flower beds lining the front porch. Spring was definitely in the air. Was love in the air also? Wyatt tried to tamp down that emotion, because he was pretty sure Caroline wasn't ready for that. He was just happy she had invited him over for dinner. They had decided on the menu on Monday when he'd helped with bingo again, and Tasha had enjoyed her role as the bingo ball snatcher. The residents loved her, and he loved her, too.

Tasha warmed his heart every time she took his hand and smiled up at him. He could hardly wait to officially be her dad. He wondered when he should have her start calling him daddy rather than "My Wyatt." He didn't want to get too far ahead of himself. All the legal stuff had to fall into place. The adoption training had started and was going well. He hoped he would be a good dad to this sweet child.

"Can I ring the doorbell?" Eager to do one of her favorite things, Tasha looked at him for confirmation.

"Yes, you may ring it."

Tasha stood on her tiptoes as she pressed the

doorbell while Ellie the elephant dangled from her hand. His heart beat to the sound of the chime. The anticipation of seeing Caroline gave him the same feeling he'd had while he sat on a bronc ready for the chute to open and the bronc to take him on a wild ride. Being with Caroline was a wild ride for his heart.

After Caroline opened the door, she hunkered down to eye level with Tasha. "Hey, who's ringing my doorbell?"

"It's Tasha and My Wyatt." Tasha grinned as she thrust the flowers at Caroline.

"Thank you. Those are lovely flowers."

"My Wyatt picked them just for you. I helped." Tasha hugged her elephant.

"From your grandmother's garden?" Caroline looked up at Wyatt with a smile.

"Yes. Tasha's suggestion. Good thing she's my social secretary."

"You have a very good social secretary." Caroline laughed, then looked back at Tasha. "Would you like to help me put them in a vase so we can have a pretty decoration for our table?"

The child nodded as she followed Caroline into the house. Wyatt glanced around at the new furnishings. He made a sweeping gesture as he took in the tan sofa and love seat accented in a geometric pattern of browns, grays, whites, and tans. The side chair had a geometric pattern in the same colors. A large print of the African countryside hung on the wall behind the sofa. Trinkets that appeared to be from Africa adorned the dark-oak end tables and coffee table that sat on a brown-and-tan area rug. The medium oak floors shone in the late-afternoon sun coming through the two windows that overlooked the front porch.

The fact that Caroline had souvenirs from Africa scattered throughout the room made Wyatt think that every memory of Kenya wasn't bad, but he didn't ask. He would hate to trigger an unpleasant thought.

"You did a great job decorating. I'm impressed."

"Don't give me the credit. My cousin Julianne is the one who helped me order everything through her variety store. She has the eye for decorating. She came over and helped me go through my things and pick out the stuff she thought would go with the room."

So Caroline hadn't chosen the accents. She had let her cousin, who didn't know about what happened to Caroline before she came home, go through her things and make the choices. But she had let them stay, so he hoped that was a good sign.

"Let's get that vase." Caroline motioned toward the kitchen.

Wyatt followed Caroline and Tasha past the peninsula bar that separated the living room from the kitchen.

"I know Tasha wasn't part of the plan for our evening, but my grandparents had some place to go at the last minute and couldn't watch her. I hope you don't mind that I brought her along."

"I'm absolutely thrilled that she's here."

Wyatt hoped that didn't mean Caroline still had

lingering reservations about spending the evening alone with him. He shouldn't think that. She had invited him over not knowing that Tasha would be with him. He should purge thoughts like that from his mind.

Wyatt held up the bag he'd carried in. "I've got the veggies and my gram's delicious homemade rolls."

"Wow! Your gram made rolls for us?"

"She had some in the freezer and suggested I thaw them out and bring them."

"That's a treat. I remember having those at church potlucks."

Wyatt smiled. He'd only gone to church potlucks because he might catch a glimpse of Caroline there. Maybe if he'd actually attended church for the right reason, she would've noticed him. Instead, he'd been in her outer circle rather than the inner circle of her life.

Caroline went to a nearby cabinet and opened the door as she stood on her tiptoes. "I have a vase up here for the flowers."

"Here. Let me get that for you." Wyatt stepped up behind her and brought down the vase. When he looked down and handed it to her, he didn't miss the tiny speck of panic that flashed in her eyes. He had stepped too close without thinking.

"Thanks." Her apprehension diminished as she smiled and hurried to the sink. "I'll just fill this with water. Then we can set it on the table in the dining room."

"Tasha, take Caroline the flowers." Wyatt stood back as Caroline lowered the vase so Tasha could place the flowers in it.

"Lovely." Caroline held the vase in front of her, then motioned for Tasha to follow into the dining room.

Wyatt stood at the end of the peninsula as Caroline helped Tasha place the vase on the round dark-wood table with the pedestal base and four matching chairs. The bright yellow and white daffodils gave a splash of color to the room with the large three-pane window on the opposite wall.

Caroline smiled down at Tasha. "Should we help Wyatt make dinner?"

Tasha nodded. "My Wyatt is a good cook. He and Gram make really good cookies."

Caroline looked his way. "I didn't know you were a cookie maker, too."

"Gram makes chocolate chip, and my specialty is peanut butter."

"Did you bring some?"

Wyatt shook his head. "Sorry. I didn't think about dessert. Do you have a sweet tooth?"

Caroline laughed. "I do, but we're in good shape for dessert. I mentioned that you were coming over to my mom, and she brought over a chocolate cake."

"That sounds good. So let's wash up before we get started." Wyatt turned back toward the kitchen.

"The hand soap is sitting next to the sink." Caroline pointed across the room to the sink that sat under the window.

After they washed their hands, Wyatt turned to Caroline. "Is the meat in the fridge?"

"Yeah. I hope I got what you wanted."

"Let's have a look." Wyatt opened the refrigerator and looked inside. He grabbed a package wrapped in butcher paper and held it up. "This it?"

Caroline nodded. "What do you need?"

"Do you have the spices I asked for?"

"Right here." Caroline pointed to the lineup of little bottles on the counter.

"Great. Let's get started."

"I'll watch, and you can tell me what to do."

"Preheat the oven to four hundred twenty-five. I need a roasting pan with a rack on the bottom."

"Coming right up." Caroline grabbed a pan from a lower cupboard and put it on the counter, then placed the rack inside.

Wyatt tore open the butcher paper. "Super. The meat is already tied. Did you ask the butcher to do that?"

Caroline smile. "I did because I wasn't sure I knew how."

Wyatt placed the meat in the pan. "Caroline, you can measure out the spices, and Tasha can sprinkle them on the meat. Then I'll rub them in."

"That's what I call real teamwork." Caroline retrieved a small stepstool out of the pantry in the corner and brought it to the counter, where Wyatt stood. "Tasha can stand on this."

"Good thinking." Wyatt picked Tasha up and placed her on the top step. "There you go. Now you can see everything that's going on and easily sprinkle the spices. Ready to go to work?"

Caroline measured the spices and dumped them into small ceramic containers and lined them up for Tasha. The little girl took the first container and tried her best to sprinkle the spice, but it turned out to be more of a dump than a sprinkle. Wyatt rubbed in the spice, then helped Tasha hold the next container as he helped her sprinkle. Then he let her do the next one on her own.

"Good job. You got it just right." Wyatt patted Tasha's shoulder. "You're a great helper."

Tasha smiled, and Wyatt's heart turned inside out. He prayed every day that things would go smoothly with the adoption plans. He'd had no idea when he'd seen the child sleeping on the bed that first day how much he'd come to care for her.

"My Wyatt, what should I do now?" Tasha asked.

Before Wyatt could answer, the oven beeped. "Right now we'll watch Missy Caroline put the meat into the oven and set a timer for thirty-five minutes."

After Caroline set the timer, Wyatt brought Tasha's stool over to the sink. "Now we'll wash the vegetables and get them ready to roast."

"Do you want to use my little counter oven?" Caroline pointed toward the corner.

"That will work great, and you can peel the potatoes and put them on to boil."

The kitchen hummed with activity as they worked together, and Tasha asked questions about everything. All this hominess made him wish this invitation to dinner could lead to a life with Caroline and Tasha. An impossible wish? A premature wish? A wish beyond his grasp? He didn't know, but he wanted to make it happen.

When the beef tenderloin was cooked to perfection, the potatoes smooth and creamy in a bowl, and the veggies roasted to the precise tenderness, they sat at the table. Caroline had folded towels and placed them on the chair to give Tasha a boost.

Caroline looked at him as she took her seat. "Will you give thanks for our food?"

He nodded and bowed his head. He gave thanks for the food and silently prayed for Caroline to find peace and healing in her life. After he said amen, he looked up. Tasha was staring at him with a curious expression.

"How does God hear us if we can't see Him?" Tasha's question took Wyatt by surprise.

He looked over at Caroline, hoping she could see his silent cry for help. "Maybe Missy Caroline can tell us."

Caroline gave him a wry smile. "That's a good question. Wyatt, go into the living room."

"Sure." Wyatt did as she said.

"Tasha, ask Wyatt something."

"When do I get chocolate cake?"

Wyatt laughed. "After you eat your dinner."

"Wyatt, you can come back now. Tasha, did you see Wyatt when you asked him the question?"

Tasha shook her head.

"Well, that's kind of like God. He's there, but we don't see him. He's always with us no matter where we are." Caroline patted Tasha's hand. "There are lots and lots of things to learn about God, and you have your whole life to keep learning about Him. Did I answer your question?"

Tasha nodded, but Wyatt wondered whether the four-year-old really understood. He was an adult, and he didn't always understand all there was to know about God.

"Okay, young lady, let's eat before our food gets cold," Wyatt said.

Wyatt dished out the food for Tasha and cut her meat into small pieces. They ate without much conversation, and Wyatt wondered what Caroline was thinking. His heart did a little tap dance every time she looked his way. He wished he could tell her how much he cared about her, but he didn't want to overstep in any way. He had to let her take the lead.

"My Wyatt, see, I ate all my food. Now do I get cake?" Tasha squinted as she looked up at him with her cute grin.

"Maybe you should ask Missy Caroline about that." Wyatt glanced Caroline's way.

"Tasha, you did a very good job eating your dinner. Do you think you have room in your tummy for cake now, or do you want to wait a little while to have your cake? That's what I'm going to do." Caroline put her fork on her plate. "We need to do cleanup before we have cake anyway."

"Okay." Tasha imitated Caroline.

Wyatt admired the way Caroline had handled that. He had dumped it in her lap, and she proceeded without the slightest hesitation. Maybe it was her years dealing with children as a teacher. Or maybe she was just wise. So many things about Caroline drew his attention. If only he could act on it.

Caroline led the way as she cleared her dishes from the table. "You two can put your dishes into the dishwasher, and I'll wash the roasting pan and other serving dishes while you do that."

"Great. Tasha and I can handle that." Wyatt helped Tasha gather her plate and cup from the table.

Within minutes they'd cleared the dishes, and the kitchen sparkled as Tasha eyed the cake sitting on the counter. What did Caroline have planned now?

"Tasha, would you like to make a drawing or color in a coloring book?"

Tasha looked from Caroline to the cake and back. "Then can I have cake?"

"Actually, if you want cake now, you can have a piece while you color."

With a big smile lighting up her face, Tasha clapped her hands. "I'd like that."

"Okay. Let me get things set up for you." Caroline disappeared into her bedroom at the back of the house and brought back a small table and a chair the perfect size for Tasha. "Let's take this into the living room. You can sit right here while I get your cake and your coloring supplies."

Wyatt stood next to the couch as he watched Caroline get Tasha settled. "Is there anything I can do to help?"

Caroline looked his way as she shook her head.

"You can just sit on the couch, and I'll bring you a piece of cake. It's the least I can do after you did most of the cooking."

"Okay. I'm looking forward to that cake."

Caroline brought Tasha a piece of cake and a box filled with crayons along with a tablet of drawing paper. "After you eat your cake, you can draw me a picture that I can put on my refrigerator. I need another one to go with the one you already drew for me."

"Thank you." Tasha gazed up at Caroline. "What do you want me to draw?"

"Anything you'd like. Make it a surprise."

Caroline disappeared into the kitchen again and returned moments later with cake for herself and him. She placed the plates onto the coffee table and handed him a fork as she settled on the couch, not next to him, but not too far away. Encouraging…

"Thanks." Wyatt picked up the plate. "This looks good!"

"I'm sure it is. My mom makes the best cakes." Caroline took a bite of hers.

Wyatt did the same. "This is good. Does your mom make cakes for friends?"

Caroline puckered her brow. "Why do you want to know?"

"Tasha's birthday is a week from Sunday, and I need a birthday cake for her."

"A week from Sunday is Easter, and my uncle Ray always has a big Easter get-together for the Keller clan. They have an Easter egg hunt for the kids as long as the weather is good. You and Tasha and your grandparents should come. And we can all celebrate Tasha's birthday."

"You're inviting me to your family gathering?"

"Yeah, there will be lots of kids there, and they can all sing 'Happy Birthday' to her. It'll be fun."

"But don't you have to run this by your aunt and uncle first?"

Shaking her head, Caroline waved a hand at him. "No. Uncle Ray always says the more the merrier. And you might have to sing. He always has his karaoke machine on hand."

Wyatt laughed. "'Sweet Caroline'?"

Caroline laughed in return. "I think Uncle Carl has worn out that song."

"I don't know about that."

As Wyatt took another bite of cake, his cell phone buzzed. He reached for it on the coffee table. Lisa Harper. His heart jumped into his throat. He hesitated to answer it.

"Are you going to get that?" Caroline gazed at him.

"Yeah." Wyatt picked up the phone. "Hi, Lisa. Do you have news for me?"

"I have a request from Shelby. She wants to talk to Tasha."

Shelby was still alive, but her request could spell problems he didn't want to deal with. Tasha had just stopped asking for her mom a few days ago. Talking with Shelby would start the cycle all over again.

"Do you really think that's a good idea? I thought

Shelby had decided after she left Tasha with me that there would be no more communication with her."

Lisa sighed. "That's what I thought, too, but they're giving Shelby less than forty-eight hours to live, and now she wants to say goodbye to her daughter. I hate to tell her no."

"Are you there with her?"

"Yes, and she's anxious to talk to Tasha."

"I don't think I can spring this on Tasha. Let me talk to her, and I'll get in touch after I do that."

"Can we do a video call?"

"I'll text you."

"Okay." Sadness sounded in Lisa's voice. "Please have compassion on Shelby. I know this will be hard."

"You can pray about it." Wyatt knew he'd have to do just that. "I'll get back to you in a little while."

"Thanks. Bye."

Wyatt punched at the screen on his phone with a vengeance and stared at the mountain landscape painting above the fireplace mantel.

"Has Shelby died?" Caroline whispered.

Wyatt shook his head, then explained his conversation with Lisa. "What should I do?"

"I think you should let Tasha speak to her mom."

"Don't you think that will set Tasha back in her progress to be without her mom?"

"It might, but I think this is the same as you asking about letting Tasha go to the memorial. It will give her a chance to say goodbye."

Wyatt let out a harsh breath. "But will she

understand?"

"Would you like for me to talk to her?" Caroline raised her eyebrows. "I used to help talk to kids on the mission field. We had a lot of orphans because their parents died from HIV. I'm not sure how much Tasha will understand about death, but I can talk to her, if you want me to."

"Yeah. Sounds like you know how to deal with this. I'd probably make a mess of it." Wyatt gave her a wry smile. "I'll just wait here while you chat with her."

Caroline nodded as she went over to the little table where Tasha was busy coloring. Tasha looked up and smiled as Caroline approached. Tasha held up the picture she was drawing, and Caroline grabbed another little chair and sat with Tasha. Wyatt's heart thumped at the sight of Caroline sitting on the tiny chair with her knees almost up to her chin. He wanted her in his life. Did he have the patience to make that happen?

Wyatt couldn't hear everything Caroline and Tasha said, but the little girl nodded from time to time. After a few minutes of conversation, Caroline stood and Tasha took Caroline's hand as they came over to the couch.

"Do you want to tell Wyatt about your mommy?" Caroline helped Tasha to a spot on the couch next to Wyatt.

"My Wyatt, my mommy told me she was very, very sick and that she couldn't take care of me anymore, and she said you would do that."

Wyatt nodded. "I promised your mommy I would."

"Missy Caroline says Mommy is ready to see Jesus

and she'll wait for me in heaven cuz that's where Jesus lives."

Tasha's earnest expression melted Wyatt's heart. "So would you like to talk to your mommy before she leaves to see Jesus?"

Tasha nodded.

"Okay. We'll do that." Wyatt texted Lisa, and a few minutes later, the musical tone on his phone jangled. Although Shelby smiled, her eyes looked tired and dull. Her words came out in a slow, calm cadence that told him the pain medication had her in a subdued state.

"Tasha's eager to talk to you. I'll hand her the phone."

Shelby nodded. "Thanks."

Tasha took the phone in her little hands and kissed the screen. "Mommy, I love you."

"I love you, too, Tasha. Are you being a good girl for Wyatt?"

Tasha nodded. "He makes me eat my vegetables."

Shelby laughed. "That's good."

Wyatt smiled at Caroline, who was stifling a laugh. Tasha continued to chatter, and Shelby's laugh sounded over the phone. They talked for a long time, mostly Tasha telling her mom about the farm, the kittens, Gram and Gramps, Sunday school, and the chocolate cake she had for dinner. Tasha blew kisses and grasped her arms in a hug. Finally Tasha grew silent and handed Wyatt the phone.

Wyatt looked down at her. "Are you done talking?"

Tasha nodded. "Mommy's very tired, and we said

goodbye."

"Okay." When Wyatt looked at the phone, Lisa came into his vision, with Shelby in the background, her eyes closed.

"Shelby said to tell you thanks. She's completely worn out. It won't be long now." Lisa's voice cracked. "I'll let you know about the memorial as soon as we have plans in place."

"Sure. I appreciate that." Wyatt tried to smile. "Tell Shelby that Tasha's happy."

"I don't need to tell her. She saw that, and now I think she can go in peace, knowing her daughter is happy with you. Thanks again. I'll be in touch. Bye."

"Bye." Wyatt touched the screen to end the call, his heart heavy.

As he sat there staring at the little icons on the screen, Tasha propelled herself at him and put her arms around his neck. He closed his eyes and held her close.

"I love you, My Wyatt."

"I love you, too, Tasha." Wyatt feared he would burst into tears, but he didn't care. How could a person's heart hurt so much and yet be filled with mountains of joy at the same time?

When Wyatt opened his eyes, Caroline sat there, the vision of her blurry in his tears. She handed him a tissue.

"How did you know I needed one of those?"

"Because *I* needed one." She dabbed at her eyes and wiped her nose. "Can I join in that hug?"

Wyatt held out an arm and brought her close, the hurt dropping away as his heart soared. She joined in the group hug as she put her arm around him. Did this mean she was getting better, that she cared about him enough to be this close? Did it all stem from Tasha's sweet declaration of love? He shouldn't examine it now, just accept it and thank God.

"You guys are squishing me." Tasha's high-pitched voice brought Wyatt out of a cloud of emotions.

Caroline laughed as she tickled Tasha's ribs. "Sorry about that. We are just so happy you're here with us."

"Will you be my mommy after my mommy goes to be with Jesus? Cuz My Wyatt is going to be my daddy. I've never had a daddy before. I like having a daddy."

Wyatt recognized the distress in Caroline's eyes. "Tasha—"

"Tasha, I would love to be your mommy, but you still have a mommy, and you need to just think about her and pray for her. You don't need to be looking for a new mommy now. Besides, Wyatt is going to be your daddy, and that's enough for now."

Tasha wrinkled her nose and let her gaze flit from Caroline to him. She narrowed her gaze as she looked at him. "Is she right?"

Wyatt was sure no matter what he said the whole thing would only get more complicated. Tasha was burying him alive with her questions. If he said yes, then Caroline would think he didn't want a relationship anymore. Maybe she still didn't want anything beyond friendship. But what was that hug all about?

"Wyatt, it's okay." Caroline put her hand on his arm.

Nodding, Wyatt smiled. She had voluntarily touched

him. Maybe he should just keep his mouth shut and pray for the best. God's plan would come about no matter what Wyatt did to mess it up. Caroline would love him if God planned it that way.

CHAPTER THIRTEEN

Plastic Easter eggs in a rainbow of colors littered the ground as Caroline stood at the edge of her uncle's backyard. While children filled baskets with unknown prizes hidden in each egg, she drank in the sound of Easter joy. A few puffy white clouds dotted the sky but didn't obscure the sun that warmed the spring day.

The day required rejoicing. Rejoicing for the risen Savior. Rejoicing for the love of family. Rejoicing for the mild weather that allowed an outdoor gathering. And rejoicing that her life had reached a sufficient calm.

This morning's sermon reminded her of how Christ had suffered for all people and anything that she had suffered didn't compare. Joy came from knowing that Jesus had risen from the dead. His triumph was her triumph. She was slowly overcoming her hurts with His help.

"You look lost in thought."

Caroline looked over at Wyatt, who stood nearby. "I'm thinking about the significance of Easter."

Wyatt nodded. "Jesus lives so we can have hope in Him."

"I'm sure that's very much on your mind today, knowing Shelby has gone to be with Jesus, as Tasha would say." Caroline gave Wyatt a sad smile. "How's Tasha doing? How did she take the news?"

"In Tasha fashion. I'm still not sure she understands, but she knows her mom has gone to be with Jesus." Wyatt sighed. "I keep wavering on taking Tasha to the memorial. It won't be for several weeks because they won't get Shelby's ashes from the crematorium until then. Tasha said goodbye last Friday, and I'm thinking that's good enough. I don't know."

"Maybe you should just ask her when the time comes. Explain to her what it is."

Wyatt gazed at her, his brow puckered. "For the rest of my life will I be wondering whether I'm doing the right thing for my little girl?"

"Probably. That's what parents do."

"And you would know how?"

"I watched the parenting decisions of the missionaries I worked with. I think they had to weigh all sorts of things while being in a distant country with a different culture." Caroline shrugged. "And every kid reacts differently to each situation. One size doesn't fit all with kids."

"You're a wise woman."

Caroline shook her head as she let out a halfhearted laugh. "I don't know about that. Most of the time I don't feel very wise."

"Do any of us?"

"I suppose not. We should get our wisdom from the Lord."

"True." Wyatt motioned toward the yard. "Looks

like Tasha isn't having any problem finding Easter eggs."

Caroline nodded. "It's just fun to watch the kids search for the eggs. Tasha's basket is nearly overflowing."

Wyatt chuckled. "She's quite the huntress. Nothing will keep her from finding as many eggs as possible. What will she find inside?"

Caroline shrugged. "You never know. Uncle Ray orders this stuff through his variety store, and he and Aunt Barbara, with the help of Julianne and Elise, spend several evenings putting the goodies inside the plastic eggs. There's always a bit of candy, but the kids are more likely to find a trinket, puzzle, gift certificate, or even a few coins."

"I'm eager to find out what Tasha has in her eggs."

"Are you going to join in the whiffle ball game?" Caroline asked.

"Are you?"

"Probably. It's been a few years since I've been here to be part of Nathan's big game. Whenever Uncle Ray and Aunt Barbara have one of their big gatherings, Nathan has to have his whiffle ball game."

"I can't say that I've ever played whiffle ball."

"You can trade in your cowboy hat for a ball cap."

Wyatt put a hand on top of the cowboy hat perched on his head. "You're telling me I can't play whiffle ball in a cowboy hat? If that's the case, I might have to sit this one out."

Caroline laughed. "You can play in whatever you'd

like, but I've never seen anyone in a cowboy hat playing whiffle ball."

"There's always a first time." Wyatt took off his hat and put it on Caroline. "You look pretty good in one. Maybe I should buy you one. Straw or felt?"

"Definitely straw. What's the occasion?"

"How about your birthday?"

Caroline eyed him. "You know when my birthday is?"

Wyatt gave her an impish smile. "I know lots of things about you. I remember your birthday from first grade."

"Really?"

"Yeah." Wyatt chuckled. "You were the prettiest girl in first grade, and I remember when you brought birthday treats for the class. May fifteenth."

Caroline marveled at Wyatt's memory. "So if you thought I was the prettiest girl, why did you call me names and throw rocks?"

Wyatt hung his head for a moment, then looked up at her, sadness in his gaze. "Because I was a dumb kid who didn't know how to get your attention any other way."

"You got my attention all right."

"I'm sure I did, but not the kind of attention I actually wanted."

"But you kept at it in high school." Caroline eyed him. "Goody-goody?"

"I was still dumb in high school. I had a lot of growing up to do." Wyatt sighed. "I wish I'd had enough nerve to ask you for a date, but I figured you'd turn me down."

"To be honest, I might have. I didn't have a very good impression of you then."

"How about now? I know we've been hanging out together at church functions, weddings, family dinners, moving, but we really haven't had a real date. Would you go out with me this coming Saturday? No Tasha involved."

Caroline's pulse raced. A real date. Yeah, she was ready to tackle a real date. "I'd love to go on a date with you."

Wyatt's smile made Caroline's heart melt. "Great. I'll let you know the details later this week. I want to surprise you, but I remember you saying you don't like surprises."

Wyatt was right. She didn't like surprises, but she wanted to go out with Wyatt. She wanted to see where her feelings for him would go. She wanted to know whether this relationship could help in her healing process. "I'm not sure about surprises, but I'm willing to take a chance on you."

"That's good to hear, since my attempts at getting your attention in my younger years were ill conceived." Wyatt pretended to wipe his brow. "I've changed a lot since those days. I appreciate my grandparents now, but when I went to live with them, I had a chip on my shoulder so big that I couldn't get my head on straight. I didn't find my way until Morgan got ahold of me and pointed me toward Jesus."

Caroline smiled, her heart overwhelmed with emotion as she swallowed hard. "I'm glad he did."

"For sure."

"Any more word from him on the job?"

"Trying to get rid of me before we've even had our first *official* date." Wyatt made air quotes with his fingers.

Caroline shook her head. "Just wanting to know your plans."

"I think you know my plans. I'm not going anywhere until things are settled with Tasha, and that takes time. I'm learning to be patient."

Caroline wondered if that included being patient with her. Last Friday had been another breakthrough for her. She'd been brave enough to join in the hug with Tasha and him. And now he'd asked her out. "Me, too. Being patient means waiting on God's timing, not our own."

Wyatt nodded. "That's a good thing to remember. Thanks."

"Now if I could just remember it." Caroline smiled.

"You and me both." Wyatt motioned toward the spot where Tasha was still searching for eggs. "I'd better check on her."

"Go ahead. Would you like me to save you a seat for lunch?"

Wyatt nodded. "Yeah. Tasha will want that."

"And we'll sing 'Happy Birthday' to her after lunch, and she can have her cake."

Wyatt laughed. "I think the Easter egg hunt has

made her forget all about the cake."

"Did you get her something special for her birthday?"

Wyatt gave her a sheepish grin. "We went a little overboard. I got her one of those little electric cars and a baby doll to ride with her, and my grandparents bought her building blocks and a set of art supplies."

Caroline smiled. "I think she deserves them. No judgment from me."

"Thanks. Now I'd better get going." Wyatt waved as he left.

As Caroline watched Wyatt trot away, Denise moseyed over. "Looks like you and Wyatt were having a nice chat."

"We were." Caroline nodded. "Is Wyatt doing okay since Shelby died? I've been worried about him."

"He's doing fine, but I think he's sad for Tasha."

Caroline took a deep breath. "Wyatt says Tasha's doing okay. Do you think so?"

"She really doesn't understand everything, but we're dealing with it." Denise crossed her arms over her midsection.

"That's good." Caroline sensed that everything wasn't good with Denise. "How do you think Tasha's adjusting to being with Wyatt, and how is Wyatt adjusting to Tasha?"

"He's determined to adopt that little girl."

"Do I sense that you're not completely on board with that idea?"

"I'm not sure what's best for Wyatt except one

thing. I don't want him involved with you."

Shock took over Caroline's mind, and she stood there with her mouth open, unable to say a thing. Her heart sank into her stomach. She couldn't wrap her thoughts around what Denise had just said. Did Denise somehow know about what had happened in Kenya? Surely Wyatt hadn't told her. She'd always been so cordial. What had changed? "Why?"

Denise narrowed her gaze as she looked at Caroline. "He's got a lot on his plate, and he doesn't need a romantic entanglement now. I know he has to stay here until all the stuff with Tasha is final, but he has a job offer in Florida. He doesn't need ties here."

Caroline didn't know how to respond. Didn't Denise consider her and her husband ties here? What was going on? "I don't understand."

"I lost my son because of a Keller woman. I'm not going to lose my grandson to one."

"What are you talking about?"

"I don't suppose you know that your aunt Marian dated Wyatt's dad." Denise's lips formed a grim line.

"I wasn't born yet, so I have no memory of that."

"Well, I remember how she tossed him aside for someone else. A farm boy wasn't good enough for her. So Wyatt's dad wound up marrying the no-good woman who ruined his life."

"But what does that have to do with me?"

Denise waved a hand in the air. "Oh, sure. Wyatt is a rodeo cowboy, not a farm boy, but he can't make you happy because he's not upper crust like you."

Denise's words pierced Caroline's heart. She just stared at Denise, not believing what was coming out of the woman's mouth. Did she think all the Kellers looked down on everyone who wasn't a Keller? Had she harbored this disdain for her family all these years? The thought punched Caroline in the gut.

"Gram, Gram." Tasha ran toward them as she held up her Easter basket. "See what I got."

Caroline stepped back, wishing she could disappear. She had just accepted a date with Wyatt. Now what should she do?

Wyatt looked her way. "Come on over and see Tasha's haul."

"Okay." Caroline did her best to manufacture a smile as she fought back the hurt. "Did you get a lot of cool stuff?"

Denise played nice as she and Caroline looked over the things in Tasha's basket. Caroline could barely concentrate on the prizes as the horrible conversation replayed in her mind. Could she make some excuse and go home? Although it wasn't anything like what happened to her in Kenya, it still brought back the shock, the unbelief, and the feeling of helplessness that inundated her then. Would something always trigger those horrible feelings? Denise was probably right. She wasn't good for Wyatt.

Caroline determined that she'd get through the rest of this day with her dignity. She would smile and pretend everything was okay—something she had mastered. She'd even get through the upcoming date with Wyatt. She wouldn't back out on that, but she would let him know there would be no more.

***

"Wyatt, we'd like to talk to you about something." Denise poked her head around the doorframe.

Wyatt clicked Submit to buy the tickets for the dinner cruise in Cincinnati for his upcoming date with Caroline. Then he swiveled away from the desk where his laptop sat. "What do you want to talk about?"

"Come to the kitchen."

"Sure." Wyatt followed Denise into the kitchen, where his grandfather sat at the table.

"Have a seat." George indicated the chair across from him.

Wyatt sat and looked from one grandparent to the other, concern knotting his stomach. "What's this all about?"

"We have some news." George smoothed back his salt-and-pepper hair from his forehead.

"That's what Gram said. So tell me."

George leaned forward and placed his elbows on the table. "We're selling the farm."

"What? When did this happen?" Wyatt wondered what this meant for Tasha and him.

"We were approached by a developer who wants the land for a big housing subdivision. They've offered us a very good price, and we'd like to take it. We're not getting any younger, and this is a good opportunity to retire." Determination painted George's face.

"Can you stay in the house?"

"No, we were hoping to retire to Florida, close to where you have that job offer."

This information crashed down on Wyatt like the ceiling falling in on him. He never would have dreamed his grandparents wanted to move to Florida. "You want to leave this town where you've lived all your lives? Leave all your friends behind?"

Denise nodded. "That's what we want. These old bones are ready for warm winter weather, and we can always visit here in the summer. The sale gives us a nice nest egg for retirement. More than we ever thought possible."

"Wow!" Wyatt sat back and ran a hand across the top of his head. "I don't know what to say."

"Say you'll take that job in Florida. It's a good opportunity for you, better than you could do here on this farm."

Tasha. Caroline. Wyatt's thoughts centered on them. What would a move mean for the adoption process? What would a move mean for his relationship with Caroline? "I can't. I've got things going on here that prevent me from taking that job now. Morgan understands that."

Denise placed her folded hands on the table. "But will you take that job as soon as the adoption is complete?"

Wyatt didn't want to make any commitments. "I understand this is a good opportunity for you, but I can't promise anything. You guys can find a place in Florida, and I may join you. I can't make a decision here on the spot."

Denise sighed. "I guess that's only fair. We kind of sprung this on you out of nowhere."

Wyatt chuckled. "You sure did. I'm so surprised by your sudden urge to move to a strange place."

"It seems like an opportunity we can't pass up."

"I suppose, but I'm not sure moving Tasha will be in her best interest. She's made friends at the church preschool. She's settling in. What will a move do to her?"

"She'll adjust. She's adjusted to being here with you." Denise held out a hand toward Wyatt.

"But how much adjusting can she take?" Wyatt couldn't help thinking about his own childhood, how losing his parents to alcoholism and going to live with his grandparents had disrupted his life. He never found his way until he was an adult. Despite his grandparents' attempts to help him, he may never have found the right path if it hadn't been for Morgan.

"I'm not sure, but please pray about it." George slowly nodded. "We probably won't close on the sale of the property for sixty to ninety days, so you'll have time to figure that out."

Praying. Wyatt had done a lot of that lately, but he wasn't sure he was getting any answers. He wanted to see Caroline. He needed to talk to Caroline. He didn't want to lose Caroline. His grandparents' news hit him almost as badly as the news that he could never compete in the rodeo again. What would Caroline say about this news? He'd find out tomorrow.

***

Water flowed over the paddle wheel as Caroline stood along the railing on the steamboat. She glanced over at Wyatt, who stood beside her. "You do know how to make a good surprise."

Wyatt grinned. "Why thank you, miss."

Caroline laughed even though sadness circled her heart. She didn't want this to be their first and last date, but how could it be anything else? Wyatt's grandmother disapproved, and that was a bigger hurdle than her own troubles, which also spelled doubts for their relationship.

"I'm glad you told me to bring a jacket. The breeze from the movement of the boat makes the air cool, but I wouldn't want to miss the scenery."

Wyatt motioned toward the shoreline. "Look. There's the All American Ballpark. Baseball season is underway. Nathan mentioned going to a game. I think Tasha would enjoy going with Ryan and Andrew."

"Really? Are you trying to make her into a tomboy?"

Wyatt frowned. "Little girls can like baseball."

"I was teasing." Caroline chuckled as she remembered her own tomboy days. She'd had to keep up with two older brothers. "I used to play ball with my brothers and their friends."

Wyatt held out his hand. "And see, you've become a

beautiful woman, despite playing baseball."

"Thank you, kind sir." Caroline gave a little bow, then pointed to the shoreline. "Do you see that cylindrical red thing over there? It's the National Steamboat Monument."

"And how do you know this?"

"When I was home on furlough, Nathan, his fiancée, my parents, and I went to a ball game, and beforehand we strolled on the Riverwalk. That's when I learned about it."

"Nathan's fiancée?" Wyatt stared at her. "You mean there was someone before Melanie?"

"Oh yeah. Andrea." Caroline couldn't help frowning as she thought of the woman who had broken her brother's heart. Thankfully, Melanie had come into his life and healed it.

"And what happened with Andrea?"

Caroline gripped the top of the boat's railing. "She knew going into their relationship that Nathan had Crohn's disease, but when things got complicated with his condition, she broke off the engagement. It was hard on Nathan at the time, but there were better things waiting for him. Melanie and her boys."

"He's a happy man."

Caroline nodded, thinking about how she planned to stop seeing Wyatt. Was she no better than Andrea? At least Caroline planned to break things off before they got serious. This way was for the best. She probably should've cancelled this date, but she knew he'd made special plans.

As the riverboat made its way down the Ohio River, Caroline watched the Cincinnati skyline fill her vision. The rays of the setting sun reflected in the water as the steamboat floated past Cincinnati on the Ohio side of the river and Newport and Covington on the Kentucky side.

"Gorgeous night. Gorgeous scenery. And I'm with a gorgeous woman. It doesn't get better than this." Wyatt smiled at her.

Caroline smiled in return. "You are certainly handing out the compliments again. You're going to give me a big head."

"Never. You deserve every compliment I can give you." Wyatt took a deep breath. "You've helped me see all the circumstances in my life in a better light. Remember when you came into my room and told me to be kind? That one statement put my life on a different course. And then you were there to help me sort through all that stuff with Shelby and Tasha."

"You're giving me way too much credit." Caroline shook her head, feeling even worse than before. How was she ever going to tell him that their fledgling relationship had to end?

She wanted to cry, but she put on her happy face. She couldn't tell him until they got back to Kellersburg. She didn't dare tell him before the ride home. That would make for an awkward trip. On their drive to Cincinnati, he'd been full of stories about Tasha's adventures, and he talked about getting her a pony after the adoption was final. The thought of not being part of the festivities placed a dark cloud in Caroline's thoughts.

"You're awfully quiet all of a sudden. Something bothering you?"

"Just taking in the sights and sounds." Caroline pointed ahead at the red sky above the trees that lined the shore. "Look at that beautiful sunset."

"It is beautiful, but I like looking at you better."

"I told you not to keep giving me compliments."

Wyatt's eyes twinkled with mischief. "I didn't think that was a compliment. Just saying what my preferences are."

"You know what I mean." She waved a hand at him.

He stepped closer, and her heart danced like the wake behind the boat. She wasn't afraid. She would have stepped into his arms and held him close, but she couldn't lead him on.

"Let's go to the front of the boat. We can see the lights of the city from there." She turned and scurried down the deck. She didn't wait to see if Wyatt had followed. She didn't want to see how this night would end. The thought pierced her heart.

"What's the hurry?" Wyatt came up beside her. "The lights of the city aren't going to disappear."

Caroline shrugged. "I know, but I wanted to get a good spot on the railing."

"The bridges over the river are a sight to take in also." He looked overhead as they went under one. "Have you ever walked across the bridges?"

"Yeah, on the trip I was telling you about." Caroline joined Wyatt in his upward gaze. "In fact, this might be the one. There are stairs that go up the bridge and a pedestrian walkway that takes you from Ohio to Kentucky and back."

"I'd like to take that walk with you sometime. Maybe when we take Tasha to that ball game."

"Maybe." Caroline couldn't bring herself to think about an event that wouldn't happen.

For the rest of the evening, Caroline forced herself to think of nothing but the present moment with Wyatt. Everything on the dinner buffet tasted marvelous. The music and dancing were fun. She'd made more progress than she'd expected since her reluctance to dance with Wyatt at her brother's wedding reception. But tonight it was all going to end. Misery seeped into her soul, but she couldn't let it ruin this date. That would come later.

As the cruise drew to a close, the lights of the city sparkled against the darkened sky along with the stars and a half-moon. A chill filled the air as they made their way to Wyatt's pickup. Caroline shivered and pulled her jacket tighter around her.

"Cold?"

"Just a little."

"Would it be okay if I put my arm around you to help keep you warm?"

Caroline looked up at Wyatt, his face in the shadows. She wanted that, and she wouldn't be afraid. "Sure."

Wyatt put his arm around her waist and pulled her close. His warmth and caring touch wrapped her in a cocoon of peace even while her heart raced. She placed her arm around him, and they walked together in step.

"Thank you for a wonderful evening. Everything was perfect."

Wyatt smiled. "I'm glad you enjoyed it. I can hardly wait to take Tasha to Cincinnati. We'll have a great time."

Caroline didn't say anything. Why did he have to bring up the future? The future for them that wouldn't be.

On the drive home, the radio played soft music. Caroline's mind filled with a dozen ways to tell Wyatt she couldn't go out with him again, but how could she do that when he hadn't yet asked her for another date? Everything she thought of to say didn't work.

After Wyatt parked in front of her house, he turned to her. "I've got something to tell you."

Wyatt's statement shook Caroline from her thoughts. She hoped it wasn't something she didn't want to hear. "What?"

"My grandparents are selling the farm."

"Wow! That's big news. Are they staying in the house or selling that, too?"

"Selling everything. They want to move to Florida and are pushing me to take that job with Morgan."

"Double wow!" Caroline's heart sank into her stomach. She should be happy that Wyatt would be leaving, but she had to admit the thought made her sad. "Is that what you intend to do?"

Wyatt sighed. "I can't do anything until the adoption process is complete, and I'm not sure how long that will take. Besides I've kind of gotten attached to you, and you don't live in Florida."

Caroline took in the last statement with dread. She took a deep breath and stared down at the hands she twisted in her lap. "I think you should take the job and forget about me. It's really best if we don't see each other again, at least in the dating sense. I don't think we can completely avoid each other."

"Caroline, please look at me."

Caroline squeezed her hands together as if doing so would keep her from falling apart. She closed her eyes to stem the flow of tears. She wouldn't cry. With a monumental effort she raised her head, but she couldn't say a thing for fear any words would bring on the waterworks.

"Did I do something to scare you? If I did, I apologize. I want this to work out between us. I'll do whatever it takes."

Caroline pressed a hand to her chest. "It's not you. It's me. You'll be better off without me. You need someone who's whole, ready for a relationship. Ready not to be worried about the next step. I'm still messed up. You don't need that. Besides, your grandparents want you to move with them. It's just better this way."

Wyatt frowned as he shook his head. "I won't be better off without you. I want you in my life."

Caroline shook her head. "Please understand."

"But I don't." Wyatt frowned. "We had such a good time tonight. You've been there for me with Shelby and Tasha. I need you."

"No. I'll just bring you down. Adopt Tasha. Move to

Florida and take that job perfectly suited to you. Find a good woman to share your life, and be happy." Caroline found her house keys in her purse and grasped them in her hand. She reached for the door handle, hoping to escape Wyatt's scrutiny. "You'll thank me."

"Caroline. No."

"Good night, Wyatt. There's no use to discuss this further." Caroline catapulted from the pickup and ran up her front walk. She couldn't get into her house fast enough.

Her heart ached as she closed the door and leaned against it. She sobbed as the image of Wyatt's hurt expression swam through her mind. He'd find someone else and forget all about her, but she would never forget him. Every day she would remind herself that he'd be better off without her. That was the only way she'd get through this hurt.

CHAPTER FOURTEEN

Laughter and jovial conversation filled the kitchen in her parents' home as Caroline stared at the chocolate cake covered in thirty candles. The cake reminded her of the chocolate cake her mother had made for the dinner with Wyatt and Tasha. The memory threatened to undo all the happiness of this family gathering to celebrate her birthday.

For the past month Caroline had managed to avoid Wyatt, even at church by coming late and slipping out early. Now he and Tasha had gone to Florida to help his grandparents look for a place to live. So avoiding him wasn't difficult. But there was still a hole in her heart from missing him.

Had she made a mistake to shut him out of her life? Part of her said yes, but the rational part said no. Even though she'd been making progress in putting her life back together, she still had no business in a relationship. And Denise's opposition made Caroline believe ending things with him was for the best. She tried hard to convince herself of that.

"It's too bad Wyatt can't be here to celebrate with you today."

Caroline turned to find Melanie standing next to her. Caroline wished she knew what to say. Wyatt hadn't forgotten her birthday, even though she'd ended things between them. Yesterday she'd discovered a box on her front porch. She'd cried when she opened it and saw the straw cowboy hat. He said he'd get her one, and he was true to his word.

"You don't want to talk about him?" Melanie raised her eyebrows.

"I guess you didn't know." Caroline tried to grasp just the right words before she continued. "I decided we weren't meant to be, since he's going to Florida with his grandparents."

"I'm sorry. I'm always the last to know things." Melanie grimaced.

"That's okay. I haven't talked about it."

"You could always go to Florida, too. I know it would be hard to leave your family here, but..." Melanie's voice trailed away.

"It's more than just the fact that he's moving."

Melanie moved closer and lowered her voice. "Do I dare ask what that is?"

Caroline loved Melanie, the sister Caroline had always longed for—someone to confide in. "It's hard to talk here."

"Let's take a walk in the yard, okay?"

Caroline nodded and followed Melanie into the backyard, surrounded by a tall wooden fence. The smell of freshly mowed grass filled the air as the sun danced through the puffy white clouds dotting the sky. The lilac bush near the back door still had a number of fragrant blossoms perched against the greenery.

Melanie went straight to the picnic table on the patio and sat on the nearest bench. She patted the space next to her. "Sit down and tell me all about it."

What was there to tell? Caroline wondered about the wisdom of relating her encounter with Denise Bayer, but Caroline supposed it had to be said if Melanie was to understand the whole situation.

Caroline slid onto the bench and put her elbows on the table as she clasped her hands in her lap. "Two things went into my decision to break things off with Wyatt. First, I'm still not over the trauma from Kenya, and second, Wyatt's grandmother said she wanted me out of Wyatt's life so he'd take that job in Florida."

"Oh wow!" Melanie's mouth hung open as she stared at Caroline. "I can't believe it."

"I couldn't either. My mouth was hanging open just like yours when she told me."

Melanie covered her mouth with her hand, then just as quickly placed her hand in her lap. "When did this happen?"

"On Easter."

"But you went out with Wyatt the next weekend."

"Yeah, because I'd already accepted the date with him, but I told him when we got home that we couldn't see each other anymore."

"How did he take that?"

"Not well." Caroline sighed. "But it's better this way. Then there won't be the chance of something suddenly triggering bad memories and making him not want to be with me anyway."

"But do you love him?" Melanie gave her a pointed look.

"Love? I don't know. I care a great deal about him, and love was something I was ready to explore."

"Then don't throw that away." Melanie put an arm around Caroline's shoulders. "Don't let someone else dictate your love life. That's what I did when Nathan and I were dating. I let Tim's parents almost ruin everything."

"You did?"

Melanie nodded. "They were so unkind and threatening to take the boys away from me. They insinuated that I shouldn't be dating, so I stopped seeing Nathan. He understood, but it broke my heart."

"How did you resolve that?"

"Your brother's a hero. He confronted Tim's parents and made them see how wrong they were." Melanie smiled. "He brought us together."

"Well, I don't see how I can fix things with Wyatt." Caroline shook her head.

"If he cares for you, he'll understand."

"I know. That's what he says, but how long can he put up with a skittish woman? I'm afraid I might never be whole again." Caroline took in a shaky breath. "I want to be, but I don't know how."

"Do you think your therapy is helping?"

"I do, but I live in fear of those triggers that take me back to that dark place in my mind."

"Are you relying on God or yourself?"

Caroline crossed her arms and hung her head.

"That's the problem. Every time I think I've handed it over to God, I find myself snatching it back rather than continuing to trust Him."

"I can see you're getting better at touches and hugs. Don't you see that?"

Caroline nodded. "But sometimes I think that's not enough."

"It's enough for now. We can pray about it. We'll see where things stand next week." Melanie gave Caroline's shoulders a squeeze. "Let's find time to have lunch next week and talk about it."

"That sounds good. Let me know when, and I'll be sure to plan that for my lunch break."

Caroline's dad appeared on the back porch. "I wondered what had happened to the birthday girl. We're ready to sing 'Happy Birthday' and have you blow out your candles."

Caroline and Melanie stood, and Caroline hugged her sister-in-law. "I'm going to thank Nathan again for bringing you into our family.

"And you know how I feel about being part of this family. A dream come true!"

Caroline led the way back into the house. Everyone had gathered around the dining room table, where the chocolate cake now sat. Her mother was lighting all the candles, and some guests joked about the possibility of having to call the fire department to put out the flames.

Looking around at the family members gathered here, Caroline knew how much she loved her family. They had helped her through the good times and the bad.

That was what love was all about. Caroline couldn't help thinking about Wyatt. She wished he and Tasha were here to share this day, but she had pushed Wyatt away. Was it too late to undo that mistake?

Her mother stepped back from the cake. "Let's sing 'Happy Birthday.' Then Caroline can make her wish and blow out the candles."

The song filled the air as Caroline took in the smiling faces surrounding her. She just had one wish. She wanted another chance with Wyatt. She took a big breath and extinguished all the flames as cheers rose up around her.

Nathan came up beside her. "I always knew you were full of hot air. Good job, sis. Looks like you'll get your wish."

"I plan to." Caroline knew just wishing wouldn't make her dream come true. She would have to step out beyond her comfort zone. She would have to toss aside her fears. She thought of the Scripture from the morning's sermon from 2 Timothy 1:7. *For the Spirit God gave us does not make us timid, but gives us power, love, and self-discipline.* She should print it out and tape it to her bathroom mirror to remind herself every morning not to live in fear.

Plans. She had to make a plans and bring them before the Lord. Maybe first on the list of her plans should be a talk with the missionaries she had served with. They needed to know about her attacker. Maybe it was too late to bring him to justice, but her statement might make the difference for another woman. Then she would seek out Wyatt no matter what his grandmother said.

***

The Florida sunshine beat down on Wyatt as he joined his grandparents on a piece of land covered in palmetto plants, cabbage palms, and old-growth oak trees. One of the canals that crisscrossed Morgan's ranch flowed nearby. The natural beauty of the spot gave Wyatt a sense of peace that he wasn't expecting. He'd brought his grandparents here to finalize their plans about a move to Florida. He had to be sure they weren't making a mistake with this sudden decision.

Wyatt removed his cowboy hat and wiped the sweat from his brow with his forearm. "Do you guys think you'd like living here? It's hot today, and summers only get hotter."

Denise nodded. "This is a pretty piece of land. I can see us building a house here."

"I want you to be absolutely sure. Morgan said he would sell these three acres to me, but before I buy it, I want to make sure you have no doubts about living here." Wyatt glanced around and tried to imagine two houses on this property. One for his grandparents and one for him.

Wyatt pushed away the thought of Caroline being part of the picture. He'd intentionally made this trip so he'd miss being in Kellersburg during Caroline's birthday, knowing he wouldn't be celebrating with her.

Why couldn't he forget her? Why was she constantly on his mind? He'd let himself dream an impossible dream of a relationship with her. It had seemed within his grasp until it had been ripped away like a Florida hurricane ripping up palm trees.

If he stayed in Kellersburg, could he get Caroline to change her mind? He'd kept his distance since the disastrous ending to their first real date. Before her unwelcome decision, he'd hoped she would accompany him to Shelby's memorial, but he'd taken Tasha alone. Although he wasn't sure what the child understood, he was glad he'd taken her, even though Shelby's parents hadn't attended. That made him sad. Sometimes he felt like the little boy in the comic strip with the cloud over his head. Did sad stuff follow him?

"Are you listening to me?"

Wyatt shook his head as he glanced at George. "Sorry. I was trying to imagine houses here."

"I can see them." George put a hand on Wyatt's shoulder. "Your grandmother and I are positive we want to build here, but you don't have to pay for all the land. We'll split with you. We're getting a very good price for the farm."

"We'll work it out." Wyatt motioned toward their rented SUV. "Let's head back to the main house and talk to Morgan. He should be able to recommend a builder. We have a lot of decisions to make."

As Wyatt drove the sand and shell road back to Morgan's place, he prayed. He hadn't done much of that lately. Too many times he didn't have any idea what to pray for. He'd prayed for Caroline to get better, but maybe his prayer had been selfish. He'd wanted her to get better so they could be together. He should've been praying that she would heal just for her healing. That was where he'd gone wrong.

As they pulled up to the house, Wyatt shut off the engine and turned to his grandparents. "I still can't believe you're leaving Kellersburg. It's been your home forever."

Denise reached her hand over the seat and patted Wyatt's shoulder. "You don't have to worry about that. Your grandfather inherited that farm from his father. It's been passed down from generation to generation. We farmed because that's what your grandfather knew, but we've never really been a true part of Kellersburg."

Wyatt frowned. "What do you mean?"

"We were on the outside looking in. Even though my ancestors came to the area at the same time as the Kellers, we were never considered founders."

Wyatt couldn't believe what he was hearing. Had his grandparents resented the Keller family all these years? There were dozens of Kellers and their many relatives in that town, but he had never felt any animosity other than what he'd created by his own misbehavior. "I still don't understand."

His grandmother sighed. "The farmers were never given the respect that the bankers, doctors, teachers, lawyers, and store owners were given. We were second-class citizens."

Wyatt shook his head, his brow furrowing. "I can't

believe you believe that."

"It's true." Denise narrowed her gaze. "Before your parents met, your father dated Marian Keller, but she dumped him for a college boy. I don't want you to be led on by Caroline Keller, and I told her so."

Wyatt's stomach sank. The news hit him as if he'd jumped off a high cliff into a body of water. He stifled his anger as he stared at his grandmother. He tried to reconcile this animosity with all the years his grandparents had interacted with the Keller family. They'd put on a facade of friendship where none existed. "And when did you do this?"

"On Easter."

Wyatt didn't say anything for fear he'd lash out at his grandmother. Why had she interfered? Didn't she realize if Marian Keller hadn't broken up with his dad, Wyatt wouldn't even be here? His grandmother wasn't thinking straight at all. But now he understood why Caroline had suddenly ended everything between them.

"Wyatt, I apologize for your grandmother. She didn't have any business coming between you and Caroline."

Wyatt looked over at his grandfather. "So you don't agree with her?"

"I stayed out of it because I didn't think it was any of our business."

"It certainly wasn't." Wyatt glanced from one grandparent to the other. "When we get back, I'm going to talk to Caroline and set things straight."

"I don't want her to hurt you." Denise knit her

eyebrows.

"Caroline is not her aunt. You can't blame her for what happened to my dad. He made his own choices."

Denise lowered her head and covered her face with her hands. "I'm so sorry. Forgive me."

"Maybe you should ask Caroline for forgiveness."

Denise looked up. "Will she forgive me?"

"She's a very forgiving person. I think your chances are good."

Worry showed on Denise's face. "Does this mean you won't be coming to Florida? That's one of the reasons why I didn't want you to get involved with Caroline. She'll want you to stay in Kellersburg."

"I don't know what my future holds. I've been trying to leave that in God's hands. If Caroline and I are meant to be together, everything will fall into place." Wyatt couldn't explain the other complications that surrounded any relationship he might have with Caroline. He had to hand everything in his life over to God. That was no easy task.

"That's what we've been trying to do, too." George nodded his head. "We originally got the offer for the farm right after you were injured. We knew we couldn't think of leaving until you recovered. So we turned them down."

"You didn't have to do that because of me."

"Yes, we did." George's determined look said so much. "We love you, and we couldn't leave you. Besides, it all worked out better in the end. They came back to us with a better offer, one we couldn't refuse."

Wyatt sighed. "And I owe you guys an apology for the way I acted while I was in the nursing home."

Denise patted his shoulder again. "That's okay. We knew you were hurting, so we took it in stride. We don't want to lose you."

"Gram, you won't lose me, because I love you, and I appreciate everything you've done for me through the years. And I'm sorry I haven't told you often enough."

Denise's eyes filled with tears. "And I'm sorry I said those things to Caroline."

"I know you are." Wyatt opened the car door. "Now let's talk to Morgan about that land and rescue Alicia and him from Tasha's constant inquiries."

Denise laughed as she followed Wyatt. "That child can talk your ear off."

George chortled. "But we love every minute of it. I'll be glad when the adoption is final and you're settled."

"Me, too." Wyatt couldn't help thinking about settling in with Caroline by his side. When he got home, he would go straight to her house and explain everything. He prayed she would listen.

***

Karaoke was in full swing at Ray Keller's annual Memorial Day picnic. Thankfully, Uncle Carl had agreed not to sing "Sweet Caroline." It would remind her too much of the Valentine party and how Wyatt had joined in the song to welcome her home. Besides that, this gathering brought back the terrible memory of Denise's pronouncement concerning Wyatt. Caroline pressed her lips together as she tried to suppress the thought of that unpleasant encounter.

So much had happened in the weeks since then— things she had never imagined. Now she was prepared to step out in faith and reach for what she wanted. She wanted Wyatt in her life, no matter what his grandmother said.

"So what's your big news?"

Caroline looked up to find Melanie standing next to one of the picnic tables scattered around her uncle Ray's yard. Caroline jumped up from the table and hugged Melanie. "Let's sit down, and I'll tell you."

"Your mom said you've quit your job at the nursing home. Is that right?"

Caroline nodded. "I never intended it to be permanent."

"So what are your plans?"

"First, let me say God works in wonderful ways— ways I couldn't even have dreamed of."

"What are you talking about?"

"When we talked on my birthday, you said I shouldn't let Wyatt's grandmother change my mind about being with him. I did a lot of thinking and praying and decided I not only had to go after Wyatt, but I had to talk to the missionaries about what happened before I left."

"Wow! Did you?"

"Yes, I wrote them an email, explaining everything

and warned them about this doctor. I told them I was sorry that I wasn't brave enough at the time to tell them."

"What did they say?"

"They thanked me and said they understood the trauma and why I didn't report it. They won't work with him again. Then they told me one of the families from the mission had returned to the States a couple of months ago and are serving at a church in Florida, and guess where in Florida?"

Melanie smiled. "Somewhere near a certain ranch?"

Caroline nodded. "About a forty-minute drive from the ranch. I called and talked to them. They are starting a school and need teachers. They want me to come for an interview, which is really a formality to satisfy regulations. Of course, I'll have to get my Florida teacher's certificate."

"What will that require?"

Caroline shrugged. "I'm not sure exactly, but I'm sure my friends will help me with that part."

"I'm sure you won't have any trouble."

Caroline sighed. "I just wish Wyatt were here now instead of in Florida. I'd call him, but I want to talk to him in person, not over the phone."

"When are you going for the interview?"

"I'm leaving Wednesday. I plan to see Wyatt while I'm there."

Melanie frowned. "Are you sure he won't be back by then?"

"I have no idea how long he plans to be gone."

"Maybe you should call him just to let him know you'll be in the area," Melanie said.

Caroline let out a harsh breath. "I don't know. He might just make nice over the phone, and then I'd feel like a fool when I see his face and know he wishes I weren't there."

Melanie smiled. "Have you ever known him to do that?"

Caroline chuckled. "I hardly ever talked to him on the phone, so I'm not sure."

"You might feel silly no matter what you do."

Caroline nodded. "I fear that might be the case, but I'm plunging ahead. If I don't, I might chicken out. I think that's why I don't want to call."

"I wish you the best, and I'll pray for a good outcome."

"I appreciate that." Caroline stood. "Let's get in the food line before it's all gone."

"My boys are saving a place in line for me. I think I can squeeze you in."

While Caroline waited in line, she took in the sights and sounds of this family gathering. She would miss these people, but exciting things awaited her in Florida. And she prayed Wyatt was one of those things.

***

Palm fronds waved in the breeze as if they were welcoming Caroline to the ranch. She slowed her rental car as she turned onto the shell and rock road. What would Wyatt say when she showed up unannounced? It had all seemed like such a good idea when she'd talked to Melanie at the picnic. Now it seemed like a foolhardy errand. Wyatt would surely think she was stalking him.

As Caroline stopped the car near the ranch house, she purged the negative thoughts from her mind. She let the encouraging words of Philippians 4:6–7 replace any destructive notions. *Do not be anxious about anything, but in every situation, by prayer and petition, with thanksgiving, present your requests to God. And the peace of God, which transcends all understanding, will guard your hearts and your minds in Christ Jesus.*

Anxiety was not her friend. God's peace could wipe out her worries, and Caroline clung to that promise. She rued the day she had abandoned God's peace while she'd been grappling with a terrible event. She'd let fear rule her thoughts rather than relying on God. Facing Wyatt *and* his grandmother would help banish her fears.

Looking around, Caroline slid out of the car and walked toward the front porch. She still wasn't sure she was dressed appropriately in her floral print sundress and sandals. No cars were within her sight. Maybe Wyatt wasn't even here. That would be a joke on her. *Dear God, let Your peace rule in my heart about what happens today with Wyatt.*

The front door opened as Caroline climbed the steps. Alicia appeared in the doorway, and Caroline's stomach churned. Caroline took a deep breath. "Hi, Alicia. I hope you remember me. Caroline Keller, Wyatt's friend."

Alicia smiled. "Of course I remember. This is a

surprise. Wyatt never mentioned that you were coming."

"That's because he doesn't know." Caroline didn't want to explain why. "Is he around? I'm here to surprise him."

"Wyatt's with his grandparents and Morgan at the property."

Property? Caroline wasn't sure what that meant, and she didn't want to ask and give any clue that she hadn't spoken to Wyatt in weeks. "Do you expect them back soon?"

Alicia shrugged. "I'm not sure how long they'll be. They're meeting with a builder to mark out the land for the houses."

"That's nice." Caroline wished she could ask where the property was located. Did two houses mean one for Wyatt and Tasha and the other for his grandparents? That was what Caroline surmised, but again she didn't ask.

"Tasha's taking a nap upstairs." Alicia motioned toward the interior of the house. "Come on in."

"Thanks." Caroline followed Alicia into the big sitting room with the fireplace. "She's actually taking a nap?"

Alicia chuckled. "She wore herself out swimming. Bella taught her to swim, and the child took to it like a fish. Now she wants to swim every minute."

"If you're going to live in Florida, you should know how to swim."

"For sure." Alicia held out a hand toward the couch. "Have a seat, and I'll get some lemonade, okay?"

"Thanks. I'd love some."

As Alicia disappeared into the kitchen, Caroline glanced around and wondered what she should say to Wyatt when she saw him. Would he be unhappy to see her but still put on a display of welcoming her? And what about his grandmother? Caroline should probably be more worried about her reaction rather than Wyatt's. God's peace. She had to cling to that and cast her worries aside. Why was she making it so hard?

"Here you go." Alicia handed Caroline a frosty glass of lemonade.

"Thanks."

"We were certainly surprised about Tasha."

"Yes, she was a big surprise for Wyatt when we got back from Florida after the wedding."

"I knew Wyatt was a special young man when I first met him. His willingness to adopt Tasha says so much about him." Alicia eyed Caroline. "And do you fit into this picture? Tasha talks a lot about you."

Caroline tried to smile. "What did she say?"

Alicia chuckled. "She told me about cakes. A chocolate cake. A birthday cake. And she said you were there when she talked to her mommy for the last time."

Caroline took a deep breath, glad that Tasha hadn't said anything about Caroline being her new mommy. "That was a difficult situation."

"I can't imagine, but Tasha seems to be adjusting to being with Wyatt and his grandparents."

Caroline nodded. "Thankfully, she took to Wyatt almost immediately."

"I can see that. He was great with your nephews when you were here."

Caroline couldn't disagree. Wyatt knew how to relate to kids and to someone like her. She should never have let his grandmother scare her away, but Caroline was here now and ready to face any obstacles. "He's the best kind of man."

"So the two of you are an item now?"

Caroline could at least tell Alicia part of the story. "Not exactly. We did spend time together after we got back from Florida, but we stopped seeing each other at my request. That was a mistake, and I'm here to rectify that."

Alicia smiled. "I hope you do. I thought you belonged together when you visited before."

"I've just signed a contract for a teaching job near here, and I wanted to tell Wyatt about it and hopefully make amends."

Alicia nodded. "And I'll do whatever I can to help."

"Missy Caroline."

Caroline turned at the sound of Tasha's voice and found the girl, so cute in her pink romper, racing across the room with her elephant dangling from one hand. "Tasha. I'm so happy to see you."

Tasha threw her arms around Caroline and held her tight. "I missed you."

Tears stung Caroline's eyes, and she blinked hard to keep them from flowing down her cheeks. "And I missed you."

"My Wyatt is with Gram and Gramps. They are

picking out a house for us. Are you going to come and live with us?"

Alicia chuckled. "This girl has ideas."

Caroline weighed her words carefully. "No, I can't come and live with you now."

"But I need a mommy."

"I know you do, but Wyatt has to decide about that."

"Why does he have to decide?" Tasha wrinkled her nose as she squinted at Caroline. "I should be able to decide who I want for a mommy."

Before Caroline could think of a response, Morgan, Wyatt, and his grandparents trooped into the house. Tasha jumped up from the couch and raced to Wyatt, who removed his cowboy hat. He picked her up without ever looking in Caroline's direction.

"My Wyatt, Missy Caroline is here. She came to be my mommy."

Wyatt's gaze swung to the spot where Caroline stood. "Is that so?"

Caroline didn't have a clue how to answer that, but she decided to be brave. "Would you like to discuss it?"

Wyatt grinned, then glanced around the room. "Looks like I have some important business to discuss with Missy Caroline. Please excuse us."

Morgan laughed as he clapped Wyatt on the back. "Don't be gone too long. We're having drinks and snacks by the pool."

"I'm going to show this lady my property, then we'll be back." Wyatt waved as he headed for the front door.

"See you in a bit." Caroline's heart raced as she

stepped onto the front porch and Wyatt turned to face her. He stood there looking so good in his faded jeans, blue chambray shirt, and cowboy boots.

"What are you doing here?" Wyatt's grin had faded, replaced with a serious look that made Caroline's bravado shrivel.

Caroline stared at him. Was he unhappy that she was here? "I'm sorry if I've interfered with your plans, but I was in the area and wanted to see you."

Wyatt narrowed his gaze. "Wanted to see me for what reason?"

What had happened to the man who had grinned at Tasha's pronouncement? Caroline took a shaky breath. "I…I came to tell you I'm sorry I said we couldn't see each other anymore. That was a mistake."

A muscle worked in Wyatt's jaw as he stared at her. "I would agree."

"Do you forgive me for making a wrongheaded decision?" Caroline held her breath while she waited for his answer.

Sadness flooded his eyes as he nodded. "Forgiving you won't change the fact that I'll be in Florida while you'll be in Ohio."

"But that's not the case."

"Seems that way to me. In a week I have a court date to make Tasha's adoption final. My grandparents have signed the papers to sell the farm and have made arrangements for their stuff to be moved here."

"I'm glad you have a court date and that everything is falling into place for the adoption and your move, but—"

"Thanks. I appreciate that."

"You didn't let me finish." Caroline eyed him.

"Go ahead." Wyatt held out a hand. "I didn't mean to interrupt."

"I'm moving here, or at least close to here."

Wyatt raised his eyebrows. "You're moving to Florida?"

Caroline smiled. "Yes, that's what I said."

Wyatt glanced back toward the house. "There are prying eyes everywhere. I said I was taking you to see my property. Let's go, and you can explain."

Caroline followed Wyatt to the SUV parked near her rental car. He opened the door for her, and she slid inside. She prayed for wisdom and strength as Wyatt climbed behind the wheel and turned her way. Where did she start? Her mind was blank.

When Caroline didn't say anything, Wyatt started the car and drove away from the house. He didn't ask her to explain, and she remained silent as she waited for him to start the conversation. So far he hadn't shown much enthusiasm about her news, which did nothing to bolster her confidence.

They drove past a house situated along one of the canals that crisscrossed the ranch. They passed a fenced-in area where horses grazed and continued through open pastures dotted with cattle. Caroline twisted her hands in her lap as she stared out the window and wished she knew if he really wanted her to explain.

Wyatt stopped the SUV near a wooded area. "This is

it."

"It has lots of trees." Caroline had a hard time imagining where houses would fit on the land.

"Yeah. We tromped through the property today and laid out the stakes for the houses and marked the trees we plan to save when they clear the land." Wyatt glanced her way. "So what do you think?"

"It looks like a lovely piece of land. I think you'll be very happy here." Caroline tried to smile, but she was sure it didn't look genuine. "When will they start to build?"

"In a few days they'll clear the land."

"How long will it take to build the houses? And where will you live while they build them?"

"Probably four or five months. Remember that house we drove by near the canal? We'll be staying there."

Caroline nodded, wishing she were brave enough to ask Wyatt if he didn't care that she was moving close by. She was afraid to hear his answer. He was making it clear that he just didn't care what she was doing. Her heart ached, but she had to plead her case. She had to quit being fearful.

"I hope you'll welcome me for a visit after the houses are done."

Without saying a word, Wyatt got out of the SUV. He walked toward the grove of trees and tangled underbrush. Caroline watched him disappear into the grove. Was he just going to leave her here? Was she supposed to follow? She wasn't dressed for traipsing through the woods, but she wasn't going to sit in the car.

Caroline exited the pickup and walked gingerly through the tall grass, trying not to get sand in her sandals. Sunshine filtered through the trees as she peered into the grove. Wyatt emerged from the shadowy trees, and her heart thumped.

"I saw these earlier and thought of you. I must've sensed your presence." Wyatt held out a handful of lavender bell-shaped flowers on long stems. "A peace offering. Pretty flowers for a pretty lady. I've missed you."

Caroline took the flowers, then threw her arms around him. "Thank you for the flowers. Thank you for missing me. I've missed you, too."

"You're good with me holding you?"

Still in the tender circle of his arms, Caroline tilted her head back and looked at him. "I wouldn't have put my arms around you if I wasn't. I've never been better, but I thought maybe you weren't happy to see me."

Wyatt pulled her closer. "I was in shock that you were here. I didn't know what to say. It all seemed like a dream. Too good to be true."

"It's not a dream. I have a teaching job near here starting in August."

"How did this happen?" Wyatt continued to hold her around the waist.

Caroline explained how the job had come about. "I want to be with you and figure out where our relationship is going."

"That makes me happy, happier than you can ever know."

"I'm sorry I ended things between us. Will you forgive me?"

"You're not the one who should be asking for forgiveness. My gram should ask for *your* forgiveness. She told me what she said to you at Easter. She's sorry, and so am I."

Caroline stepped out of Wyatt's arms. "She told you?"

"Yeah. I wanted to be sure they weren't making a mistake in leaving the only place they've ever lived. That's when she confessed she had always felt inferior in Kellersburg and not a true part of the community. And she was afraid you wouldn't want me to come to Florida. That's why she told you to stay away from me." Wyatt shook his head.

Caroline nodded. "Yeah, she kind of said as much. I couldn't believe it. But I'm at fault for letting her dissuade me from being with you. I admit I used her warning to feed my fear. Fear that I would never get better. I have to lean on God and quit living with fear. You are a good man, Wyatt, and I love you."

"I love you, too. I had planned to see you as soon as we got back to Kellersburg, but you beat me to it." Wyatt pulled her closer and held her tight. "What do we tell Tasha?"

Caroline swallowed hard as she leaned into Wyatt's arms. She didn't want to overpromise anything. "I love you, and I love Tasha, but I'm not ready for marriage. Not yet."

Wyatt held her at arm's length. "Maybe by the time

the houses are ready, we'll have that figured out."

"Then you're not unhappy with that?" Relief flooded Caroline's mind.

"I'm good with working through this. I have hope that we'll get there."

"Me, too, but will Tasha understand? After all, right before you walked in the door, she told me she should be the one to pick out her mommy, not you."

Wyatt laughed. "I'm sorry I missed that. Now I know what to tell her."

"What's that?"

"This is a joint decision. Her and me. And she can't decide before I do."

Caroline smiled. "Do you think she'll go for that?"

"She'll have to because I'll be waiting on you to tell me when you're ready for that big step."

"So you'll want me to propose when the time comes?"

"Sure. After all, you're the one who said 'I love you' first."

"And I do love you. More than I can say. You have helped heal my broken places."

"I want to keep doing that and loving you."

"Then I think you should kiss me."

"Gladly." Wyatt pulled her close.

Still holding the flowers, Caroline put her arms around Wyatt's neck as he bent to kiss her, a kiss with a promise toward the future. A future without hurt. A future without fear. A future with love to share.

□ □ □ □ □

Dear Reader,

Thank you for reading *Hometown Cowboy*. I hope you enjoyed Caroline and Wyatt's story, the fourth book in my Kellersburg series. New beginnings is a theme throughout the books in this series. This story shows that a person can start over, even when things seem bleak and unattainable. God promises to always be with us. As the characters in this story learned, we can rely on Him through troubled times.

This book deals with a difficult subject, and it was sometimes hard to write. When the idea first came to me, I wanted to dismiss it. But I went ahead because I believed God gave me the idea that I wasn't looking for. He knows that someone somewhere needed to read this story.

I would love for you to let other readers know what you think about *Hometown Cowboy*. You can do so by posting an honest review wherever you purchased this book and also on Goodreads or Book Bub.

Please consider mentioning *Hometown Cowboy* on your social media sites, especially where you talk about reading! Word of mouth is the number one reason people pick up unfamiliar books. Every review and mention helps.

This series is dear to my heart because the setting is based on the small Ohio town where we lived when our two daughters were born. Although Kellersburg is fictional, I drew on my experiences from the time we lived in Ohio. If you haven't read the other books in the series, I hope you'll look for them. Although each book can be read without having read the others, I enjoy connecting the books through characters and settings. Please check out the other books in the Kellersburg series, *Hometown Promise, Hometown Proposal, Hometown Dad,* and *Hometown Hero.* If you would like to get information on my upcoming books, please sign up for my newsletter.

Blessings,

Merrillee Whren

ABOUT THE AUTHOR

Merrillee Whren is an award-winning and a *USA Today* bestselling author who writes inspirational romance. She is the winner of the 2003 Golden Heart Award for best inspirational romance manuscript presented by Romance Writers of America. She has also been the recipient of the RT Reviewers' Choice Award and the Inspirational Reader's Choice Award. She is married to her own personal hero, her husband of forty plus years, and has two grown daughters. She has lived in Atlanta, Boston, Dallas, Chicago and Florida but now makes her home in the Arizona desert. She spends her free time playing tennis or walking while she does the plotting for her novels. Please visit her website, www.merrilleewhren.com or connect with her on social media sites.

https://twitter.com/MerrilleeWhren

https://www.facebook.com/MerrilleeWhren.Author/

Puppy Love and Christmas Cookies

Other Books
Miracle Baby
Second Chance Christmas

Village of Hope
Annie's Hope
Kirsten's Mission
Melanie's Resolve

.   .

.